BEYOND THE TRUTH

A BEYOND SURRENDER NOVEL

NICKY F. GRANT

THANK YOU FOR READING!

Thank you for choosing BEYOND THE TRUTH! Have you read BEYOND THE MASKS? This is the start of it all and I wouldn't want you to miss out on the all the action that led you here. I highly recommend starting with Book One - BEYOND THE MASKS. Available NOW!

And never miss a release! SIGN UP for my newsletter! www.NickyFGrant.com

DEDICATION

For all survivors of addiction and those in recovery:
Life is worth second chances. Stay strong and remember to love your-
selves along the way. You are worth it.

ONE

"Hey, what's all this?" Jolene asked, setting her prized guitar and blue IKEA bag on the entryway floor. Mild chilies, cilantro, and garlic aromas wafted past her nose, and her stomach growled with delight.

"The first meal in your new place," Marcus Smith said. With precision, he lifted a mountain of steaming roast beef and bubbling cheese with a spatula and placed it on ciabatta bread. *Delicious.*

Marcus possessed an array of talents—like singing and the ability to play any and all musical instruments as well as being a great cook. She would be jealous if he weren't one of the most important people in her life.

"I'm only staying here, remember? Your parents own this joint."

"You live here now. Take a load off. Food's almost ready." Using a knife, he pointed to a spot on the couch. He did this thing when excited. The way his mouth curved on the side when he smiled. A very attractive man, the ladies fell to their knees every time he took the stage. It was a shame she didn't feel the same. To

1

her, he was her music partner and best friend. Her safe haven from the world she'd left behind.

She plopped her body on the futon and stretched the length of the cushion. Sore muscles groaned their displeasure from a long journey.

The crunch of toasted bread sounded as he divided the sandwiches in half. "How was the flight?"

"Good. But why the airlines make you go all the way to Florida from North Carolina only to come back to New York seems ridiculous."

"It's a conspiracy to make you feel uncomfortable." He laughed, handing her a plate.

Her mouth salivated in a rush of hunger, dismissing a discussion of her travels. As she bit into the giant concoction, a kaleidoscope of flavor burst onto jubilant taste buds. *Damn, he could cook.*

She swiped a thumb along her lips and sucked the chipotle aioli from the tip. "I missed your world famous sandwich."

"Thought you might." He washed his food back with a glass bottle of Coca-Cola.

A few months had passed since they'd temporarily parted ways. He'd returned to New York City to get things settled and set up for their music pursuits. A man determined to make her comfortable and appointed himself to the role of her "protector", he was the only one she'd let close enough to understand the magnitude of leaving home behind. He'd helped her move forward and keep the dark whispers of her past from tempting her back to hell.

"Thank you." She squeezed his hand.

He swiftly cupped her wrist and turned the underside to the ceiling. A callused thumb scratched along the bubbled scar on the skin. "How are you?"

She swallowed the last bite of her meal. A clang of the plate against the coffee table alerted her of her quick movements when she discarded it. Marcus freely accepted her self-inflicted scars, but her stomach still churned with the knowledge she would always be damaged goods.

"Not bad." She stretched the hem of the sweater sleeve to hide the reminder. "Can we not talk about that right now?"

"Talking is a good thing. Helps bring perspective. You can't shut down and forget everything your therapist taught you at rehab."

"If something was wrong, I'd tell you. I'm fine, really."

His lips thinned as he followed her gaze. "Do you want help unpacking?"

"I don't have much." She considered her small pile of possessions resting by the door. "I pack light, remember? I can handle it."

"I know." His hand squeezed her knee.

His soft vibe and caring tone didn't spark the sexual thrumming she'd experienced with other men. She'd questioned why a relationship as lovers with Marcus never worked and learned she used sex as a tool to gain traction and false control. Besides, love never existed with sexual partners meant only to give her a warm bed for the night. And she was incapable of feeling it.

"Paige has a closet full of clothes you can use."

The quick remark about his sister didn't come without sorrow in his eyes. He missed her. She was victim of drug abuse and a resident of the same North Carolina facility Jolene had lived in. She'd met Marcus there when he visited Paige on occasion.

"You sure she won't mind? Especially since I'll be living in her completely furnished room and eating her brother's home-cooked meals?" She smiled to lighten the mood.

"She's not coming back to New York." He grimaced. "Too many traps to fall into. I get it. So unless she is magically cured of addiction or sends for her things, I'm sure she won't care. Besides, you and she have similar tastes, and I'd hate to see the clothes go to waste."

"Thanks. For everything. I mean it." She hugged him tight.

"That's what I'm here for." He tapped her shoulder. "Are you ready for Monday?"

Anxiety flowed through her at the mention of their pending record deal, and she hurled her butt onto the futon. "Of course. It's everything we've been working for."

"No need to get defensive."

This was her shot to prove to her father she could achieve great things without polluted agendas. The key to freedom dangled like a freshly washed carrot waiting to be eaten. Nevertheless, she'd rather starve than eat from a garden she didn't want. She tucked her feet under her bottom and fished the phone from the woven pocket of her sweater, flicked the screen, and aimlessly let it take her away.

"Jolene, look at me. Don't pull away."

A quick glance and she caught the concern in his eyes. The prior balloon of excitement from her arrival deflated in response to his current expression.

"Just nerves." Her thumbs floated over the keyboard. Before she finished typing the name, Google prepopulated the search.

Gavin Mayne.

A stampede of horses pounded the lining of her stomach. Butterflies would be an insult to the wild strength a herd of stallions could offer. Her skin flushed hot as a picture of him at some music award show filled the screen. Smooth dark hair sliced in a hard part framed his extraordinary jawline, his wide lips apparently refusing to smile. The stormy blue of his eyes cut through her as if he'd leap off the picture and have his way with her. *Oh wow...*

The power radiating from his fine masculine fierceness never wavered each time she took a peek. It consumed her in areas she'd walled off to men. Her gaze traced the outline of his luxurious tuxedo, unbuttoned to show his massive barrel chest trying to escape the confines of a white pleated shirt. The gleam of his bow tie caught the flashing bulbs of a celebratory night. She sucked her bottom lip inward. *Jesus.*

"You're obsessing about him again, aren't you?" Marcus pushed the phone to her lap, bringing her back.

"He was the one."

"No, he wasn't. Gavin Mayne is a creep and sleazy businessman."

A hard swallow to quell the defensive words heightened the ache in her heart. Gavin Mayne, the past Talent Director for Omega Records, was supposed to carry them into the music industry. A successful connoisseur of hidden talent snuffed out like a cigarette burning from the wrong end. Too soon. Too fast.

"He's a risk taker. We were this close to working with him before all that shit came out about him and his boss. He discovered us, so yeah, it's a little hard to let go."

"His *assistant* discovered us."

She narrowed her eyes. "Same thing. He'd hired someone with a golden ear or he would've done it on his own. Why couldn't I have gotten better faster? We'd be on our way by now."

"You needed time to focus on yourself. And look at you." His hands motioned along her front. "You're healthy, vibrant, and able to focus on your talent now. Being swept up into a record deal too soon could've made you spin out of control."

The light from the phone screen urged her to take another glimpse of Gavin's unearthly eyes.

"When will you see? Omega Records hasn't had a hit in a year, and they lost most of their artists when the CEO left. We would be starting over again. Now we know what Gavin is, and it probably saved you from some asshole predator."

She tilted her head. "Allegedly."

"It was all over the news, Jo."

Gavin Mayne's reputation held darkness from what the media reported. *A non-consensual attack on a woman.* Not just any woman. Shane Vaughn, his former boss and CEO of the record label. A night of hot sweaty sex at a notorious BDSM club, The Resort, caught on video and leaked to the masses. At least that's what she'd read.

"And never proven. Shane Vaughn left town to manage some pop star and Gavin disappeared. *Also* blasted on the internet."

Marcus snickered, collecting the plates and stomping into the kitchen. "I thought you were past this."

A million pounds of soggy regret sat on her chest, pulling her back to earth. "I'm trying."

"Let's say he's still around. Why put yourself in a situation where he might take advantage of you?"

"Who's to say he would? Plus, I'd never let him. You know I have issues with sex triggering my need for acceptance. It would be an invisible barrier I wouldn't cross."

He drummed his fingers to a nondescript beat against the linoleum countertop. "I want to believe you. And I do. I'm more worried about what *he* would try. If someone tries hard enough, they can still get what they want."

Marcus was right; she would know. When she wanted something bad enough, she always searched for an edge to find a place to stay or a high to chase. She would've done anything to get either one if it meant giving her body to achieve her goals.

"You can't protect me all the time. I'm going to fuck up. But I'm smarter now. I can spot the red flags." Lava bubbled from her gut, waiting to explode. Sure, his fears and feelings were in the right place, but she needed space. Two years of being watched over had worn thin. "It's about his business smarts, Marcus. He brought every—"

"Every band he managed to number one on the charts. You're starting to sound like a bad infomercial for washed up talent directors."

"Doesn't make it not true." She narrowed her eyes.

"He's gone, Jo. And the sooner you let go of the idea he's *ever* going to manage us, the better. The road is paved in gold for us with Eco Recordz. It's the safest route and the one we're taking."

The hot sting of tears crested her bottom lids. Not from sadness but pure frustration from fighting the girl ready to leap into danger in exchange for a small thrill and a line of powder up her nose.

Your old normal.

She breathed in and out slowly. *This is the new normal. A new life.*

"I'll be over it by Monday."

The promise oozed over her in a blanket of disappointment. She gazed at the phone again. No new articles on Gavin's whereabouts. Over a year and nothing. It was time to let go, and only one thing could put it to rest.

TWO

"What's in the box, Jolene?" her therapist had asked.

"What you told me to bring." The contents rattled around the box as her knee bounced out of control.

"This is to help you. A way to let go."

"I know, but it's more than that."

"Explain it to me."

"These were more than meaningless rendezvous." She lifted the box, flicking a glance to the trinkets inside. "I connected with them. Even if for a night. I can't forget what they did for me."

"What did those men do for you?"

"Accepted me." She toyed with the keychain marked Bud's Tavern *surrounded by a half-smoked pack of cigarettes and a deck of cards. All trivial items no one would miss.*

"Why do you think that?"

"Because I could never accept myself, and they were willing to take a short one-night chance on me," she breathed, the exhaustion from years on the run released into an invisible trace of air.

"Did you think it could be more?"

She shrugged with a breaking heart. "Yes."

Every time the last shuddering breath escaped and a man

toppled over her, she'd listen to their heartbeats sync to a matching rhythm, praying the melody would end on a high note and they'd ask her to stay. But the note never came and neither did the invitation. She'd taken the mementos to remember when someone might have cared, no matter how fleeting the time.

The memories of many men hammered in Jolene's head with each step down the sidewalk. Men were used for one thing. A warm bed in trade for a quick fuck. A small payment for a night of temporary acceptance. Each man kept a piece of her and so did she—through trinkets and consuming memories of passion and regret.

As the warm summer breeze blew, her hair stuck to her face. She flicked it away with each ancient memory.

When her purple Doc Martens met the staircase at her destination, her face burned.

This was wrong in so many ways. Three days spent trying to forget Gavin only intensified her stalker-crazed obsession to locate him. Her sweaty hand fisted around two smooth metal rods in her pocket. Two important tools her ex taught her how to use to gain entrance into a person's house.

But she never broke in to take the owner's belongings. She'd use them to pry into a life she'd never know. She'd gape over their worldly possessions, examine family portraits, and imagine herself living in a *home* someday.

Her finger hooked the bent end of the tension wrench.

What's the harm? He's probably not even here.

She cast her eyes on Gavin's Brooklyn Brownstone. The afternoon sun blasted the front of the house in warm heat. Off-white exterior stone and white trim burned her sight. She shifted her gaze down the block. His dwelling stuck out like a thorn from the brown houses lining the street. Was he deflecting or staking his claim? *Claim.* He owned this block. A powerful force emanated from the structure to the hot pavement rising up to swallow her body whole. *He probably owned everything he touched.* She puffed out her cheeks to expel the pressure tensing her gut.

A squeaky sound drew her gaze to a stake planted inside the small garden area next to the stairs. It waved at her as it moved in the breeze. *For Sale.*

The pinch of pressure from biting her bottom lip screamed, *"It's over."* And her sigh replied, *"I know."* Her purple Doc Martens ignored the mocking voice inside her head and marched up to the door. Nerve endings woke and vibrated with each step like a drug addict's high for a fix.

"Turn around, Jolene. You are past this part of your life," she whispered. Her gut fought her addicted brain.

She pulled out the metal objects, and they caught the light in a shining ray of invitation. *One last time and you can move on.*

Her hand shook when it lifted and pressed the doorbell. *Bing Bong!* She straightened and rolled her neck. Light conversations from passersby on the street and a rush of moving cars soothed her nerves.

With a professional criminal's movements, Jolene jammed the tension wrench into the lock followed by the hook rattling each tumbler with a *click, click, click.* A quick jostle and *snap!* Her heart leapt to her dry throat, and she tried to swallow it down. She turned the knob and...*voila!* The door opened a crack. *Easy.*

She crossed the threshold and her mouth opened as she shut the door. She was greeted by stark white walls and sporadic onyx décor spread about the open living area while slate gray hardwood ran to the kitchen. A mystery. A blank slate. A man without a heart or love.

A lemony scent pierced her nose. Flashbacks from the hospital threw her back in time. Sterile. Gavin was as obscure and detached with his own space as he appeared to be in person. There had to be something to reflect his virility and power. A piercing curiosity tugged her forward.

A clean kitchen and pristine dining area with a barn wood

table and seating remained untouched. She pivoted to face the living room, and her eyes zeroed in on a retro turntable and a stack of records leaning against the console. Frank Sinatra's smile gleamed on the album cover. She knelt, picked up the album, and traced a palm over Ol' Blue Eyes. When her heart rate ticked to an acceptable level of calm, she placed it back in its spot.

"Where are you hiding, Mr. Mayne?" She tapped her hands on her thighs and found the stairs leading to the second floor. A grin stretched her mouth wide. *Gotcha.*

She took two steps at a time, and her heart crescendoed a climactic score when she reached the top. A closed door at the end of the hall called to her, and she pressed her palms on the cool wood, followed by her ear. Gavin's energy zipped through her skin like wildfire. Her heart thumped for permission to enter. The door creaked open.

"Who am I to deny that invitation?" She skipped through the entryway.

Light seeped through the window dressings, reflecting planes of sunshine onto the hardwood. Copper accents and green tones danced around Gavin's domain.

He does have a life.

The massive bed, the focal point, commanded the room. A terracotta accent wall gave a hint of Gavin's hidden sexual vibe. Rich and fascinating. A timber headboard had been mounted to the bed. She ran her fingers along its flaws.

"I'm getting closer to finding you," she quipped.

She plopped down and lay back, enjoying the texture of the duvet under her palms. Luxurious and expensive. Fucking sexy. She snatched a pillow against her face and inhaled. Anise, cloves, and a hint of dangerous. Her favorite kind of man. She squeezed her thighs as images of what he'd look like sleeping naked flooded her mind. Did he sleep in the center or prefer one side? Did he bring home many women? What if he brought her here?

Shit, Jo. He's dangerous and not the good kind. You are here to say farewell! Get it over with.

Jolene sprung up and smoothed the imprint her body had left on the bed. She frantically glanced around for something to take. The long dresser against the wall revealed a picture frame lying flat on its face. She flipped it over. A vibrant little girl with white bountiful curls laughed as Gavin held her in his arms.

"He has a daughter?"

A bright smile, wide and carefree, radiated from Gavin's expression, and the child's eyes sparkled the same blue as his. She shivered. She used to look at her mother the same way, with adoration and love. She shut her eyes, fighting the faint image of her. As the years passed, her mother's face had faded as she clung to her memory for dear life. She placed the frame right side up and brushed the photo with a finger.

The scent of cologne moved her thoughts aside. Anise. Cloves. Goosebumps fizzed above the surface of her flesh. "Getting warmer, Jo…"

This is what she needed to relieve her obsession. The bottle was a pleasant weight in her hand as she brought it to her nose. Her eyes rolled back as the scent fogged her mind and ran its course to the apex of her thighs. She had finally achieved the desired high she'd been searching for. Gavin was as real as the men she'd slept with.

Her thumb smoothed over the gold embossed script on the green bottle. She couldn't take the bottle with her, only a ceremonial trinket to help her release the infatuation. At least she hoped. The cologne spritzed in the air with a push of the nozzle. Falling beads of liquid tickled her wrist. The earthy, potent smell of licorice against her hot skin pulsed the smoldering ache between her thighs. *A small piece of him. It would wash away later.*

She snorted at the moment of insanity. Her therapist would be upset. But no one could understand how taking a trinket, no matter how small, cooled the raging thoughts in her wild imagination. Gavin would never be in her life. And for good reason. Her heart plummeted to her knees with the fall of her hand and the bottle thudding against the dresser top.

Time to go.

"Ba-ba-ba-daaa..." The smallest melody forced itself from Jolene's mouth. She dragged her wrist across her nose as the high diminished into a humming euphoria. "God, he smells good."

As she took one step at a time down Gavin's front stoop, the beat in her head blended with the vibration of rushing cars on the street and hollers from somewhere, a cacophony of music laid out for her to write down. Strangely enough—it was a happy tune.

"Can I help you?"

Mid-sniff, her feet froze. A man's baritone timbre sounded less than pleased. She blinked and followed the voice rippling her insides awake.

"Holy fuck..." she gasped.

Gavin stomped around the front of the car and halted when his blue gaze raked from eyes to boots. A flicker of curiosity— was it? As she gripped the cast iron railing, her ring clinked the metal, and dizziness smacked her silly.

Jesus, pictures did him no justice.

A sculpted tight jaw, shaved close, accentuated wide lips as they thinned in displeasure. When he flicked his palm over meticulously styled dark hair, the refined gunmetal sheen of his suit reminded her of a shark in the water hunting for prey.

She squinted from the blaring sun, or maybe it was his bright cornflower blue dress shirt peeking from a matching vest, his heated eyes illuminated against the matching color. Full and round and angry. Her hand gripped tighter along the stinging hot metal of the banister as her chest rose to force her forward. He stepped closer with gleaming shoes, which nearly captured the reflection of her astonishment.

"Hi, Gavin…"

"Do I know you?" Jolene focused on his voice, allowing every syllable to wrap her in its sensual tones. A wave of anise and clove floated with the city breeze to her nose. *Wow, even better on his skin.*

"Damn…you're…" She tilted her head. What was he?

"Yes?" he prompted anxiously.

"Beautiful…" *What the fuck!* "I mean…oh shit."

"Okay…"

She put her hands up and walked toward him. "I mean, no. You don't know me."

He shook his head and turned toward the direction of his intended escape.

"Wait." She snagged his bicep, and it tensed into a mountain of contained muscle under his jacket. A zip of pleasure electrocuted her arm. "I'm Jolene Harrison and—"

He stepped back. "The story's been told. Tell your newspaper, blog, or whatever I have no comment."

She chuckled, and his eyes narrowed. "Sorry, I didn't mean to laugh, but I don't work for anyone.

"Then what do you want?"

"I'm a musician and I wanted to talk to you about managing me and my partner, Marcus Smith."

He marked every cell of her existence. "Not a good idea."

"It's not like you have a long list of clients right now. From what I've read, you—"

"From what you've read?" He craned his neck forward. "Or what you've seen?"

"So what if I've seen the video. Who hasn't?" *Liar!*

She'd safely tucked the sex tape away on her tablet for future viewing. Many nights of temptation racked her mind, but she couldn't allow images to tarnish her opinion of him. She desperately wanted to believe the release was a mistake.

"And you still want to work with me after what I did to that woman?"

"It was a private moment accidentally leaked."

"That's what you think?" A glimmer shone in his gaze. Maybe relief or his way of examining the situation.

"I want to work with you because of your business sense. You take artists to a different level, and honestly, I need to make something happen fast."

"Who put you up to this?"

She jerked back. "No one."

He snickered, shoving his hands in his pockets. "You willingly show up on my doorstep to chase me down and tell me you want *me* to manage you?"

She smiled even though she wanted to shrink into the cracks of the sidewalk. "Exactly."

He lowered his voice. "I'm a failed talent director responsible for taking down a multimillion dollar record label. Smells like a setup."

A million and one thoughts to convince him otherwise dissolved on her tongue. She shook her head and straightened. "Don't you remember me? The name at least?"

"Remember you? God…" He furled his fist and tapped it on his mouth. "I don't want any trouble. Whoever put you up to this can go to hell. Sorry, Jolene. I'm not in the market." He stepped onto the bottom step.

"Wait, please. Didn't your assistant tell you about me?"

He froze. "My assistant?"

"Yeah, last year before…well, you know what happened…he said he would get you in touch with us and then nothing."

"He?"

"Tall guy in a suit."

His head tipped back until he found the sky maybe in the

hope God would throw down a lightning bolt. "You have the wrong guy, Jolene."

She touched his arm. "No, I'm sure of it. He said: Gavin Mayne is in the market for new talent, and he would make sure you would see us perform."

"First…" He held up a finger, shaking her grip away. "I've never had a male assistant. And second…" His fingers formed a V. "I don't send assistants to do my work. If you were anyone special I would have heard of you. That's how good I am. Trust me."

"Was," she murmured.

"Yeah, *was*," he repeated walking up the stairs.

She wilted. How was he different than what she'd hoped? Sure, he was a "get to business" kind of guy, but somewhere her obsession had muddied her perception of him *after* the fallout, like suddenly he would be a humble man. Shame coated her insides, and the familiar fight feeling burned deep.

"If you could, for one minute, get past your egotistical defense mechanism, you would see I'm your big break. No one else is calling, and in fact, I'm glad…no, thrilled you're like this. It makes me realize I'd never work with someone like you."

A dog yipped at her heels in agreement. Walking by, the owner stared them down.

Gavin's eyes twitched in sadness, and his barrel chest rose and fell.

"It's for the best." He jingled the key ring from his pocket, unlocked the door, and stepped inside his home.

Her heart broke in two. She understood the walls he'd built to shield his jaded image. Those same walls reconstructed themselves daily around her heart.

Gavin was unattainable in *every* way possible.

THREE

Did karma give Gavin a good thing, or did a wolf in sheep's clothing dressed like a gorgeous blonde musician land on his doorstep? And why the hell did she smell like him?

He rolled the office chair forward, and his fingers struck the keyboard to search *Jolene Harrison*. Nothing came up. *Some musician. Not even a social media page.* Warning bell number one. When musicians sought a manager, they at least had a presence showing their ability to self-promote.

He deleted the search and typed *Jolene and Marcus*. Still nothing. What the hell? It had to be a setup, and maybe Jolene wasn't her real name.

He leaned back in the chair. Flashes of her green eyes melded with her tight, curvy figure on display beneath the army green midriff shirt. Her round breasts had attempted an escape over the scooped neck. And her hair. *My God.* The mermaid-like waves flowing down to her waist met a sparkling belly button ring he wanted to suck. Whoever she was stirred a desire he'd never experienced with a woman he first met. He stared at the computer screen.

Warning bell number two. Who would dangle a beautiful girl

to see if he would take her on? No one even knew he had returned to New York. How did she know he'd be here? Paparazzi were probably crouched across the street like a committee of vultures waiting for him to pounce.

The headline would read: *BDSM Lothario Claims Another Victim.* The dark side of his dominant nature gripped his chest. His fists curled on the armrests of the chair. The image left him reeling in his desire to tie her up and spank her ass cherry red for calling him out on the sidewalk. *"It's not like you have a long list of clients..."*

"Fuck." *What kind of animal are you?* "Stick to the plan. You have a job waiting for you. She's nothing."

"This will be your office." The co-founder of Eco Recordz, Corrine Sinclair, slid the frosted glass partition along the metal track like the door to a jail cell.

Gavin stepped past the threshold. Murmurs of conversation spilled over the gap between the industrial ceiling and the top of the modular walls. The shoebox-sized area held minimal furniture: a drawer-less desk with metal legs, a black ergonomic chair, and one visitor's chair. *Thank God the steel toilet and sink wouldn't fit.*

"No filing cabinet or phone?"

Her wide smile followed, showing all her teeth. "Your cell phone will be connected to the switchboard. Economizing equals employees using their own devices. And did I mention we were paperless? Everything is digital. Your laptop should be here soon. IT is setting it up on the network."

"Thanks," he grunted.

"You betcha! Coffee is in the common area and our team meeting starts in..." She flicked her wrist. The square screen on the blue rubber watchband illuminated. "...ten minutes. And lose the suit." She bounded out of the room and clanked the cell shut.

Plopping his body into the chair, he rubbed his eyes. This is what life had come to: four walls and a desk in a start-up company with barely enough cash to give him a minimal wage to keep him a float.

The record label prided itself on the ability to offer cheap streaming radio through eco-friendly power channels. Wind and solar. What a joke. Who bought into this shit?

"The hipsters. A new wave of Earth-conscious Millennials," Corrine had answered with a toothy grin when he interviewed.

Musicians cared about record quality and uninterrupted streaming, not the *how*. Corrine had attempted to convince him the stored reserves of solar and wind power from several sources would keep the servers for their streaming app going. But he had no choice. No other record company was knocking on his door, and he needed this job to help his only friend.

He picked up his phone and dialed. The dreaded shrill of doom echoed into his ear.

"Well, look who decided to call." The emotionless voice of Ethan Pax—friend and past business partner—chilled him to the bone. He'd hoped for frantic and angry. This wasn't good.

"I'm sorry, man."

"Fucking *video cameras*? Do you even care how bad things got after you disappeared? The subs you took advantage of freaked out and wanted to know what kind of dirt you have on them. Like, Selene. Remember her? A fucking councilwoman. How long have you been filming them?"

"Just Shane," he admitted. He'd installed the cameras to capture his boss in a vulnerable moment for blackmail.

One goal: Get her job.

Outcome: A broken heart and two collapsed businesses.

"That poor woman lost everything because of you. *I've* lost everything because of you. Our members have refused to come back after the goddam paparazzi tracked down the entrance to the club making *no one's* identities safe. Way to out all of us."

He pressed his tear ducts and swallowed. *The anonymity.* He couldn't see past the end of his dick when he'd made decisions. His MO used to be: Plan every move. Understand the outcomes. Know the exit strategies, including who would be affected. But his tunnel vision around becoming CEO, then falling in love, dragged everyone through his wake of selfish determination.

"Are you gonna speak? If the community was still here, we'd stake you to a Saint Andrew's cross and have our way."

"I wasn't thinking."

"You never think about anyone but yourself." Desperation and damage wrapped each word and fell like an anvil in Gavin's gut. "Is it your lot in life to push everyone away?"

It appeared he'd succeeded in his so-called life's mission by segregating those who were assets and those who were liabilities into buckets of people he could use or immediately discard. Gavin had learned at a young age, thanks to his father, how to clear the forest with napalm.

"What can I do?"

Ethan laughed. "You've done enough. Without our...*my* members, I'm finished. The club is dead." A familiar *beep* and the snap of a lock ascended his spine. Was Ethan in his room at The Resort? "The only thing left is your mask."

A black mask. A shield of false protection. It had been intended to preserve anonymity; however, it hid more. The carved grooves over the face reminded him of scars, and the vacant eyes matched his dark and lifeless soul behind them. Hollow dominance.

A real Dominant had limits. A true Dominant understood the meaning of gaining the trust of a submissive. Gavin had used the title and authority for his own ulterior motives for a taste of ultimate power, and now he'd forever regret it.

"I thought you'd want to keep it to remember her by," Ethan said.

Shane Vaughn. A woman built for love, and she tried to show him he was too. Turns out he wasn't. After he fucked it up, she ended up with the man who deserved such things. *Jacob Andrews.*

"Right," Gavin paused. "I can't change what I've done, but I can help turn it around."

"There isn't anything you can do."

A pang traveled from his heart to his gut. It churned and turned over, folding layers of truth and fear within itself.

"Start by removing my name from the deed and the business ownership."

"There isn't a cent to buy you out." Each word was clipped like a pistol releasing bullets into his chest.

"Forget about the payout."

"Gee, thanks. You're a swell guy, leaving me with a pile of bricks and no cash." He could envision Ethan's blue eye, a deep navy, and the other a light hazel, fighting against an intriguing juxtaposition of colors. Angry and forgiving.

"I always knew you were fucked up, but I turned a blind eye. I always took the stance that, as long as it didn't affect me, I'd let it go. I should've known your bullshit would eventually come barreling in my direction. Christ, we were tight, man. I knew everything about how your family abandoned you, and I helped you pick up the pieces after Nicolette died—"

"Don't mention her." Gavin sucked in a breath at his daughter's name. Nicolette had been another victim to his selfish ways.

"You're going to listen this time. You can't keep pushing people out of your life."

"I wasn't going to go through with it. The blackmail, I mean, but the video got out anyway, thanks to my ignorance. I didn't mean for this to affect everyone."

"You never do. But your bullish attitude still finds a way to run interference. You wanna revive my club and find me new members? The Resort meant more than money."

"I know."

"Do you? Because you took your power to different realms with those women."

"It was only Shane."

"One sub or several, it doesn't matter. You broke our sacred code as Doms. We offer them protection, and all our members expected a safe place away from the pressures of the world. Now it's all gone." His voice lowered as he took a deep breath. "This place was my life."

Ethan, a victim of the foster system, never had a family to call his own. The Resort offered him a place without judgment. It accepted him and allowed him to follow his desires and talk with people aligned with his ideology. The BDSM community filled his void. Now he'd forced Ethan to find a new location or drop out of the business altogether.

"I fucked up, and I'll do whatever is necessary to serve my penance. For nothing more than to get back what I lost for you."

"How are *you* going to convince the members to come back?"

A laundry list of unanswered possibilities flipped like a Rolodex in his mind. The *For Sale* sign popped into his brain. "I have a job and..." He breathed deep, hoping to release the vise around his chest. "Come to the house and I'll explain."

"You think you can turn this around, huh?"

Gavin rubbed away the soreness in his eyes. The mental exhaustion of getting Ethan's life in order shook him to the core.

"I will get the club back for you, Ethan."

FOUR

ORGANIC COFFEE SPUTTERED OUT OF THE COFFEEMAKER AND INTO a mug. A cartoon feline mocked Gavin with a fangy grin and condescending message: *I like your cattitude*.

"Jane's mug." Gavin turned to see some jeans-wearing kid, no more than twenty-two. "Kyle." The short hipster held out a hand, which lacked part of two fingers.

"Gavin Mayne." He shook.

"Ah, the new hotshot supposed to take Eco to new places. I work in production down the hall." He pointed with a short-knobbed finger.

"Not a hot shot. Who's Jane?"

"Jane Popper. The cat lady talent manager before you. Lasted three months. Didn't end well. Guess her 'cattitude' soured like warm milk."

He lifted the cup in the air. "Maybe this is cursed and will take me next."

"Funny guy. I like it."

Employees—all twenty or so—sauntered into the commons area discussing the upcoming season of *Game of Thrones* and Netflix. They sat at tables, on beanbags, and on the edge of a pool table. A calculator tallied the overhead costs in his head. These kids had more playthings than work things. How did they get any work done around here?

"Okay! Monday. Up! Up!" Everyone stood and Corrine clapped a beat. Beat boxes and cymbal crashes sputtered from the mouths of the employees. A song appeared somewhere through the noise. Kyle "Little Fingers" whipped out a kazoo. A fucking *kazoo*. The buzzing noise set his nerves ablaze as the shock of hot coffee burned his throat. No way would he be participating in a fucking chant session. Ever.

And why had he turned Jolene away again? He could go out on his own. Visions of Jolene taking the stage with her long legs and unique style made for the perfect spotlight musician and revenue to pay Ethan back. A shot of heat struck his groin and his hands went clammy. *Okay, maybe a chant was better.*

Loud applause erupted and Corrine said, "Awesome guys. Thank you for indulging me. We have our newest employee—number twenty-eight—joining us today. Gavin Mayne!" She circled her hands toward her, urging him forward.

"If you play your cards right, you'll get to keep the mug," Kyle joked.

The mug hit the counter and meowed its retort as Gavin slid to the front of the room. He'd rolled up his sleeves, having left the suit jacket in his office. Public humiliation didn't scare him and neither did a room full of barely post-pubescent adults.

"Gavin was the leading Talent Director from Omega Records and will pivot our revenue stream from subscription-based streaming to talent acquisition."

Was the leading Talent Director. An avalanche of hard stone shifted in his stomach. So much for his prior track record. Time to start from ground zero.

"Say hello!" Corrine clapped his back like they were old buds.

He rolled his neck and channeled the old Gavin, the one with balls the size of Everest. Once Ethan got on his feet, he could move on to other things.

"Hello," he said roughly.

"Tell them about yourself."

Which part? Where he crashed a record label? Where the industry assumed he raped his boss?

"I have a track record of finding the best artists and executing a strong plan to forge their talent to the forefront of music." Crickets sounded. Blinking eyes and tilting heads questioned. They all knew what he'd done.

"And he has a *cattitude* for success!" Kyle yelled from the back followed by snickers and chuckles.

He cracked a small smile, thankful for the ice breaker. "First thing. This is a business. I expect long hours and dedication from those on my team, for which you shall be rewarded. If you believe in this company you will believe in what I can offer."

A slow clap started from the back of the space, and Corrine chimed in, leading the room in a thunder of cheers. "Employee number twenty-eight y'all!"

Gavin fled to his office and swiped a palm over his damp forehead. Had he joined the Twilight Zone? Number twenty-eight? He wasn't sure if he hated being a number or that he didn't belong.

Sink your life into work; it's never done you wrong, and don't fuck it up this time.

He slid the door of his office open to find his brother, Liam, sitting in the lone visitor's chair.

"Who let you in?"

"I'm checking to see if you're still alive." Liam tugged the cuffs of the white-striped oxford from his navy suit coat. His onyx ring caught the recessed lighting from above.

"Don't look so disappointed." The chair creaked as he sat. "How the hell did you get me this job anyway? Is this some kind of special torture?"

"I'm on the board and Corrine is Kate's niece. Something, isn't she?"

"And so is this place. Am I supposed to believe you felt the urge to help your little brother? How's your wife, by the way?"

"Gone. Kate wanted kids knowing it was never on the table." He crooked his thumb over his shoulder.

"She left and you owed her a favor for a clean divorce," Gavin said flatly. Three failed marriages all before the age of forty. "Why get married?"

"Tax breaks."

"And a mountain of alimony."

"You know me better. Pre-nuptials. Anyway, I owed it to her." He grinned. "You happened to be unemployed while Eco desperately sought out a Talent Director. Simple decision."

"Simple decision to keep your wife out of your hair. Why the hell did Corrine agree to this? I'm sure she reads the industry news."

"Didn't matter. This place is sucking cash like an elephant's trunk in a small bucket of water. She had no choice."

"Way to put the company's success in my hands."

"You'll get over it." He shifted a disappointed glare over Gavin's seated form. "So, a viral video of your boss and you in a BDSM club? Didn't the Maynes teach you to keep that shit behind closed doors?"

"Like Dad did all the years when he cheated on Mom?"

Liam shrugged. "Dad still talks about the day you left the family."

"He disowned me."

"Because you stirred trouble. You told Mom about those women. Maynes don't rat."

Gavin locked his jaw. He'd escaped Liam's conceited holier-than-thou approach when they were younger and listening to it now would only cause a scene. They had a healthy distance, and he vowed to keep it that way, even though he worked under Liam's niece.

"Mom deserved better."

"Dad gave her the life every woman dreams of: money, expensive clothes, and social status. She read the rulebook. She understood it."

Blood boiled from his toes to his head. The defensive urge to slam Liam's smug face for his mother's sake shocked him. *Strange.* He'd left all concern for her wellbeing on the doorstep of his childhood home when he left it behind.

"We weren't always rich," Gavin reminded. "Dad was a measly salesman—"

"With an aptitude for success. He carved the family name in stone. If not for his business acumen and drive, the Mayne name would have been nothing."

"Still sticking up for the man. So like you."

"He made me who I am. It's a shame you didn't stay around to gain his wisdom. It appeared going rogue with the Mayne ammunition proved to be a failure."

Gavin pounded a fist to the desk. "I am this way *because* of him."

Liam mocked him with an arched brow and bored smile. "I see nothing's changed. You are still the hotheaded spoiled brat, blaming the world for your problems. I saved you, remember?" Hot air pushed out of Gavin's nose to temper his emotional outburst. "Now with the pleasantries out of the way, I'll tell you why I'm here."

"There's more? I should've known," Gavin sneered, walking to the small window.

"Mom's sick."

Gavin turned, blood draining from his face. "Sick?"

"Cancer. I understand you wouldn't have known, given your stance on family matters."

He waited for the sadness to roll in, but anger and relief argued for a space in his chest. The silence between him and his mother had spanned half a lifetime—sixteen years of missed opportunities—without a second thought. To him, she died the day she chose her cheating husband over her son.

"You should go see her."

Gavin narrowed his eyes. "She made no attempt to reach me after all these years."

"Suit yourself. Don't say I didn't tell you." He walked to the door. "And Gavin..."

"What?" he bit out.

"I had to pull a lot of strings to get you this job. Keep your dick in your pants and the video equipment locked away. Okay?"

As his brother's final attempt to peg him to the wall of shame worked, Gavin dipped his head between his shoulders and into his hand. He was too raw and too unsure of himself to ever portray the man he used to be. After Omega Records crumbled and he disappeared, he'd left his self-righteous armor on the battlefield. Whether he liked it or not, he was a changed man. If not for Ethan, he'd never have to show his face again.

"Oh, I'm sorry Uncle Liam," Corrine said from the hallway.

"How's this guy treating you?" Liam asked.

"Good so far."

"If he gives you trouble, I want to hear about it." He winked at Gavin and left. Was he going to have to deal with him daily?

"Gavin, your first act is here and ready to sign." Corrine crooked a thumb toward the conference rooms.

"Thanks." He followed.

"Jane vetted them, and since she's not here any longer, you will be taking the lead. Obvi." She rocked her head from side to side and rolled her eyes.

"Great. Who are they?"

"A duo from North Carolina. Sick sound. Indie robust. I think you'll like them." She opened the door and his heart stopped.

The blonde sitting at the table lifted her head. Her vibrant green eyes rounded and her red lips parted.

Jolene Harrison.

FIVE

A blazing red sticker etched with *Sign Here* marked the area where Jolene would be taken to another level in her musicianship. She wiped her palms on her high-waisted shorts.

"I can't believe this is happening."

"You should. It's meant to," Marcus said.

"Are you sure this is what you want?" She pulled her long hair to the side.

"Yes, are you?"

"It seems strange without Jane. I don't know. My chakras seem off. Maybe we shouldn't go forward with this."

He laughed, and his confidence exuded from his pores. If they'd been more than friends, she'd lick them to ingest his infectious self-assurance. "I think it's fine. Corrine did say this new guy topped a few charts with past talent."

She regarded Marcus' signature. *Do it for him and stop obsessing over Gavin.* She gripped the pen and breathed out. The ink flowed smoothly, imprinting her name on the white sheet. This was her way into the world.

"I hope he's as easy to work with as Corrine and Jane."

"I'm sure he will be." Marcus squeezed her hand.

The frosted glass panel of the conference room rumbled open, and when she turned, a tidal wave of heat awakened deviant desires in the pit of her stomach. Gavin filled the entryway like a god in a bespoke shirt and slacks hiding a hard body and masculine virility. His wide lips thinned, and the energy pumped off his barrel chest in waves, threatening to pull her into the undertow of dark and sinful rage. The iciness in his blue gaze pierced holes through her, searching for clues as to why he'd found her roaming his doorstep a few days prior. *Oh shit.*

Corrine bounced through the doorway. "Jolene and Marcus, this is your new manager, Gavin Mayne."

"You've got to be kidding me," Marcus murmured.

"F-fu—" Jolene sputtered trying to catch her breath. He was here and *he* would manage them. Elation tamped down the guilt swarming through her brain from snooping around his house.

He entered as though he owned the space and held out a hand. "Marcus."

Marcus shook. "Gavin."

What. The. Fuck.

She swallowed, and her heart pumped what felt like a million liters of blood through her veins in a heated rush. She didn't understand up or down with Gavin in the room. One minute hot, the next minute angry, and the seconds in between amounted to joy. No other human affected her this way. Not her ex, Zane, and not even Marcus when they were together. A tripping exhaustion of emotional instability split her brain in two. Like him or hate him?

Hate him! He's an ass. He wouldn't listen to you.

"And Jolene." Her name puckered off his sexy, bitable lips with tight authority.

Okay, like him. He was protecting himself.

She stared at his attempt at a cordial gesture, the gateway to the rabbit hole. All things mystical, consuming, and frightening. His impressively sized hands were corded with tendons spiraling up his exposed forearms. She wouldn't mind having those mitts all over her. *Jo! Concentrate!*

She took his hand. It embraced hers, wrapping it in warmth and triggering a wave of prickling hairs up her sweater-clad forearms. Did time stand still? His face softened for a moment, and she could swear she glimpsed a smile in his hardened eyes.

Corrine clapped her hands, breaking the moment. "Gavin has joined us from Omega Records and is a top talent director in the industry."

Marcus snorted. "Was…"

"Yes, I was with Omega, and I'm here to bring Eco Recordz to the top."

"I…I…" Jolene stuttered. Her words evaporated in a mixture of unease and embarrassment.

"I'll leave you to it." Corrine went to step out.

"Wait!" Jolene yelped. The chair skidded across the carpet when she bolted to the door.

Corrine turned when they met in the hallway. "Hey, you okay?" Her soft blue eyes scanned the length of Jolene's body, no doubt seeing her bare knees shaking.

"He's our manager?"

Her light-hearted smile faded. "You know about him."

"Yes, I know. I watch the music news. I mean, who *doesn't* know?"

Corrine softened. "I would never want to put you in jeopardy. I may be young, but I get it."

"Do you?" Jolene squeaked.

"I do. But his references checked out."

"References? Like who?" Her spine snapped straight.

"A board member and Shane Vaughn."

"His boss from Omega?"

"Yeah, her. Although unhappy about the video release, she said their relationship was consensual, and the person behind releasing the video had been taken care of."

She blew out a breath. This information unlocked the burning question of whether Gavin would intentionally force himself on someone. A sudden giddiness took over with a laugh. "Employers tell you that sort of thing?"

She gritted her teeth and whispered, "Off the record." Corrine touched her shoulders. "We can rescind the offer. I will understand if you walk away."

"Walk away? As in, there is no other choice in a manager?"

"Unfortunately, not at this point. We have a lot riding on him, and with you and Marcus being our flagship duo, I know we will be a success."

A bomb hit her chest. Corrine's eyes pleaded while holding a strange confidence. In the brief interaction Jolene had with Corrine, she appeared to be a woman who followed her gut.

"And if *he* doesn't...?"

"Work out? One wrong move on his part and he's gone."

"Thanks, Corrine."

"Sure thing, Jo. Listen, I have your back, and this is a learning process for all of us. Consistent check-ins and an open-door policy, means you can come to me at any time."

She swallowed. She wasn't worried about Gavin overstepping; she was concerned with herself. How would Corrine feel about losing her "flagship" musician?

"Great, thanks."

"Let me know how things go today. One step at a time."

Yeah, the twelve steps. She'd learned all about them. However, admitting powerlessness over her addiction—Gavin Mayne— would be an impossible feat. She returned to her chair, keeping her chin up and her back straight.

"It's nice to meet you."

"Again."

She swallowed. "Right. Again."

Marcus' eyes widened, and Jo wilted with a *did I forget to mention I stalked him?* expression. His lips drew a fierce line while Gavin's burning vision never left hers. His anise-laced sweet cologne sent her into a fugue of hypnosis.

"Not a set-up," he remarked harshly.

She gritted a smile at Marcus and back to Gavin. "Surprise."

"How do you know each other?" Marcus shifted in the chair.

"Shall I tell him?" Gavin arched a slanted brow.

"Yeah, sure," she said.

"Jolene stopped by my house to ask for my management skills on your duo."

"You what?" Marcus stared her down with rage and disappointment.

"I...I wanted to tell you but I thought: What was the harm? He said no. And here we are."

"What the hell? We talked about this, Jo."

Gavin's alert signals seemed to rise. "Talked about what?"

She shrank under the watchful glare of her music partner and the intense, silent anger of Gavin's. "He's a risk taker. We deserved one last ditch effort."

Gavin laced his fingers. "Jolene, tell me why you sought me out."

Finally, an open forum to discuss her obsession. "Your established record proves itself. You somehow managed to get all of your artists to number one." She paused, thinking back on his repertoire. "Well, all except one."

"Halst." His head tilted slightly as his eyes focused in on her understanding of his entire history in the industry. Halst had been the only band he failed with. His jaw flexed. "We'll get to that. What can you do for Eco Recordz?"

She jerked back, slightly confused by the question.

Marcus chimed in, "We can bring you a fresh feel and vibe to the noise running rampant on the airwaves."

His eyes finally left hers to meet Marcus. "I asked her."

Marcus smirked and sucked his teeth with his tongue. Jolene could have sworn he mumbled *jerk,* under his breath.

She set a hand on his thigh to stop the erratic bouncing. "I don't understand," she said as Gavin glanced at her hand. Calculating. Observing.

"I don't take on anyone. I need to know what you're willing to give me to make this worth my while."

What a prick! The vetting process had been completed. He needed them as much as they needed him. No musicians had come knocking on his door; she knew that for sure. Why would any band risk their reputation? Why would she?

"Not sure that's relevant." Jolene skidded the contract toward him.

He spun the thick stack of stapled papers to face him. The black ink radiated off the page.

"It's relevant. Jane Popper vetted you, not me. And it doesn't mean you're right for our catalogue. Consider this a probationary period."

"What catalogue? We *are* it. And what are you going to do for *us?*" Marcus lurched forward. Gavin lifted a hand and motioned for Jolene to take the floor. Marcus plopped back. "Unbelievable."

It was time to speak her heart. Although terrifying, she had nothing to lose and this meeting couldn't get any worse.

"I…*we*…would give you our art. Everything we've composed. The music is yours to promote, record, and profit off of."

The practiced declaration bubbled over in a torrent of mumbled words, all fighting to escape. A twinge of dread gripped her insides. What if he turned them away because of her past?

"I don't like rehearsed answers, Jolene. If that were the case, *Jolene Harrison* and *Marcus Smith* would have a presence on the internet. Jane didn't do her research. A musician looking for representation would have an established platform by now." He narrowed his eyes.

"You looked us up?" She couldn't contain her stupid girly smile.

"After the uninvited meeting on my doorstep, I checked things out. Why the mystery of your group?"

Her smile faded to a frown. "There are reasons." Tears slickened her throat, a strange occurrence since arriving in New York City. If Gavin knew why she shielded her life, he'd never commit to her baggage when he owned suitcases full of drama.

"What reasons? I require an answer, Jolene." The controlled cadence in his baritone voice boomed past the layers of protection she'd built. Her glass house shattered to the floor.

"She's telling the truth," Marcus jumped in. "And she's not comfortable explaining."

"Marcus, it's okay," Jolene said. "I'll tell him."

Marcus sat back. Jolene straightened her spine, allowing her shoulders to fall. Maybe Gavin would appreciate her glass house.

When her gaze met his, his gorgeous arctic irises seemed to conceal...heartache?

Who are you kidding? He's gathering information for the company not you. The risks she presented could wreak havoc on a growing label, and she respected his direct line of questioning to protect himself and the business.

"I'm an addict with a history of overdose." She cupped her hand around her wrist and rubbed. The desire to bolt out of the room fought her desire to stay. Would he understand? "There wasn't time for a social presence."

Gavin nodded, and his rigid stance caved a millimeter. "Why the rush? You mentioned it the other day."

"I want to show my parents they can be proud by proving to them I can do something good versus bad." A silent prayer to her mother crossed her thoughts.

Gavin's blue eyes clouded over, looking past her and into the distance. He blinked.

"Are you two in a relationship?"

"What does that have to do with anything?" Marcus scoffed.

"I've worked with too many musicians who think they can work through this." He shifted a finger between them. "The focus needs to be on the music, and relationships get in the way."

"That wouldn't happen with us," Marcus countered. Why didn't he confirm they were just friends?

Gavin's serious jawline softened a bit. "Halst, or Hal and Stephanie as I knew them, could write, and the more they fought, the better the music. Their angst was their muse, not each other. The issues they faced played into their survival as musicians and lovers. Once the fighting stopped, their relationship ended. They didn't even make it through a single tour."

"We aren't like them," Marcus defended.

He continued looking at Jolene as if Marcus wasn't in the room. The atmosphere in the room stilled as the white noise from the AC system silenced. It was just them. Manager and artist. *Gavin* and *Jolene.*

He cared about Halst, from what she could tell, and perhaps it broke his heart when he couldn't keep them together. The unnerving need to bite his lips and devour his entire being spiked a craving of sensual lust through her body. She wanted him to care that deeply for her beyond a professional relationship.

"Looking back, I wished I could've seen it coming," he continued. "But I became blinded by the money the label could make, and I never interceded to keep them on track." He leaned back, the sudden reverie gone. "I'm not about to make the same mistake."

"We're not in a relationship," she confirmed. Marcus opened his mouth, and she shot him a look.

An awkward silence simmered around them when the men

stared each other down. It was more than jealousy, at least from Marcus. He was protecting her.

"There are things to consider here. I look to be fully committed to my musicians and need time to consider everything. I will be in touch." Pausing to take her in, he stood, and before she knew it, he was gone.

"What an asshole," Marcus chided.

"Yeah…sure." She smiled.

SIX

JOLENE STRUCK THE WHEEL OF THE CIGARETTE LIGHTER. THE FLAME flared and ignited the tip of the incense stick. The billowing smoke of lemongrass curled relaxation into her nostrils when she blew it out. It eased her racing mind as she jammed the end into the wooden holder.

She shuffled through her blue IKEA bag and pulled out the knickknacks she'd kept through the years. Her collection inspired peace and confidence about her future. She hoped the items would help her find the higher power the rehab clinic encouraged.

"Find a higher power. It will be your source of strength."

She placed the Buddhist and palmistry hand statue on the cloth runner of the distressed vintage dresser. Would they help her find *balance* and *strength*?

Finally, Floyd, her pet cactus made it to his new home by her bed.

"Hope you enjoy the new scenery."

Marcus had surprised her with it, telling her she had a hard time letting people in. He said the cactus had a protective layer of thorns around the soft part of the plant, like her. The yellow flower pursed from the top like a crown. *Maybe there is hope for you yet.*

"The beauty within can still sprout from the most jaded of beings," she whispered Marcus' words.

She snagged a finger on a thorn. It hardly stung given her callouses, but occasionally it caught, leaving a sharp discomfort coursing through her. It woke the misery from its slumber with a warning to keep moving forward. Marcus taught her to feel something even if it hurt. By allowing the emotion to come to the surface and release through the wound, other good stuff came with it. Happiness, normalcy, and maybe someday—love.

"California Dreamin'" sang from her phone. She dashed to the vanity and hit the speaker button.

"Elliot!"

"Hi, Jo." A small twinge of Carolina twang slipped from her brother's lips. "How's the new digs and music coming?"

"Awesome. Seriously, I can't believe I'm here." Taking in her room, her heart bloomed. The distressed hardwood floors ran the length of the space, and in the middle, a metal Bombay bed, with swirls of embellishments on the foot and headboards, grounded her. A little girly for her taste, but it beat a mattress on the floor or no bed at all. "As far as the music, it's good. Marcus has helped to push the muse along."

"You really lucked out with him."

"I don't believe in luck. This was *meant* to happen."

"Oh, here we go," he chuckled.

At the age of twenty-seven, most people could hardly afford a closet-sized apartment with multiple roommates. She, on the other hand, had ample space to stretch her legs. "Do you believe in fate?"

"I guess."

"Think about it. I know my hiatus from life sucked for you and Dad."

"Sucked is a light word."

Regret stabbed her heart. Would there be a time when the black cloud stopped lingering? *Only if you can prove to them you can achieve something great.*

"Shit, Elliot. I'm sor—"

"It's okay, Jo. Things were tough, and if it hadn't been for that asshole you hooked up with, it would've never happened."

"He wasn't the asshole, I was." Her skin prickled at the mention of her ex. Everyone saw what they wanted regarding Zane. Sure, he could be rough around the edges, but he never harmed her. Not really.

"You need to start seeing him for face value. It worries me you still blame yourself for what happened."

She pulled her robe down and stared into the mirror. Scars ran up her arm and down her chest from a night that almost killed her. Her fingers met two circular divots and swirled to the path of the tattooed vines and flowers covering her skin.

"I would be dead if he hadn't saved me. *I* made us hide away because of my drug addiction. That's why Zane never came around. I wouldn't let him. But I get it; you witnessed the aftermath and assumed he put these scars on me."

She heard a screen door open and shut as she imagined Elliot on the wraparound porch. He loved to sit out there, said it helped him think. "I get this weird feeling…"

"He's gone. A closed chapter, right?" A chapter earmarked with a bent page. *Where did he end up?*

She walked to the window and slid the lace curtains to the side. Muffled sounds of horns filtered into the room. A woman rolled a utility cart down the street, attempting to sell handbags to any tourists passing by, hoping to lighten the load one step at a time.

"How's Dad?"

"He's Dad."

Distant and matter-of-fact. "What's he been up to?"

"Working. Keeping busy. The insurance game never stops," he

chuckled. The phrase mocked the one their father said when he would work late nights selling insurance to his customers. "He met someone."

She straightened. "What? When?"

"It seems pretty new from what I can tell. Maybe in the last week. Unless he's been keeping it a secret."

She smiled behind a pang in her chest, souring the moment she'd wished for her father. Maybe it wasn't new. Maybe he'd kept his daughter's secrets from the woman. Quickly, the pang hardened into an encasement of steel, pulling her chest forward as she rested along the window. *Baggage.*

"Sounds like he's finally moved on from Mom. Do you remember her?"

"You always ask me this. I was only two." He exhaled. "Everything you've told me and the pictures I've seen makes me wish she had a few years left before she died."

"Me too."

"Wow. This conversation got deep." He laughed nervously.

She spun to sit on the windowsill. *Mom would be proud of you.*

"You okay?" Elliot asked, pulling her back.

"Too much change in a short period of time."

"Do you still have my gift?"

She smiled and tugged at the ball chain around her neck. She cupped the silver guitar pick charm. The inscription read: *Music Heals.*

"I never take it off."

"Good. Don't until you're ready. I believe in you."

Her eyes met the water-marked ceiling. The armor she wore pierced in *one, two* heartbeats. "Don't even think about making me cry."

"Always the tough one. But when you're not, call me. I'm here."

"I know. And tell Dad hello for me."

"Wanna talk to him?"

The stone in her gut held her still. "No. Tell him I'm safe, okay?"

"Sure. Love you."

"Love you." She tapped the glass and stared at his name as it faded from the screen.

She sauntered over to the folded-up contract from Eco Recordz on her vanity and flipped it open. Her signature held promise as a stepping-stone toward success and a future everyone could be proud of. *Step eight: Make a list of all you harmed and make amends.*

"Someday you will be proud of me." Would her father feel the weight of the expelled words? An image of Gavin blipped across her mind. *Strange.* Why did she care what her conceited manager thought? She would prove him wrong too.

"Who's that?"

She blinked to find Marcus. "Elliot called."

"No. Who do you want to be proud?"

"My dad...again." Her phone clunked against the vanity where she tossed it. She snatched her lotion from her nightstand and squirted the creamy substance into her hands, then sat on the edge of her bed and smeared it on her legs.

"You can't control how he feels, and he is proud of you."

"How can you say that? He didn't even say goodbye, Marcus. Jesus." She raised her hand then let it fall.

"He cares."

"You need to back off." She knotted her fingers in her lap.

He crouched and shifted his head side to side to gain the avoided eye contact.

"It's gonna be all right. This will take time for him to adjust. He saw you in a hospital bed with burns and detoxing from a major overdose, Jo. Of course he's not thrilled to see you go off on your own."

"How do you know so much?"

He shrugged. "With Paige being in and out of rehab I saw it

with my parents, and I still feel it, even though she's doing great. The worry never leaves, only dissipates. Give him time."

"You sure?"

"Yeah." His smile could melt the panties off any woman, and she wished he had the same effect on her. She craved fireworks with a man she'd hopefully settle down with, and Marcus simply supplied embers. Not because he lacked skills in bed, rather she lacked skills to love.

"Do you ever think about us?" The saturated neediness on each word made her stomach recoil.

"How?"

"Like forever, Marcus. Do you want to be with me forever?"

"Be with you? Shit, Jo." He paced the room. "I would like to be your friend forever, yes. But together, as in a couple?"

His hesitation eased her tension a bit. She walked into her closet. "Forget I asked. I'm flailing right now and trying to get my bearings."

"Stop." She pulled the hanger from the shirt and it snapped upward on the rack. "I said stop. What's this about?"

Gavin. Our career. My life.

"I'm nervous, okay?" She gazed at the signed document on her vanity. His eyes followed. "Life's getting real. Disappointment is my friend and attached like a shadow. Can't we get a fucking break?"

"We have our break and even though I fucking despise Gavin, this is it. It feels good, right? For the first time, you are living."

Was living feeling every twist and turn like a never-ending rollercoaster? If she had to say yes, it sure as hell was better than being numb...*comfortably numb*. Heroin had brought her to the womb of comfortable despair, desensitizing the bad emotions and transforming them into a sea of nothingness. Now, although hard, she welcomed the sting of pain, the heat of anger, and the dread of sadness. Even during the brief encounter she had with

Gavin, desire and curiosity spilled over in ways she'd never felt for a man.

Damn. Even his brooding angry side turned her to mush. How did one man contain all the assertive and primal energy he exuded? How did he relieve it? A liquid smoke of desire curled her insides with a come-hither motion. She glanced to her tablet on the bed, the video calling to her.

"It does feel good, in a shit-covered sundae with a hidden cherry kind of way." She picked up the contract and waved it between them. "Let's find the cherry, Marcus. Let's pretend for a moment this contract holds its weight. Let's put it into the cosmos and believe it will happen."

"You and your weird belief shit..."

"Anything you put into the universe will come back. And what you mean is: *Law of Attraction.* What you reap is what you've sown. Trust me. We can tolerate Gavin, and I hope he continues to be an ass." *For my own good and our future.*

"Answer me one question. Why go through with this?"

"For you. You deserve this big break. You've done so much for me, and this is our time to shine."

His lips thinned as his chest rose and fell. "I talked to Corrine earlier to clarify this probation thing. She said Gavin had a point with Jane's vetting process and all, but not to worry. She gave Gavin a demo of our stuff to get up to speed. We'll win him over in no time."

"That's wonderful! Are you okay with this? Like, really okay?"

He rubbed the "A" of his Nirvana T-shirt covering his heart. "He's the real deal in promoting new bands."

A smile crept on her face. "You researched his professional history."

"He is undeniable on a resume. But if he fucking touches you, we walk."

"Agreed." She hugged her best friend and he left.

She clicked the door closed. Marcus would always have her

back, and he was right. Gavin—all delectable and dangerous—couldn't be denied, no matter how much she tried.

Jolene unlocked her tablet and landed belly down on the bed.

Let's see what the asshole holding your progress hostage is all about...

Could he give a probationary period on their contract? It didn't matter; she needed to get the demanding gorgeous man out of her head, and watching the video resembled emotional cutting in a way. *Get the pain out of your system and all will be okay.*

A few deliberate clicks on the screen and the video popped up from her downloads file. She hadn't seen it but had saved it from some pirate site in case she got curious or whatever.

The white arrow called to her like a flag of surrender. He was everything she should avoid. From his essence of controlling behavior to a self-centered sexy man...*with a nice body who could brood for days...*

"Get it over with!" She smacked the play button. Leather slapping skin had her fumbling for the volume. She clutched the device to her pounding chest and listened for any sound of Marcus coming toward her door.

Peeling the device away, she witnessed the primal fierceness in Gavin's eyes. With each swing of the flogger in Gavin's hand, Shane Vaughn moaned, crying out in, what...agony? Another slap against flesh and a groan escaped her lips, followed by a reprimand from Gavin. Jolene flinched, feeling each punishing blow.

The rope bound to Shane's wrists loosened from overhead, elongating her sensual form on a bed of silver satin. A smile pulled on her lips as the red marks from the flogger brightened.

Jolene picked up Floyd from the night table. She pressed a finger into its needles, and a sharp slice of discomfort ran from her fingertip and up her arm until it faded. She hissed until warmth replaced the icy edge of pain.

Was it the same? Was his boss looking for pain to alleviate

tension in a stressful world of nothingness? Did it tell her she would survive?

The cactus pot thudded on the night table when she set it down. *No. This had to be different. Gavin's world was different.*

Everything—the room, their masked faces, the implements of torture—meant it was different. Floyd never provided the level of desire matching the smile on Shane's face.

She squinted to focus on Shane's eyes. Why wasn't she telling him to stop? Desire sprang from every dormant cell of Jolene's body. Shane *enjoyed* it, and in turn, Jolene could feel her vibe and wanted to consume it. Jolene's clit throbbed and wetness soaked her cotton panties.

The flogger smacked the floor with a hard thud, and Gavin stripped his boxers and his cock sprung forward. Jolene gasped. *Holy mother...*

It was beyond huge. Frightening...well, almost. A shaft of power and masculinity only seen in porn, shocked her core. Her sex clenched, wondering what it would feel like inside her.

Her eyes widened as he prepared his cock to take Shane. The nerve endings tingled around Jolene's opening and her muscles tensed in delight.

"Take it off. The mask. Please, Sir," Shane whispered.

He did, shedding the last bit of protection she had. She was beautiful, flawless, and aware with clear eyes and a wide smile. Shane was enamored with Gavin, from what Jolene could tell. And he was with her, too.

Maybe he hadn't forced his boss.

Maybe he had second thoughts.

Maybe Gavin could love a woman.

His hand stroked Shane's face gently. The demanding man from seconds before melted into a vulnerable, romantic, loving person.

Did inflicting pain take him there?

Did receiving pain allow his boss to connect with him?

Could pain be the path to freedom?

Jolene paused the film and tossed the device. She sucked in air as her hands wrapped around her face.

"No, no, *no!*"

The temptation to satisfy her body to orgasm strung her out. Her sweaty hands curled as she attempted to cool her flaming body and steady the rapid breathing. She gripped the comforter and squeezed until the pressure to give in dissipated. How could sex resemble her weakness for drugs? Her muscles twitched, coated with a fever pitch to get a fix.

Maybe he wasn't the man the media made him out to be. Now she would be in for a fight, working alongside a man who enjoyed inflicting pain because she was a woman who invited it.

Gavin would no longer be her obsession...

He would become her addiction.

SEVEN

SURROUNDED BY A MOUNTAIN OF PAPERS, GAVIN SCRAWLED HIS
name on the last line to give up the house he'd purchased through
hard work and achievement. But as the hollow walls and shaking
foundation reminded him, not all business deals were won fairly,
rather through taking power to the extreme.

"Here." He clicked the pen and slid the stack of papers to his
real estate agent.

"I'm not surprised the house sold so quickly." Sheila straightened the papers with dollar signs in her eyes.

The buyer—some holdings company in Manhattan—paid
more than the asking price due to a bidding war. Sheila said they
insisted, given the location and the real estate market in the area.
He didn't question it because Ethan needed the money.

"Closing will be in forty-five days—"

"Sooner."

"I'll see what I can do." She shoved the folder into the leather-
bound briefcase and held out a hand. "Wonderful doing business
with you, Mr. Mayne."

He returned the handshake and walked her out. "Thank you."

Gavin shoved his hands in his pockets and took a long look at the vacant white walls. A veneer to the real life that had constructed them. He exhaled sharply, hoping to close the bleeding wound in his chest.

It was only a hunk of bricks and somewhere to stash his things, unlike his Uncle Rick's home, a place where he'd felt protected and loved even in the short time he'd stayed there before college. Rick, with his caring and attentive nature, had been night and day compared to Gavin's father. Escaping the confines of a house filled with anger and betrayal, Gavin felt welcome around his uncle. Loved, even. A reunion was way past due.

He turned up the sound system from his phone app. The demo of Jolene and Marcus played, and her evocative voice soothed him in an invisible embrace. Her melodies left a prodding nudge in his side, as if she inhabited his space somehow.

After a quick knock on the front door, it opened with a *whoosh*.

"Hey, man." Ethan tossed his backpack and motorcycle helmet on the kitchen island. "What's up with the *For Sale* sign?"

The welcoming face of his close friend helped the day fade away. "I'll fill you in. Beer?"

"Yep."

Gavin pulled one from the fridge and handed it to him. Ethan twisted the cap and pulled from the longneck. "Who's this?"

"Jolene," he grunted.

"What's up your ass?"

"Nothing."

"Okay, who is Jolene? Some hottie you have tied up?"

"Please. My dominant days are over." Every encounter as a self-proclaimed Dominant had been steeped in a pool of agendas so deep, he could never associate with it again.

"You can't shut it off. It's hardwired." He looked at Ethan as if to say, *dare me.* "I get you used your powers for evil, but it will never go away. Even if you find a sweet girl, vanilla will become bland and unfulfilling. You're smart enough to know that."

"Whatever."

"So spill it. Who's the chick with the sexy pipes? She sounds hot and talented."

He couldn't disagree. He no longer listened to test her level of musicianship and craft. She was a twenty-seven-year-old lyrical veteran. Her melodies struck deep from the provocative rasp in her voice and the cryptic verses piqued sheer curiosity. What had her life been like? Why the struggles at such a young age?

Damn her for making him desire to know her more and, worse, want to swap stories of their lives. A spark of hope ignited.

"A musician Eco Recordz signed."

"That's a good thing, right? Talent directors need musicians to stay employed. How do you like it there?"

"It's fine." He walked back into his office with a file folder as Ethan followed. Sitting at his desk, he turned down the multiple speaker sound system while Ethan plopped down on the couch along the wall.

"Not even in the job a week and already discovering treasures."

He arched his brows. "I didn't. She found me."

"Really?"

He and Ethan never shared stories, per se; they only discussed business. Clean cut and to the point, all because Gavin shut everyone out. And here Ethan was being a *friend,* and it felt good for a change to get into a complicated conversation.

"She showed up on my doorstep the other day asking for representation. I said no way. And the next day, she appeared, sitting in Eco's conference room with wet ink on a recording contract."

"She stalked you."

"She didn't stalk me."

"Shit, you are the only guy I know who can do what you did and *still* get the ladies to track you down."

He exhaled harshly. "It's not like that."

If it were that simple, turning her away would be easy. Now he fed her some stupid excuse about a probationary period—which would never hold up. He was stuck with her.

"How is it then? Does she know about the video?"

"Who doesn't?"

He whistled. "She found out where you live, heard what you did, and still wants to work with you. Is she nuts?"

"No, she's strong willed and confident and..."

"Hot."

Gavin found his friend's smirk. "I didn't say that."

"It's all over your face. You like her."

Gavin snatched a wad of Post-its and wailed it in Ethan's direction. "I'm her manager."

Ethan swatted it away. "Isn't this interesting. Karma—like the bitch she is—came back with a bushel of forbidden fruit."

There was no way after his last office relationship he'd ever cross the line again. He could be professional. "This is temporary. I can get her where she needs to be, and then I'm out."

"See, she's probably smokin' based on your willingness to walk away from a career." He whipped out his phone and clicked the face.

Because I don't trust myself. "She's not right for the catalogue."

"Bullshit!" He flashed the screen at Gavin, displaying a picture of Jolene leaning up against a brick wall covered in New York's best graffiti. Marcus hung to the side. The banner read: *Jolene and Marcus. Tonight.* "You're scared you might get involved with this girl. And for good reason."

"Can we get on with it?"

"Sure. What's all this?" Ethan flicked through the paperwork Gavin handed him.

"The house sold."

"And?" Ethan's eyes widened when he stopped on a particular page. It must have been the selling price.

"And when it closes the money's yours."

His multihued eyes narrowed. "What do you mean, *mine?*"

"This is to help you get back on track after the club went down. It's not a loan, consider it payment for damages."

Ethan rubbed the back of his neck. "I don't know what to say other than I can't accept it." He slapped the folder down on the desk.

"What do you mean? I owe you, Ethan."

He feigned tears, wiping an imaginary droplet from his eye. "That's really sweet, man. Taking the bromance to a new level."

"Shut up."

"I'm not looking for a payout or charity."

"You're taking the money."

Ethan held up a finger. "No. You're going to do this the hard way. I want your blood, sweat, and tears in this. I want you to crawl and beg and *earn* your success even with temptation nipping at your heels. A taste of your own medicine, maybe? I think you need to submit to me."

"Keep dreaming." Gavin smirked at the amusement of his friend's dealings.

"Here me out. You take this Jolene girl on one-hundred percent and make her number one, then I'll consider taking your money and possibly forgiving you."

"I'm not—"

"Ahhh…have you thought about her outside of a professional arrangement?"

Visions of bondage, spanking, and fucking her appeared in his mind. "Yes."

Ethan's jaw moved around as though he was chewing on Gavin's answer. "What happened when she came over?"

"God, you're relentless."

"You aren't getting something for nothing."

"Fine. It was weird, and I'm not sure but she smelled like me and…"

"*Smelled* like you?" He nearly choked on his beer, wiping the liquid from his chin.

"And things were moved around my room."

If Ethan's eyebrows shot up any higher they would have disappeared beyond his hairline. "She *is* a stalker! Seriously, that's hot. You have a little crazy one on your radar."

He spit a sigh of frustration. All the muscles in his body constricted with want for a girl who *could* be a criminal. Call *him* crazy, but he liked it.

"There's something about her. She's a tough one. I'm totally fucking twisted over it, and I should be weirded out, but I'm not."

"There's a story there." His grin widened in mischief.

"Oh, no."

"Oh, yes. The insane ones make for the wildest times. You need to find out more. We're going to her show."

"Fuck no." Gavin left the room before his friend talked him into his hard limit. *No sleeping with the artists.*

"And I won't let you pass up a chance to meet someone who sticks it to you!" Ethan yelled.

Ethan's voice echoed off the hollow hallway and into the cavern of his heart.

EIGHT

Gavin and Ethan suited up at the bar of a smoky nightclub in the East Village. The torn leather chairs reeked of cigarettes, and the water-ringed tabletops gave the rugged club its charm. It used to be Gavin's favorite place to locate undiscovered artists. Three acts emerged from here and became huge hits for his past label.

He leaned on the Formica bar top and sipped the bourbon Ethan had ordered. The burn settled into his stomach.

"Other than the obvious hesitation with managing Jolene, what else is up?"

"Her music partner and her past."

Marcus made him feel uneasy about his odd hold on Jolene. Apparently, their musical relationship had kept them together, but something else existed. He couldn't put a finger on it.

Ethan bent the straw over the lip of his drink and took a sip. "Jealous?"

"Fuck no. I don't trust him; there's a difference."

"Keep telling yourself that. And the past makes the person."

"You're the one guy who can say they came out of a shitty situation on top."

When Ethan had turned eighteen, his mentor taught him about extreme sports and entrepreneurship, which provided him a balanced scale of pursuits. Freedom and control. Traits Gavin wished he possessed. But *all or nothing* reigned as his motto.

"Everyone is capable, my friend. Even you."

Feedback squealed over the speakers, and Gavin and Ethan faced the stage. Two microphones accompanied matching stools, and the sound monitors edged the front.

"Ladies and gentleman, please welcome our first pair of musicians. From North Carolina, Jolene and Marcus."

Gavin straightened. A tingle of excitement chased away any apprehension. Jolene walked onto the dimly lit stage. Her oversized sheer tunic and flowing skirt hid her tight form. Her familiar Doc Martens peeked out from the hem as she sat on the stool. They were sexy as hell, and he pictured her nude, wearing those fucking boots.

Cradling the guitar on her lap, she slung the multi-hued strap around her neck. A wide, messy braid crowned her head and disappeared into the luxurious curtain of hair. Her bow lips were decorated with vibrant red lipstick, and her green eyes flickered beyond her wing-tipped eyeliner. The shadows of her rounded face accentuated her bright smile. *Stunning.*

Ethan handed Gavin another drink. "Damn, she's better in person."

An assured confidence radiated off her. It washed away her toughness in the filtered light, illuminating her true being. The strings came to life with a flick of her fingers to test the capo she'd placed on the neck of the guitar. She was in her element.

"Hi, everyone." The small crowd whistled. "Hold the whistles, you may not like what you hear." Her laugh melted him to the floor. She gestured to her music partner raising the mic stand to meet his mouth. "Say hi."

"Hello," Marcus said in a low mocking voice.

Gavin's misplaced envy soared when Marcus looked at her in a way only lovers could.

"Hope you guys enjoy these little ditties we've been working on for a while." Her voice rasped through the microphone, and the diamond in her nose caught the light when she looked toward the ceiling. "This one's for you, Mama. Ready?" she asked Marcus.

He nodded as he strummed the beat to their first song, "Tiny Dancer." She picked up the melody with her hands, plucking each string with thoughtfulness.

Gavin fell back onto the stool. Her husky voice floated over the crowd with a gritty and raw sound. He'd compare her to a Janice Joplin meets Joss Stone type. And she did this cute curl of her upper lip when she sang a higher note. Her front tooth protruded a bit to make her smile crooked. It fit her face perfectly, and he wanted to inhale her voice and bite that lip. He spun to face the bar.

"You okay, man? I haven't seen you this horny ever." A huffy cackle of contagious laughter escaped Ethan. Gavin hit his friend in the chest. "Just saying. I mean, look at her. And man, her voice makes my dick hard."

"Watch it," Gavin barked.

"Already staking a claim?" Ethan's white teeth sparkled off the house lights.

Ethan loved to poke the bear, especially with a challenge he assumed he'd win. Planting the mere idea he'd approach Jolene made Gavin's dominant alert signals rise like wildfire.

"I don't mix work and play. It's too important. And that means you too. No touching the merchandise."

He placed the bent cocktail straw in his mouth and chewed. "Hint taken."

An hour later, after traveling through Jolene's tormented mind, he set the empty glass on the bar and kept one eye on her. A red blast of heat rose in his chest when Marcus' hands rested at the small of her back, and he laid a kiss on her forehead. Gavin snagged Ethan's Henley by the elbow before he ripped Marcus' lips off. "Let's go."

"You should say hello. It's good PR. Work for it, man."

Gavin gazed over to find Jolene had rested her hand on Marcus' chest as they celebrated a great set. There was more to them than she let on in the initial meeting. His story about Halst rang true. Any group in a relationship never worked. And why should he care? If they were sleeping together, he could keep it strictly business.

The grinding of his teeth must have alerted her, even over the sound of the club. She shot a look in his direction, and he was sure he was staring like some sort of brute across the cigarette-smoke clouded club. Her mouth formed an "O" in surprise.

"Looks like were staying. Lou, another round please," Ethan called to the bartender.

Jolene sauntered toward them with her hands tucked behind her. "Mr. Mayne. What are you doing here?"

"Soda with lime, Jolene?" Lou called from behind the bar.

Her eyes darted to the bartender. "Yes, please. Coming to spy on me?"

Sharp amusement twinkled in her mossy eyes under sweeping long lashes. "This guy"—Gavin crooked a thumb at Ethan—"brought me."

"And are you going to manage us all the way?" She swayed side to side, and her crooked tooth made an appearance. Confidence manifested from her musician's high, causing his cock to twitch.

Marcus came up behind her and rested a hand on her hip. "Mayne. What a surprise."

"Marcus." He nodded, curtly.

"Here ya go, darling," Lou shouted as he handed her a drink.

"Thanks." Her lips wrapped around the straw and sucked. *Good lord.* "Who's your friend?"

Gavin shook out of his trance of jealousy and lust. "Ethan Pax."

"Great set. Did you write all of those songs?" Ethan asked.

"All except 'Tiny Dancer', of course. Marcus and I have been working together for a few years now." Her neck craned back to look at her music partner. "Can't seem to get rid of him. He's too damn good at what he does."

They all laughed except Gavin, who was planning on pushing Marcus into the crowd and dragging Jolene out of the place and into his bed. *Fuck, this was wrong in so many ways.*

"She's being modest. I add the harmonies," Marcus said.

"A solid match, then," Ethan said, lifting an eyebrow to Gavin. He could read his friend, seeing the possessive storm brewing around them. "Marcus, let me buy you a shot. Jolene?"

"No thanks, I'm good." She lifted her glass of soda as Marcus sat on a stool.

"Where were we?" she breathed.

"You asked if I would keep you on with Eco Recordz." Relief washed over him as they settled into a conversation.

"What did you think?"

"Of the show?"

"Yes," she said, drawing out the word.

She smiled with one side of her mouth. He wanted to plant a kiss at the corner of her lips. He swallowed. He couldn't rightfully manage her with this much attraction. Fuck it; he'd find another way to help Ethan, go out on his own maybe. Many good musicians lived in New York.

"Let's talk where it's quieter," he suggested.

Every grain of his desire to work with her caused a tectonic shift inside him, the compulsion to touch her, screw her senseless, and keep her for himself magnified ten-fold. He touched her elbow to lead her to a table. She jerked back with a sharp intake of breath.

"You okay?"

Maybe he could take her on as her manager. The obvious reaction meant she didn't share the same attraction. And if she kept this up, he would never cross the line.

Her eyes darted to the exit door behind the stage. "Follow me."

Her hips rolled in her long skirt as the dim lighting of the club flirted through her see-through tunic. Why would she hide her slim figure?

They entered the green room and closed the door. A black, beat-up leather couch rested along the wall, and the smell of incense permeated the air. Jolene set her drink on the end table under a lamp with a pink scarf placed on the shade to mute the light.

"Much better." She exhaled.

"The show was impressive."

There was her corner smile again. Her hands slapped together in a praying position. "Really? You think so?"

"I don't lie about good music."

She tilted her head. "You only lie about other things, Mr. Mayne?"

She was a bold one, unafraid to air his dirty laundry. A possible sign of a savvy business-oriented musician.

"Gavin, please." He strolled closer, and she stepped back. "You should know I've never lied to musicians about their art. If their music is crap, I tell them. If it's good, I acknowledge their craft. And if it's exceptional..." His mind wandered as his train of thought jumped the tracks. Captured by her closeness, he licked his lips and his gaze followed her blonde braid. He flexed his fingers to keep from pulling each rope of corn silk strands from the braid until they fell to her succulent breasts.

"Then?" Her chest rose and fell, and her eyes became hooded as he took one more step closer. Her back hit the wall.

"Then I make them mine."

"Oh yeah?" Her tongue darted out to moisten her lip. As he

towered over her, her desire-saturated eyes called to him. Her breasts lifted and fell when her gaze reached his mouth. One kiss and the tension would be over. But then what? Would there be more? His mouth went dry, and he swiped her drink from the table. He sipped from the straw to calm his eagerness to ravage her and to allow his half-mast dick to relax.

"Yes. I sign them."

Her cheeks tinged with pink as she moved her hair over her shoulder. "You have a little…" Her chin motioned.

He wiped his mouth and red lipstick smeared on his hand. "Thanks."

"Okay. We've established you sign exceptional musicians. What can I do to convince you to take us on?" The twinkle in her eyes faded, replaced by a guarded shield. Her lower lip skidded against her teeth until it plumped to fullness.

Kiss me and let me fuck you, Jolene.

"Time. I need to understand you better, like where you get your sense of inspiration. When I commit, it's for the long haul. One-hit wonders don't make my repertoire. I won't half-ass this."

"I see. And what about you?"

He smiled at their tango of business and desire. "What about me?"

"What are you all about?"

"Business."

She sat on the couch, patting the spot next to her. "I'll be the judge of that. This interview for partnership goes both ways. Come here and give me your hand."

A shock of heat shuddered him awake from the fugue she wrapped around them. "Why?"

"I want to understand you."

"By my hand?" He laughed as he settled next to her.

"You strike me as a man troubled with"—she tipped her head back and forth—"sharing."

"My artists are on a need-to-know basis about me, and you

already know more than most. The media wasn't gentle with my intentions."

"I'll make my own assumptions."

"What if I did blackmail my boss?"

"And what if you didn't?" she countered quickly.

"Don't answer a question with a question."

She sighed. "Whether any of what happened is true or not, I choose to make my own determination. Nothing else in your past, from what I've researched, points to malicious behavior. People make mistakes. I've done things and haven't been shunned from society. Everyone deserves a second chance, right?"

A martyr for a better life. Could he have a second chance at his career without fucking it up?

"How can you be sure I won't do it again? Assuming those were my intentions."

"I can't. That's something you need to deal with. It's a choice between repeating history or changing the way you approach life. Now, give me your hand and let me figure this out." His brows quirked up. "I dabble in palmistry."

"Readings?"

"I prefer discoveries."

What information could she discover that he didn't already know? He was a failure, a man in limbo, and nothing in the creases on his palm could reveal the future. He held out a hand.

"Is this your *dominant* one?" she asked with a delightful chuckle.

He retreated. "This isn't a good idea."

"Oh, hush." She snatched his hand and pulled it to her face. Her touch sent an electric pulse to his chest. "Now the other." Slowly, he unfurled his other fist. She spread the tight fingers wide with a brush of her soft palm. "Relax. It won't hurt."

"What does it say?" His head tilted to the side.

"There's no hope for you."

"Now someone tells me." Expelling a breath into the incense-soaked air, he laughed.

"See here?" Her fingertip grazed the long line running straight down his palm, leaving a tingling wake. No woman made him this wildly uncomfortable. "Your career is very important to you. You work hard and enjoy it." She said this like it surprised her. "Success drives your life forward."

A hot moment soured by the word *success*. What did it say about his fucking failures? "Are you sure you're reading that right?"

"The palm never lies. Have you ever done anything outside of work?" Her finger ran up and down aimlessly, driving him to the edge of insanity. The lump in his throat caught and became impossible to swallow as she examined every moment of history marked on his skin.

"No, it's the only thing I can control. It is my life."

"Things can change. See here?" She flattened his other hand. "The line is less prominent. This could mean you are unsure or experienced some misfortune."

Could someone have misfortune when his intentions were doomed from the start?

"Can we move on?"

Her face crinkled in jest. "You sure? You seem nervous."

"Yes. I'm sure." What was it with her?

"The love line it is then."

He quickly rubbed his palms on his jeans. "Let's not. It's not in my gene pool."

"Everyone is made for it. We're human. It's a choice. Maybe some of us choose to save it for someone special." Her green eyes softened.

"Okay, quickly please. But I'm telling you there isn't anything there."

"I don't know about that. See how this is wavy and darker

than the other? You have the potential to love very deeply and openly. Is it possible someone had your heart?"

"No. Never." *Unless you count the false reaction to love with my boss.* With her lips folding over her teeth, she paused. The deafening silence made him squirm. "What about you?"

She turned her palms to the ceiling. A bouquet of masculine cologne matched his own, like a DNA helix connecting unanswered thoughts. *Why does she smell like me...again?*

"My love line stretches to the forefinger." She exhaled. "It doesn't make sense. Doesn't add up."

"Why?"

She scrutinized the twists, turns, and indentations squiggling along her beautiful skin. "I don't have an abundance of love to give. I lack in that area." She curled her fingers into a fist.

He held her wrist and a zip of understanding and comfort warmed his palms. "I've heard your songs, Jolene. Your music says otherwise."

Her eyes met his. "No, it doesn't."

Their fingers laced in his lap, fusing their pasts together. He fixated on her lips. They gave way to the future through an unknown doorway of pass or fail. If only he could kiss them for answers. But they held more than an invitation. They telegraphed his demise.

Her hot breath on his lips granted entrance as they parted, and he let go of the questions floating through his mind. His hand lifted to her cheek, and she leaned into the caress. Before he could change course, his lips slanted over hers and held. The world ceased to exist beyond the walls of the room, his failures evaporating at the spark of electricity in her touch. Her lips were soft and timid, the exact opposite of the tough girl she portrayed. He opened ever so slightly to feel the brush of her mouth on his. She whimpered, and his dick went hard. His hand shook when he cupped her cheek as if he'd never kissed a woman.

She opened, exploring the tender tissues of his lips, possibly searching for undiscovered territory. It was magnificent.

He groaned, "Jolene." His tongue darted to catch hers. Tips curling, nudging, and merging, unsure yet begging to be unleashed.

"More," she whispered.

He licked her lips. His tongue caught her tooth, fighting every urge to grant her request.

It was too much.

More meant seeing a future with a girl he should run from.

Because he wasn't worthy to grant her a life she deserved.

NINE

A FELLOW ADDICT IN NORTH CAROLINA HAD STOOD UP IN FRONT of the room and said, *"My first time trying heroin can only be described as the best time of my life. It was the taste of all the bad things my brain will forever crave."*

"Oh...wow," Jolene muttered as Gavin backed away.

His kiss—a million times more powerful than any drug—pumped her desire sky high. It was a drug so potent, her mind would forever crave more. She rubbed her hands along her skirt to dry her clammy palms. The ache was too powerful to stop the high from taking over her body.

"Holy shit, Jo." He shot up to face the wall and leaned forward, placing both palms on the surface.

The sudden ardor evaporated into the space, bringing her crashing to earth. She tugged the sleeves of her shirt to hide her hands. "I'm sorry. I don't know what happened. Well...I know. This has happened a lot, actually. I get all wrapped up and I can't...shit. Never mind." Her lips creased and she closed her eyes tightly to fight the aftershocks of pleasure ravaging her body.

The door scraped open and Marcus' head popped in. A

proverbial bucket of cold water doused the flames engulfing the room. "There's someone here to see you, Jo."

"Who?"

"It's Zane."

She frantically got to her feet and swiped her beverage, sucking down its remains. "Tell him I'll be right out."

Marcus nodded and flashed a look at Gavin before he disappeared.

"Who's Zane?" he asked turning to face her. A telltale bulge evident in his jeans.

"Someone from my past." She tried to flash a genuine smile when she reached the door. "I gotta go. Are we good?"

"Monday?" he gritted.

"Absolutely."

Jolene escaped the vortex of troubled pasts and unchartered futures in a rush. She welcomed the chill of the air-conditioned club on her hot skin. *God damn it. Why can't you leave the need for sexual exploits behind? Gavin is your manager not an agenda.* The familiar feeling of fighting desire over what was right pulsed through her blood. She clenched her jaw, demanding the impulses go back to the cage she'd built for them.

"Thanks, Marcus."

"What's going on in there?"

"We were hashing out details for Monday. Where's Zane?" She looked past Marcus' shoulder as a spike of adrenaline took her out of her haze.

"By the stage entrance. Do you know why he's here?"

"To see me, silly. I can't believe he found me. I haven't seen him since the hospital. Oh, Marcus…this is…"

"What? Exciting? This isn't good."

She scoffed. "Don't tell me this isn't good. He's the only guy I've ever actually loved. He saved me from my own mistakes. I wouldn't be alive if he hadn't taken me to the hospital. Jesus, do I have to explain this to everyone?"

"I didn't tell him you were here." His face fell.

"What do you mean?"

"Yes, he knows you're here, but when I saw him come in I came back to find you. Look, let's get out of here. We had a great night, and I don't want this ruining everything."

Her classic defenses rose as if Zane had carried them into the club. "Ruin everything for you, you mean."

"Knock it off; you know that isn't what I meant."

"Then let me go. You can't keep shielding me." She stomped toward the stage entrance, following the dim lighting of the club spilling through the curtain. When she pulled it aside, she found Zane sitting at a small table, sipping on a clear drink. *Water.* The man never drank a day in his life, nor did he do drugs. He'd provided heroin to her because it was the only drug he sold and she demanded it. It was her fault they failed.

His brown eyes savagely took her in as he stood. She finger waved.

"Jolene." He opened his arms wide.

"Hey, you." She fell against him. His hug reminded her about all the missing pieces she'd left behind in North Carolina. Flashbacks of their bad romance shocked her soul, resuscitating her past.

"You look…wow. You look amazing."

"What are you doing here?"

"Hold on. I want to take you in." His eyes cleverly marked each area, leaving a burning trail with each beat of her heart. He still owned her, deep within her bones. "I've missed you." He hugged her again, squeezing the air from her lungs. "I was so worried."

"I'm fine. Better than fine. There's so much to tell you, but where did you go?"

"Our place."

"The one we were going to run to?"

He nodded. "It's all fixed up, Jo. You should see it."

"Really? Why? I thought you left me."

"I told you at the hospital I couldn't be that guy for you. I hurt you and made you do things I'm not proud of, so I left, and our little trailer called to me. I put a lot of work into it and thought about how you would decorate it. It's not much, but I needed to show you how much I love you."

Her heart leapt at his words. "You didn't do those things to me. I did. I used you."

Looking back, she'd used him for his connections to heroin, and in return, she gave him her mind, body, and soul. Hidden chains locked their hearts together. She slumped forward. She loved him too.

"No, you didn't. I didn't know any other way to care for you. I fucked up, and I'm here to tell you I'm better and maybe...I don't know."

"What?" Did he want to try again? Her bond to him came back in a rush.

"Wanna take a walk?"

He rubbed his tight buzz cut and the tattoo on his right arm flexed. The inked Virgin Mary covered the entire space. She held a rosary made of screaming souls as the bottom dripped into a fiery hell and beyond. Mary searched the heavens in bliss as if to say: *"I'm sorry"* to the Lord for choosing the alternative to heaven because fighting the devil had become too much. And when Jolene stopped fighting, her soul had slipped into a world of possession and protection. *Zane.* If that wasn't love... Well, she had nothing else to compare it to.

A prickling at her nape caused her to turn. Gavin stood at the stage entrance with fists at his sides and a gleaming distaste flashing in his eyes. Then he walked away, like every other man who'd had a taste of her damage.

But for once, it was okay. They were professional partners who couldn't afford a detour toward a relationship or one-night stand.

"Sure."

As they headed out the side door and down the lit sidewalk, Jolene avoided uneven cement as Zane tucked his hands into his pockets.

"How've you been, baby?"

"Hanging in there. You know, the life of a survivor and addict. One step at a time."

He stopped and faced her. "I was a coward for leaving you there, especially when you needed me."

"It was for the best."

"Are your...?" He brushed a hand down her left shoulder and she flinched.

"Yep. All healed up. I can't believe I did that."

"It was scary."

"What happened, exactly? I have a hard time remembering bits and pieces." A flashback of her sniffing powdery snow up her nose blurred her vision.

"You were out of control. We fought about Trip because..."

The name, Trip, slammed her still. "You *made* me sleep with him. And I'm not sure if it was to pull off your stunt or to test my loyalty. So yes, I did sleep with him, and I did it for you." As humiliation coursed through her veins, she grabbed her middle.

Zane had wanted to put a plan into action to escape to their trailer north of New York City. In order to do so, he needed money, and she required a stash of heroin to make it through. Jolene had to distract Trip the only way she knew how. She'd gone as far as giving her body to another for a man she'd loved.

"Right. You did. I see that now, and if I hadn't been so insecure, you would be unharmed. Right before you passed out, you fell on our dresser with all your candles burning. I felt helpless to stop it, Jolene." He took her by the shoulders. "Our entire time together ended because of me."

She flinched at the tightness of his grasp and the grit of his gray teeth. But the agony in his brown-colored eyes touched her heart.

"I never blamed you for what happened."

He drew her in, and she inhaled the faint smell of cigarettes and convenience store cologne, flinging her back to their time together. "I miss you."

Dread gripped her heart and bones, triggering her alert signals. Shouldn't she want this? "I missed you too. For a long time."

He pulled away. "You don't anymore? Tell me I'm not too late."

She brushed his peppered jaw, the stubble giving the slightest friction against her palm. Sorrow mingled with fear in her gut. Could she let him go? "I'm not ready to jump back into things. I need more time to figure everything out and understand who I am."

He rubbed his mouth. "This is not how I pictured this."

"I didn't either."

"Jo!" she heard Marcus shout from the club door.

"Be right there." She held up a finger. "I gotta go."

"But Jo, I love you. Let me make this better." His voice cracked and her heart felt heavy.

"Give me time. I'm sorry." She walked to the club.

"You all right?" Marcus asked.

"No. But this is a start." She wiped her tear and showed him her wet hand.

He smiled. "Purging the pain will allow all the other good things inside."

TEN

"HI, I'M KYLE DAVIS." THE HIP PRODUCTION MANAGER STUCK OUT his left hand. Itty-bitty guitars were printed on his shirt, buttoned to the collar. His sporty jeans were rolled up to show off his rugged Chukka boots.

Jolene juggled her guitar in one hand and shook with the other. "Jo. And this is Marcus,"

" 'Sup, man." Marcus shook.

"The studio's this way. It's not much, but it's a start. We're excited to hear you record. Corrine's got high hopes for you."

Jolene smiled so wide her cheeks ached. "We are excited to be here."

As they shuffled down the hallway, employees greeted them with nods and salutes on their way to conquer the world of alternative music streaming. She bit her inner cheek. *Yep, not dreaming.*

Once inside the small recording area, her guitar case clopped against the floor when she set it down. An upright piano rested against the far wall, and recording equipment, guitars, and other musical accouterments had been strategically placed to make the most of the area while amplifying a wide range of desired acoustics.

"So it begins!" She high-fived Marcus with a loud slap before he shifted behind the drum kit. He whipped out his drumsticks and tapped the snare, then tightened the heads with the drum key hanging on his key ring.

"Is this the whole space?" she asked.

"So far. There's an offsite place we use occasionally for certain tracks, if we can't get the main songs done here." Kyle flicked on the monitors and sound equipment in the adjacent room with a glass window.

"It's perfect."

"Glad you like it. Marcus, there's someone I'd like you to meet." Kyle moved to the door.

Thump, thump. After two bass pedal hits, he followed. "You coming, Jo?"

With eyes wide, she said, "I'm good. I want to get tuned up."

"Cool."

She swiped her guitar and sat in a powwow area with a couch and beanbag. The guitar came to life with a strum of a chord. Her fingers ached as she pushed the strings. She tightened the tuner with a creak and tested the sound again.

"Whenever you were near, with Tiny Dancer in my ear," she sang softly as her fingers barred the transition chords. She closed her eyes and lost herself in the words. The remaining song came to her as she embraced her mother's spirit. *Finally, Lily arrives.*

"That's good stuff."

She blinked to find Gavin blocking the doorway. The suit covering his hard body intensified her frenzy to be touched by all of his hot maleness. His charcoal vest and matching pants complimented the richness of his blue shirt, which he kept open at the collar.

"I didn't know I had an audience." She rolled her neck, hoping to dissipate any weirdness from their kiss. She looked at her fingers on the strings, attempting to memorize the lyrics before his presence cast them away.

"Is it about your mother?"

"Yep." The sweetness of the question zinged her like he understood the longing behind it.

"Has she ever heard it? It's beautiful."

She cringed inwardly. "I hope so."

"Do you talk?" He stepped into the space, taking the last of the air from her lungs. The smell of him, earthy and sweet, suffocated her in a cocoon of safety and nervousness. He seemed relaxed even though they'd crossed the line at the club. *Okay...*

She propped the instrument against the couch. "All the time. In my dreams, when I'm awake, and always when I need her." Gavin's brows quirked. "She's dead."

"I'm sorry."

"It's cool. It was a long time ago. You wouldn't have known."

He sat on the far side of the couch. "About the other night..."

Here it comes. The explanation of why things needed to be platonic. She laughed. "Are you apologizing for something that wasn't your fault?"

The way his eyes flicked across hers held so much emotion. Was it concern or a little guilt? "You know what I am, Jo. I crossed the line and refuse to have what happened interfering with your success."

She strode across the room. A dagger of regret pierced the callused wound on her heart. "I don't like rehearsed answers either, Gavin. You mean *your* success. We can't have the big bad King of Kink out to hurt the young unassuming artist. Please. I've handled a lot more than you."

He swiped one palm over the other, and the sound of friction floated toward her. "Please understand, it's not what the media said it was, and as much as I preached control at one time, it's apparent I have none."

Fissures of hot lava disseminated from her center to her skin, tingling to escape into the atmosphere. Images from the video overtook her sight. The echoes of slapping leather and sexual moans rushed to her ears.

"There's a lot we didn't mean and the other night was a perfect example," he confirmed.

Maybe you *didn't...*

"Great. And right, I didn't mean it. Not one bit. I get carried away with men. It's a problem I have." She toyed with the drumstick lying on the speaker, rolling it back and forth until the sound steamrolled the old Jolene away.

"Glad we are on the same page. You're in good hands with Kyle today." He moved toward the door.

"You're not going to stick around to listen?" She shifted her ankle, bending it side to side. The strap of her sandal cut into her skin.

"I'll follow up at the end of the day and listen to the tracks." He grasped the steel knob.

"I thought you said: *In for the long haul*," she chided him.

His gaze captured her lips like it had before. The murkiness, now sharp with color, rimmed the edges of his irises to a brilliant sapphire.

"Are you wearing my cologne?" He shifted into her line of sight. Each hand precisely flattened on either side of her head, caging her in a womb of savage desire. The idea of getting caught pitched the game higher and hotter.

She straightened, the old Jolene winning the battle. "Yes. All over my body."

His Adam's apple bobbed. "You were in my room, at the house, weren't you?" He leaned closer to smell her trepidation and arousal. "And you moved the picture frame."

"Yes. And I laid in your bed to feel you."

Her body went rigid with the admission. Right from wrong battled with wanting to be with him as a fling versus needing him to help her career.

"Feel me? Are you...?" He hit the door just loud enough to make her flinch.

"I'm a girl you will soon forget after all this is done."

His jaw tightened. Yes, she should've avoided the A train to Crazyville, but the throbbing pulse in his neck told her he wasn't angry, only holding back.

"What were you looking for?" His hot breath hit her face. Mint and Gavin. She wanted to taste him again.

"Nothing." She scrunched her face, wishing she would melt into the carpet, hoping he would kiss her. "I wanted..."

Why was this so hard? She'd never had an issue with flirting with men to get what she wanted. And that's who he was—a hot, gorgeous man.

"Tell me, Jo." His low growl opened up a world of possibilities. It matched the commanding nature he had with his boss in the video. She wanted to be Shane, all flawless and successful. But she wasn't.

Her mouth parted and the words escaped in a whisper. "To say goodbye."

The humming of the recording monitors, his breathing, and the sound of her heart screeched to a halt. *What a mistake.* Why couldn't she be normal?

Then his finger touched her chin, like iron crackling against flame, and a blazing heat radiated down her neck to the apex of her thighs. A flood of arousal coated her underwear. She peeked through closed eyelids.

"Goodbye? We'd never met before." He frantically scoured her face in confusion.

The lump in her throat swelled to the size of an egg as she forced out the words. "I held onto you for a long time in my mind, believing we would work together. Your assistant told me we would meet and then nothing. I searched for a year and came up short. It became...abnormal. But looking you up online everyday helped me escape my thoughts while in rehab so I pushed on. When I got to New York, I stumbled across your door and had my chance to say goodbye."

His blue eyes closed and he shook his head like a pinball hitting the tilt button.

"You stalked me." He pushed off the door and paced the room.

"Stalked is a harsh word. I prefer visited."

"Is this what you do? Be cute?"

"Is that what you like?" Her hands gripped her *Music Heals* pendant and tugged the chain.

"What I like? *Jesus!*" He caged her again, and she butted up against the door. "Fuck, Jolene...what I *like*?"

"Yeah." She cringed even though her hot buttons were dialed to the max.

"What I'd like is for you to stop acting like this."

"Like what? I'm trying to be whomever you want me to be."

Officially the words rang clear. Everything she'd ever felt for a man all coming out in a rush of honesty. Her talent for conforming and becoming the girl men wanted had helped her win the game. But this game ended a long time ago. Their attraction meant more than agendas.

"I mean, I want..." She cupped his face, and a frown marred his beautiful features. "I want you to do things to me. *Hurt me.*" Desperation suddenly exposed an ugly darkness she'd tried to conceal. What had she done? Her back slid down the door.

He gripped her elbow and pulled her up to meet his face. "You're making this difficult," he whispered along her temple. Their combined anise and clove scents wrapped her in sinful pleasure. "It's like you're baiting me on purpose. Why are you doing this?"

"I want to—"

"Fuck?" The velvety smoothness of his declaration rolled off his tongue. Her need to act out the definition of the word, right there, against the door, wobbled her knees.

"I was going to say *have sex*. But *fuck* is a good word too." She practically panted.

"I promised myself"—their foreheads met—"I wouldn't touch you."

"Promises sometimes get broken." Her breasts pushed against her bra with need, nipples demanding to be pinched. Her one track minded goal to musicianship had been swept away by the raging rapids of desire slickening her pussy and caging her heart. She hungered for one thing. *Him.*

His eyes met hers again, the brilliant blue shifting darker as his forearm moved above her head. Their heat intermingled and it felt as though he'd suffocate her with his power.

"You're curious. Is that it?"

Curious, horny, wanton. All of the above.

"Y-yes."

A finger danced along her face, sending a tidal wave of goosebumps along her shaking knees and spine.

"Me too." His mouth covered hers gently. Her hands glided around his neck, and he lifted her around his hips. "Jolene."

"Shhh. I got you."

She opened her mouth, and he pushed his tongue inside like he'd die without her kiss to feed the animal inside. He yanked her hair, and she looked at the ceiling. Erotic pleasure tightened with his grasp followed by warmth as his tongue grazed her neck.

She closed her eyes to feel everything he gave. His hips shifted, hitting her throbbing clit through her shorts against his length. "Gavin…"

"Shit," he said harshly.

"What the…?"

He set her down and pulled his phone from his pocket.

"Oh." She leaned against the wall to save herself from becoming a puddle in the middle of the floor. He paced the room and adjusted his pants to accommodate the sheer size of his erection. She smiled in delight.

"Gavin Mayne...yes..." His face went passive, shutting away the desire radiating from his body. "Getting Jolene set up for the day. Tell him I'll call him back." He tapped the phone screen and shoved it away. "Well, call the HR department because I've crossed the line to unemployment." He smoothed her hair and straightened her blouse where it had ridden up her midriff.

"We can't do this."

Her heart plummeted. "What?"

"Not here. Not..." He flattened his unruly hair with his hand and backed away. She must have made a face because he touched her chin. "Let's talk. Later. We need to get on the same page."

"Okay. But know I'm a pro at chasing down a high to become ensnared by addiction."

"Is that what you think will happen?"

She took a long look into his eyes. "You might be a victim of my highs. I'm not sure I can handle it but I want to find out. Am I crazy?"

"I think we passed crazy when you broke into my house." He brushed his mouth against hers and a zip of pleasure hit her sex.

"You've only seen the beginning." She rose up on her tiptoes and licked his bottom lip. He grunted with a shiver of tight muscles, then leaned his head back slightly, the sheen of her saliva glistening off his succulent lip.

"This is work. Get tuned up. We'll reconvene when I take you home."

"You're taking me home?" A thrill curled her toes.

"It's only fair, since you've seen my place."

She slid away from the door, sucking the faint taste of him off her lip. A quick glance and he left.

How could she work after that?

ELEVEN

A BUCKET OF WATER COULDN'T ELIMINATE THE FIRE BREWING FROM Gavin's toes to his head. Jolene's fucking honesty drilled him. She was smart, talented, and undeniably wicked. A goddamned stalker and it spurred him on. He'd fantasized about her kiss and thought he'd gotten past the night at the club. He was wrong.

"How's it going so far?" Corrine asked behind him.

He turned and noted she had a laptop in her arms as she left a co-worker's office.

"Good."

"Awesome. Kyle's excited, couldn't wait to introduce Marcus to a member of the team. How's Jolene?"

A layer of perspiration dotted his forehead. "She's good, I guess. Ready to go."

She cocked her head and a chunk of short brown hair bobbed in front of her cheek. "You guess?"

"First day jitters. I've seen it before. Nothing to worry about." *It was a minor slip up. They'd discuss it.*

"Okay…just making sure," Corrine said. Gavin turned and took a step toward his office. "Oh, and Gavin?"

"Yes, Corrine?"

"How about breakfast tomorrow at the diner down the street? There are a few things we need to tackle."

He cracked a smile. "Absolutely."

"Hello?" A gravelly voice came through the receiver.

"Rick, it's Gavin. You called?" He tapped his thigh.

"I heard you were back in town." Rick's loving tone left a blanket of comfort over his body followed by a tinge of guilt for not reaching out sooner.

"I am. I should've called."

"You're a busy young man. I'll make this quick. You know your mom's sick, right?" His voice cracked as if telling him the news about his dying mother was a bother.

"Yes, Uncle. I know."

"She said you haven't seen her. You should go before it's too late."

During the time he lived with Rick, he'd never heard from his mother. Not a call. Not a note. Now, with her on her deathbed, she expected him to stop his life to say goodbye?

"You still talk to her?" His hackles rose. Rick was her brother; of course he spoke with her, but Charles Mayne had strained their relationship, all because Rick had taken Gavin in without question. If anyone didn't obey, submit, or go along with Charles' commands, he made their life a living hell.

"Sometimes." He paused. "You're her son, and I wouldn't be a good relative if I didn't tell you. She misses you."

Fuck that. She wanted to make sure she left the world without guilt. "I appreciate what you're trying to do, but she's *never* made an effort, Rick."

"Do it for me. I know it's hard for you to forgive, Gavin. But she's your mother, and I don't want you to regret it. You were always the tough kid"—he chuckled—"and I understand why.

Charles is… Well, he is what he is, and Marie had her reasons for staying."

Rick could never speak ill of anyone. Even when prevented from seeing his sister, he remained the purest of all human beings.

"And what about you? Did Charles get off his goddamned high horse to let you say goodbye?"

"Not in person."

"Let me guess, Mother couldn't stand up to him and snuck away to call you. Her own fucking brother…" He swiped his face.

"This isn't about me and Marie."

"It's about all of us. *We* owe her only what she gave us. Nothing." A headache throbbed behind his eyes.

Gavin sat with one hand clutching the phone while the other gripped his temples. No sound came for a long time, except the background of doors opening and closing, a quick strum of a guitar, and low voices. Rick must still be working for a music studio as a sound engineer.

"Sometimes what happened in the past can't be forgotten but we can choose to forgive."

"Why do you feel the need to make this harder?" He breathed out, softening to his uncle's request.

"It's not a need, Gavin. It's a duty."

A duty.

"Why are you like this?"

"Because I love you, and I care about your mother."

Rick did love him. Unconditionally.

The time had come to pay him back.

"I'll see what I can do."

Twelve hours passed in a blur. Marketing and branding had kicked off with creative brainstorming meetings, and several interviews had been scheduled to start placing Jolene and Marcus into the forefront of the music industry. They would be the flagship duo of Eco Recordz Talent Acquisition sector, and it excited him.

He had to hand it to the employees. They knew how to hustle, and the creativity behind the initial marketing sketches was impressive. The lack of barriers and mountains of red tape for approvals allowed them to pass the marketing plan without a hitch.

This job could work.

A muffled piano and voice seeped through the walls as he entered the back entrance of the recording studio. The analog clock on the wall read nine o'clock. Enough time had passed to ease the hunger he had for Jolene and afforded him time to think about their discussion.

"How's she doing?" he asked.

Kyle was slouched over the workstation. He stuck his short finger up and slid the knobs down and up on the mixing board.

Jolene commanded the piano across the room as a light *thump, thump* of the dampers hit the strings from the petal. Her eyes were closed as her red lips kissed the mic guard.

> *You came on strong,*
> *you swept me through.*
> *But when the demons arrived,*
> *I was bonded to you.*

The tortured song drifted through the internal speakers, sending a shiver through his body. Jolene wrote about hard life experiences from what he'd heard. Who did she feel bonded too? Was it the guy at the club?

> *Destined to be die-monds, we fade to black.*
> *Die-monds and black.*

The song faded as she let her fingers fall solemnly on the keys until the final note rang out in silence. No one breathed until Kyle clicked the loud speaker.

"Perfect, Jo. We got it."

With a swipe of her hand across her cheek, she flipped her head back. Her flushed face met the light as she made her way to the sound booth.

"Are we good?" She poked her head in and her eyes widened at Gavin.

The rush from hours before ran through him and he straightened.

"Yep. Great work. It's been a pleasure." Kyle smiled, and her lips did that sexy fucking curl again.

"Thanks." She backed out of the room and closed the door. His gaze followed her as she packed her items.

"Where's Marcus?"

"Left a few hours ago. We didn't need him for this last part." Kyle stood and leaned back on the soundboard before slapping a yellow legal pad down. "She's great. A natural, except for this one. This is her hit single; I know it. We tried recording it a few times, but she's holding back."

Gavin leaned over and read the title: "Mother."

"You have an ear for this stuff." Gavin smirked. "She sounded good this morning on this one."

"Whoa. That cat mug must have you giving out compliments." He laughed and pointed to the tablet. "You heard her on this?"

"I caught a part of it, in passing." *And so much more.*

"You have to get this out of her. She's locking up."

"Good to know." His eyes went to Kyle's blunted finger tapping away on his phone. "Sorry to ask, but what happened?"

Kyle lifted his hand. "With this? Shark attack." Gavin's brows lifted. "Okay, sounds cooler in my head. It was a stupid accident with a fishing line. My brother says he feels bad about it, but I like to give him a hard time."

"That's why you're a sound guy?"

"Yep, sliding decks come easy with a missing finger or two." He performed a show and tell as he moved up two sliders, missing the center one. "See?"

Gavin chuckled. "You've got it all figured out. So what's with the kazoo?" A burning question he'd held since meeting Kyle at the coffee lounge.

"Won it in a contest at a corporate event. I was this close to being in the Guinness Book for the longest run on a kazoo when my lips gave out from the vibration."

"Sounds like a personal problem."

He laughed, sliding his phone into his back pocket. "Totally. Anyway, Corrine and I met there, and she gave me the kazoo as a consolation prize and hired me."

Jolene poked her head in again. "You ready?"

"I'll be right out."

"You're taking her home?" Kyle asked.

He pushed out a breath, seeing the apprehensions of his history all over Kyle's face. "She shouldn't go home without an escort. She's an asset now."

"Does Corrine know?"

"Text her. I'm sure she'll agree." His stomach turned, unsure of Corrine's reaction. "It's not what everyone thought, Kyle. Shane and I—"

"It's cool." Kyle snatched his backpack. "Not testing my boss. But word to the wise?" Gavin nodded, feeling a trusted bond with him. "People talk and perception is everything. See ya tomorrow."

Kyle's young age didn't match his maturity. Before the fall of Omega, Gavin never gave two shits about what other people thought. Now, living under daily scrutiny of his past choices, he had to remain focused on rebuilding to become a different *him*. And keeping Jolene away was a first priority.

"What did you think?" he asked Jolene as they walked out of

the studio.

She shuffled her guitar and bag, and he took them from her grip. "Thanks. Overwhelming."

"How so?"

"I wrote these songs so long ago, and now they've come alive. I thought I'd put those skeletons to rest, and now it's time to"—she air quoted—"face the music." She flashed a bleak smile.

"I can see that." He unlocked the door to his Range Rover and helped her step in. After packing away her items, he climbed into the driver's seat and turned over the engine.

"I wasn't expecting to feel this way, but using my songs to purge the past helps." She leaned on the door, apparently taking in the passing row houses. His heart sank as a few moments of silence passed. His raw emotions wanted to meld with hers.

"What did you think of my last track?"

"It was exceptional."

"Will it ever get old hearing those words? *Exceptional. Great. A natural.*" She shook her head, still gazing out the window. "I sure hope not. Anyway, maybe we could lay an additional harmony track with Marcus on 'Die-monds and Black.' It needs something, and I think he has the touch."

"Sure. Where to, by the way?"

"I live next door to Electric Lady Studios. I touch the marquee everyday as a reminder of why I'm here and not to forget my goals."

When her vulnerability slipped through, he ached to know more. As the car moved, he peered over at her long legs, curvy middle, and tits so succulent he wanted to torture them for hours. He slammed on the brakes, almost coasting through a stop sign.

"Whoa, you okay?"

He cleared his throat. "Let's work on 'Mother' tomorrow."

She placed an elbow on the door. "Sure."

"You don't want to?"

"It's not that. I feel I *have* to. It's not ready. It hasn't marinated up here long enough." She tapped her temple.

"It's ready. You're a natural."

"There's that word again." A husky laugh filled the space. "Well, this one's a little different."

He accelerated to the Brooklyn-Queens Expressway. "What happened to your mother?"

"Cancer. It seems to grab the best and take them too soon. You would think I'd be over it by now. She died twenty years ago. But I still feel her or at least what's left of her. It's like, if I dwell in the void of not having her, I can embrace her memory a little longer."

The corners of his heart pinched at the thought of his own mother dying. He couldn't forget his younger years when she was the most precious thing he knew.

"I'm so sorry."

"Thanks. It's just...her song will never be perfect enough to capture the love I had for her."

She plunged a hand between her knees and rocked them back and forth. She'd been robbed of her mother's love too soon and here he chose to close the door on his own. All because he didn't agree with her choices.

"You will."

She peered over at him. "You're so sure of me, aren't you?" She took a deep breath and settled her hand on his, where it rested on the gearshift. He grasped the knob—all blood flooding his groin—as her dynamic touch shocked his dead heart to life.

"Someone needs to be." She slipped her hand back into her lap, and the loss of her touch pierced him. How the fuck could he work with her?

"I don't want you to be that person."

The SUV charged over the Brooklyn Bridge as the city lights created a soft glow in the night sky. "What person?"

"Someone who feels the need to hover while putting all this pressure on me to be great."

"I'm only telling you what you need to hear."

"I get enough of that from my brother and Marcus." Her strained voice cracked as they fell in line with the sea of brake lights in the middle of Manhattan. "It's been a long day. I'm sorry to put all this on you."

"It's fine, Jo. The manager takes whatever comes their way. If our business relationship can become stronger by getting to know each other, we all win."

"But do you?" She cocked a perfectly arched eyebrow at him.

"My friend needs me to get his club up and running, so in a way, yes. We need to keep this shit in check." His sweaty palms slipped along the steering wheel.

"Why fight something that's natural?" She drew a knee up on the seat, facing him straight on. Her hand brushed his arm, sending a straining need to his fingers to touch her back. "What happened today made me feel alive, Gavin. I can't ignore it."

His stomach squeezed with the intensity of a vise to fight his Dominant shadow hovering in the background, waiting for him to give in. "We can't, Jo."

"You're afraid of what happened before. I get it. I can talk to Corrine. We can do this together."

"You have no idea what happened. Why are you testing me on this?"

"Because you're here to help me. I haven't figured out how, but I want to look outside the false claims of your situation. The truth lies beneath the surface of what happened, why you did it, and how it affected you. Maybe it's the lunatic in me talking, but I feel it in here." She held her hands close to her chest.

Her declaration was everything he'd felt in the last year. The shell of his former self—the mask—threatened to realign after arriving back in the city. Her enigmatic honesty ate away at him.

"We can't."

They lucked out, coming down her block with an open spot right outside her building. He parallel parked and turned off the engine.

She peered at the key ring on his finger. The green in her eyes flickered with mischief. "Are you asking to come in?"

"I'm walking you up. I need to be sure you're safe."

"Lame." She feigned annoyance and opened the door. He retrieved her bag and guitar and followed her up several flights of stairs, her ass swaying from side to side. *Behave. This is to see her to the door.*

She unlocked the deadbolt and the main lock and stepped inside. The keys clanged off the distressed entryway table where she tossed them. He stood at the doorway as she set her shoulder bag on the couch.

"Well?"

"Well, what? You're home safe." He leaned the case against the table.

"Come in, silly. You came all this way, and I'm starved." She picked up a to-go menu from the end table. "Pizza?"

His stomach growled. Was it starving for her or at the mere mention of food? "I said we can't."

Her chest deflated with a quick huff. "People eat together all the time. Nothing will happen, okay? Besides, I want your take on today's recordings." She pulled a flash drive from her back pocket and handed it to him.

"Sure." When he closed the door, a wave of spicy incense hit his nose. Her apartment—a colorful array of hodgepodge furniture and random art on the walls—had the perfect blend of masculine meets feminine.

"Go ahead and order. And don't lose that flash drive!" She disappeared down the hall.

How did she know he lost the USB drive with the sex video? The one responsible for shattering two hearts and a multimillion dollar record label? She was smart, but no one knew about what happened except him, Shane, and Ethan. *Ethan, maybe? No way.* Did she know more than she was letting on? He flipped the USB in his hand.

Coincidence, man.

An hour later, with a notebook filled with ideas and suggestions on Jolene's album, Gavin leaned back into the futon.

A bone of crust clunked against the cardboard pizza box on the coffee table. "Stuffed," Jolene groaned. She extended her bared legs along the space between them. Her toes wiggled near his thigh. "Thanks for staying and hashing this out."

"Sure."

She leaned her head along the sofa back. "Tell me about her."

He blinked. "Who?"

"Shane Vaughn."

"I think we've covered enough today."

"Yeah, business stuff. I respect we need distance, but I still want to know who you are and what I'm working with. You know my past, so spill." Her big toe, painted glittery blue, pressed into his thigh. The area flooded with warmth.

"She was my boss. I took advantage. End of story."

She narrowed her eyes. "No way. The story continues since no happily ever after came out of it."

He snorted.

"Fine. I'll tell you about my shitty ever after. I went to rehab after I overdosed and met Marcus at the facility and we"—her one shoulder moved up then down—"hooked up and made music. The sex stopped because I wanted him more as a friend than a lover." She creased her lip with her teeth and mused, "Never had one of those before." *Pause.* "Anyway, a year later, we left North Carolina and came to New York."

His eyes widened. She *had* slept with Marcus. Jealous wildfire spread along his chest. *None of your business.* "And here we are? I think you skipped the part where you stalked me and broke into my house."

"You know all that. You are my 'wonder what might happen' ever after." She smirked.

"Wonder what might happen? I manage you. You become famous. Happily. Ever. After."

"Did you love her?" she pressed on.

Love sat in his stomach, mixing with spicy sausage and too much cheese, threading itself among all the shit to be digested. He scooted forward and popped the flash drive from her laptop and handed it to her. "You tell me."

She took the device and stowed it in the pocket of her sweater. "Tell you what I think?"

"You seem to know way more than you let on."

"How?"

"How did you break into my house, exactly?"

"A tension wrench bar and hook. Easy peasy. My ex taught me."

"And you think breaking and entering is okay?"

"I only entered," she defended. "Besides, there has to be a reason for entering someone's home. Not just to steal something."

"Explain."

"I used to enter houses to get out of the elements, but I always left things in their place. On occasion, I'd *visit* to understand what it was like to have a family, where the mom and the dad were together. I'd sit in the middle of the floor, close my eyes, and hope it would spark love."

He sat back and narrowed his eyes. "And what did you find in my place?"

"Truthfully?" She gnawed on her bottom lip.

"Yes."

"It was cold and vacant. Seemed like an expensive place to stack belongings you have no attachment to."

"Who says I have no attachment?"

"Do you?"

"Okay, fair." He shuffled in his seat. She could read him too well. She had to know more. "How did you know about the USB drive?"

"What do you mean?"

"You told me not to lose it before disappearing to your room."

"You lost me." She twirled a finger in her long blonde hair.

"How much do you know about Shane and me and what happened?"

She laughed, "The video, of course."

"*And?*"

She pushed off his leg and pulled her knees to her chest. "And the internet. The story was all over the place."

Did she know and keep it to herself? Was she lying? The news didn't break the whole story, he knew. He checked. After the video had been exposed, he'd kept everything under lock and key to keep from exposing Shane further. When she decided not to press charges on the woman who exposed them—against Gavin's advice—he promised her he'd handle it all. He took the entire fall, because he did love her as much as he knew how.

"Jo, I need you—"

"Wait," Jolene whispered. His eyes lifted from the floor in a haze of fresh memories to meet her forgiving ones. "Did you *lose* the jump drive? That's how your video got released? By someone else?"

He remained stock-still. A learned muscle memory he'd honed in on as a past-agenda-making son-of-a-bitch.

"You did."

"This conversation is over." He stood abruptly and cruised to the door.

"Gavin."

Sucked in by the pity dripping from her tone, his hand stayed poised on the knob. "Don't feel sorry for me. I'm not the man you stalked, idolized, whatever. I'm someone you need to keep clear of. This is a business transaction, Jolene. Nothing more. What happened today stops. I won't—"

"I don't pity you."

"What?" He spun to find her standing.

"I'm enamored of you."

"You're insane."

"I know," she said simply with a corner smile. "You *loved* her."

"Don't be ridiculous," he lied.

"You protected her from whomever released the video. You practically admitted to losing the jump drive."

"I didn't protect her." Seeing Shane's face in her office that last time, told him he'd done everything wrong. From trying to blackmail her for a job, all the way to falling in love. Blair Grayson, the woman who leaked the video, was nothing but a catalyst to the unplanned demise of Shane and her record label. All as a result of his actions.

"You tried. A case of 'out of your hands and conceal the aftermath.'" She strutted to the kitchen and leaned against the counter. "At the height of my using, *life* was out of my hands. I couldn't stop it. That drug…" She paused. "…became a life-form in itself. I'd do anything to get it. The last night I used, it landed me in the hospital. The aftermath had been concealed by my father to make sure I was protected from all of it, even myself."

"Jolene…"

"What? Are you gonna tell me it's not the same thing?" She narrowed her gaze. "We all fuck up, Gavin. No matter how. No matter when. But what counts is getting past bruised egos or"— her hand skidded over her sweater and down her arm—"burnt skin to change our future. We need to forgive ourselves for being at the highest or lowest point of our lives to realize it. And that's okay, I guess."

He pushed out a sigh as her declaration permeated every cell in his body like a healing serum.

"It was all I had left to give her," he admitted.

"Yeah..."

She glanced toward her bedroom at the end of the hall, a flicker of unease running through her. He knew the look. Right from wrong. Desire against denial. As a former Dom, he understood the signals; however, as a man, he wanted to calm her mind.

"Jolene, we can't."

"I know. And I'm fighting against my old self. The one who would make you fall for a split second because that lining comforted me, a false moment of truth only to find the morning sunrise mocking my insecurities." She stepped forward. "This is different. I can't explain it, only feel it."

She slid the wool sweater from her shoulders like she was shedding a part of herself. The reflection from the track lighting glinted off her scars in an array of white and pink now covered with tattooed flowers and vines. His muscles shook with the desire to wrap her in his embrace.

"You should go." Her lips thinned and she went to her room.

TWELVE

"WHAT THE FUCK? GOING BACK TO YOUR OLD WAYS?" JOLENE mocked, her brain running on a loop.

She stripped her high-waisted shorts, sidled up to the dresser, and rummaged through the top drawer. She yanked out a pair of sleep pants and waited to hear the front door shut. No, *slam* shut. Gavin had made it clear he was off limits, and she *should* be happy about his decision because she couldn't risk ruining her career. This was a job. Eco Recordz was a new way of life, a way to change course.

"Take your own advice, Jo. Change *your* future," she whispered.

"Jolene."

She jumped, feeling the burn of Gavin's eyes on her. Clutching the pajamas in her hand, she spun, and her skin flushed at her partial nakedness.

He shoved his hands in his pockets to keep from touching her, but the outline of his cock behind his slacks showed the desire he kept hidden beneath his smile.

"What am I doing?" he asked.

"Not leaving?" *Yippee!*

As he made his way to her double dresser, each sinew of tight muscle rolled and flexed beneath his shirt, stealing the speech from her tongue. Even when hesitant, he manifested a sexually primal male who could bring a woman to her knees. He slid onto the dresser's top and gripped the rim. Engorged tendons weaved down his exposed arms in an attempt to harness control.

If she wrung the fabric of her pants any harder it would cut off the circulation in her hand. Sex and attraction were easy, and the *old* Jolene had most certainly taken the night off. She never showed a nervous card when it came to fucking. *Is that what they were going to do?* Her body thrummed a solid *yes* as the lump in her throat tried to say *no.*

"Not what I meant." With his eyes flickering back and forth over her body, she waited for him to make a move. After several excruciating seconds, he didn't. Why wasn't he having his way already? Where was the man in the video? It's what she craved after all, and a small part of her wanted to understand the feeling of letting go in his sin-filled embrace.

"You mean us?" How could a powerful man like Gavin look so lost and unsure? She tossed the pants on the bed and approached him. "I don't know."

One hand rubbed his eyes. "I feel it too, Jo. You fill my bones with a need I've never had. When you asked me to hurt you? I wanted to, badly, in ways you would never understand, and it scares the living shit out of me. It's like my past is coming back tenfold for all the mistakes I've made."

"I get it..." Floyd's needles shimmered in the light of the bedside lamp. When her fingers moved over them, each pinprick mirrored lifelong mistakes she couldn't outrun. She pushed a finger against one, hoping it would remind her why she should make Gavin leave. A gasp escaped her from the searing heat of pain shooting up her arm, leaving a dissatisfied reaction. She still wanted more.

His eyes glazed over with a haunting iciness. "Do you really?

Because I'm breaking inside, and you keep coming at me with this." He snagged her bleeding finger. "Is it the fantasy? Because if it is, I'm not capable of giving it to you. I won't see you hurt because of me."

She pulled away and sucked the blood from her finger. "You can't hurt me. Not in the way you think."

"You don't even believe your words. I see it. You admitted to stalking me, practically obsessed over finding me until you succeeded. Then fate slapped me in the face after *you* were the one signing with Eco. Now I see how much you enjoy pain. Jolene, don't you get it? I should be running away, but I fucking can't." He swallowed so loud she heard the gulp. "And here I am, purposely putting myself in the flames."

He folded forward to grip the roots of his hair. The constant see-saw between right and wrong ate away at him too. This appeared wrong in many ways but felt right compared to the other men in her life. They never held back in order to advance on an *easy* sexual encounter.

This was far from simple. It was pure agony.

Watching him struggle made her want to jump into the flames with him. She stepped between his knees and they shifted apart. He straightened, casting an angsty gaze over her until it met her exposed shoulder.

He brushed a hand down her scars, looking into her eyes. The intensity of the blue in his gaze expressed trouble as his fingers flexed her skin with heat and compassion. "Who did this to you?"

"I did. It was the cost of jumping into the flames to come out a different person."

"We shouldn't," he breathed out.

Shouldn't didn't mean *wouldn't*. He left the door cracked open for her to step through.

Her body burned with need. If they walked out of her room without another word, she believed their bodies and souls would become helpless and remain alone, never finding a way to be whole again. She wouldn't let this moment pass her by, and she'd be damned if she would let him either.

"Let's," she said, hoarsely.

She cupped his face and licked the frown from his beautiful lips. He sucked in a breath, and his hands found her waist, tugging her closer. His lips parted, and his tongue slipped between hers. It was soft in contrast to the fierceness in his body, so much so she wanted to eat him alive.

"More, Gavin. Give me more. It's okay."

It was as if a gun had gone off at the starting line, and he charged toward her. With his whole body, he pushed through the kiss. He touched every crevice, tissue, and nerve ending his tongue could reach inside her mouth. She gasped when his lips released hers to meet her neck. The room spun in a cyclone of heat and lust. She climbed into his lap in an attempt to embrace all of him. The dresser crackled under their weight, and a few items clanged and rolled, bouncing off the floor. Her feet hooked around his back, and she rubbed her cleft along the hardness beneath his slacks. She leveraged her hands on his shoulders.

"Oh, God, yes…"

"Fuck," he bit out, shifting her hips up and down. Her clit rubbed against the delicious friction of clothing, pulsing with each pass. He tugged on her hair, exposing her neck. When he bit the skin there, the resulting high was like the first blast of powder in her nose. It was…beautiful.

"Tell me too stop, before it's too late," he grunted as her hard thrust against his erection almost sent her over.

"Oh…God. We're…past too late. Fuck me…make me come. Please."

Before her mind could catch up with his movements, he stood and placed her feet on the floor. Crouching, he stripped her panties. His dominant switch clicked on full, and the man in the video appeared. He paused for a moment, inspecting her nakedness.

"Oh, Jolene." A devilish grin met his sex-fueled gaze when it landed on her mound. "Show me how wet you are."

She panted and blinked downward. Her arousal had coated the hairs of her unshaven pussy. "W-What?"

He stood. "Your cunt. How wet is it? Show me."

The word cunt vibrated through her body with obscene delight. His top lip curled without apology. Shame kissed her flesh and seeped into her core. Darkness and filth lived in his mind, and even though she might only get a glimpse tonight, she'd push him to the brink.

The cool surface pressed along her naked bottom as she slowly shifted onto the dresser. She propped each heel on the edge and spread her legs. His eyes narrowed, and she parted her slick folds to expose her desire. Humiliation shook her bones as she braved a look into his smoldering eyes.

"It's very wet."

He sucked in a breath. A part of her wanted to crawl into a hole and weep from the fierce mortification of being told to show her arousal to a man. But his cock tenting his trousers and the beads of sweat on his brow told her how much she'd provoked him.

"Taste it," he ordered, spurring her to continue.

A shaky hand slid past the coarse hair and dipped through her folds, coating her palm with fluid. She lifted it to her mouth. Even with her eyes closed, she could feel his lust matching hers. One slow, leisurely lick of the fluid on her palm and her hot body fell deeper into his command.

"Are you a dirty girl, Jolene?"

"Yes…" she moaned. Her hand touched the swollen nub at the apex of her pussy and swirled. His voice made her embrace the bad girl she'd been. She gasped at the exhilarating feeling of being watched.

"Dirty girls don't come unless given permission."

The formidable dominance from his lips seeped into her

pores and defiance took hold. She didn't follow orders but being *told* sent a thrill through her. She arched her back, succumbing to it like a drug-induced high.

She sucked choppy air through her teeth. Feeling the heat from his eyes and the swirl of her hand through her juices, she nearly tipped. He slapped her hand away and slammed two fingers into her pussy.

"This is a taste of the fantasy." Her eyes rounded to find the vulnerable man from moments ago, gone. Gavin the Dominant had fully arrived.

"Oh, God…" The pain fluttered from her pussy into a hot core of pleasure and warmth. It was perfect. "Yes…harder."

Her hands flattened on the dresser and she undulated on his fingers. Wet sounds filled the air as he jammed a third finger into her. In and out, stretching her wide as her muscles had no choice but to adjust.

"Jesus…" he hissed. "You like being used, don't you?"

"Always."

A belt jingled and smacked the floor. "Why?" He pinched her clit, and the force of it made her climax scream for release. She yelped, and he pulled out his cock from his boxers. *Holy shit. How was that going in her?*

"Condom. In the drawer." She pointed to her nightstand.

Her core twitched with relief when he left to prepare himself, which allowed her to take a deep breath. He grasped a condom and ripped the foil. His stance radiated superiority and mastery, even when half dressed, as he efficiently rolled the prophylactic over the purple crown of his cock. In one quick movement, he pushed her against the wall. The jewelry box cut into her back.

He smacked the head of his penis on her sensitive clit. "You want this?"

She whimpered a weak response. "Please."

"Tell me why you like being used." *Smack, smack.* She craned her chin up to meet his gorgeously savage face. A smoky spark of doubt flashed behind his eyes for an instant.

"Because I'm a...."

"You're a what?" He coated the tip of his cock on her wetness.

"A wh-whore..." The word left her mouth in a rush of relief and shame. A word she'd heard from men and believed it. But in that moment, with Gavin commanding her and touching her, her admission pulled all raw wounds to the surface, and it started to heal.

"Yes you are, Jolene... *Fuck...*"

His hips shoved forward, and in one motion, they were connected. The pain shattered her core as it stretched her, breaking the meaning of the word *whore* to bits. "Make it hurt, Gavin. Please..."

He didn't break his stride or allow her to accommodate his invasion. She'd asked to be hurt, and he would inflict pain.

With each thrust, her slick pussy swelled. Her mind disconnected any lingering thoughts of right and wrong. She only wanted the pain and the words every man used to describe her, all to achieve pleasure and acceptance. Then maybe she could live knowing who she was without the dark cloud shrouding her evolution to normalcy. She wrapped her legs around him, and hot air from his mouth beat against her ear. Sweat slickened his neck. She braced tighter, snagging the collar of his shirt.

"You like it rough?" *Slam, slam.*

"Yes..."

The dresser screeched and knocked against the wall. Her head fell back as she lost control to hold him close. He pinched a nipple over her camisole, and she gasped as the piercing ache flooded all over, carrying her higher. How was she this fucked up?

Long passes of his cock relentlessly butted up against her sex. "You're amazing," he said. "Taking it all with your pussy, aren't you?" A hand stroked her neck. "So beautiful."

"Yes." *Beautiful...* How is a whore beautiful?

"Do you want to come?"

"Only for you. I touch myself thinking about you. And now..." He shoved deeper and she crested to orgasm on an explosion of stars behind her eyes from his succulent torment between her legs. She screamed.

"Now what, Jo?" he grunted, pumping his hips and not allowing her time to fade. He wrapped his arms around her and squeezed the admission from her lungs.

"I have you..." Her bones turned to jelly as her hands slipped from his neck. His back arched with one last powerful thrust.

"Absolutely fucking beautiful. Your cunt...you...want it all... You *fucking* whore." He rutted with such force another orgasm rolled and rolled until a dark haze of ecstasy took her body completely. *Whore* seethed from his lips with a bite of satisfaction running through her weak body. How could one man make an abhorrent word alluring? His debasing prose showered her with delicious humiliation, utter shame, and distant beauty. She swallowed to hold in the sobs racing to her euphoric brain as Gavin held her close, shockwaves ravaging his large frame.

After a while, she managed, "Gavin?"

He released a long breath from his mouth and the strained muscles in his arms loosened around her pinned body. Her eyes rolled back in exhaustion as he carried her to the bed. She heard a zipper as he dressed.

"Where's the bathroom?" he asked, gently.

She pointed in the general direction, too sated and high to talk or open her eyes. This was bad. If every time was this way, she'd lose the life she'd fought so hard to regain.

Moments later, using a warm washcloth, he wiped her sex with gentle strokes. Not rough. Not even a "see ya later." Was he cleaning her? Her chin quivered as she fell from the sky. Hard. Reality sank in, confusing the normal routine associated with fucking a man. She rolled over and gripped her pillow.

"Let me clean you up."

"It's fine." She pushed his hand away from between her thighs.

Shouldn't she be flying to the moon or floating on a cloud? Or should she feel empty? Why sadness? A balloon of fear filled her chest and burst with a sob.

"Jolene, look at me." The mattress dipped and tears tickled her cheek on their way to their destination.

"Marcus will be back soon, and you shouldn't be here." A black cloud of guilt swarmed her body and exhaustion wracked her bones from the ongoing fight to settle on an emotion.

"Jo." His lips touched her forehead and the warmth of his body enveloped her. Gavin shifted her into his arms and lay with her as she cried, her cheek pressed against his chest and their unique scents intermingled. He stroked her from face to back then arms.

The last thing she heard before slipping under was: "I'm so sorry."

Stench creeps into Jolene's nose. She twitches and tries opening her eyes but the sweet heroin womb sweeps her deeper. She coughs and gurgling follows a heave of her stomach threatening to double her over, but she can't move. Singeing noises and flaming heat yank her away with a scream...

Jolene jackknifed up. The sheets stuck to her sweat soaked body. The pitch-black room granted the specters permission to hound her sight. The smell of burning flesh saturated her nose and the screams howled through her ears. She fumbled for the lamp and clicked the switch.

"Fuck," she whispered. The blinding light scorched away the lingering nightmare and magnified her nail-driving headache. She snatched her phone by the bed and pressed the home button.

Almost two a.m. It dinged with an incoming text from a number she didn't know.

Z: Baby, it's Zane. I can't be here without you. I need you. Call me, please.

His tenor voice ghosted past her ears, matching the viciousness of her dream. An instant tightening of her chest shot through her.

I need you.

Somehow his declaration, no different from their past, managed to suck her back in. She slapped the phone face down on the nightstand.

A stirring brought her to peer over her shoulder, and the entire evening came into focus. *Oh, fuck. He stayed.*

"Hey," Gavin said, sleepily rolling to his side. A man undone, with his wrinkled charcoal suit pants and shirt, and his hair spiked in competing angles. Stubble underscored his sculpted jaw.

"I'm sorry about last night. I didn't mean to cry." She pulled her knees to her chest and became engrossed in the stitching of the cream quilt.

He propped up, leaning his back against the headboard. "I couldn't leave you. I hope that's okay."

"It's okay." She rubbed her arms. *No one ever stayed.* Rather, she left.

"What time is it?"

"Almost two. You should go." She flipped the comforter and the cool morning air bit her naked skin from the waist down. She promptly snapped up her pajama pants and pushed her legs through the holes.

"Are you okay?" he asked, unmoving from his spot. Why did he have to look so devastating?

"Last night was fun."

Interesting. Humiliating. And don't forget hot.

She bent beside her dresser and picked up the incense box, along with its spilled contents of wooden sticks, and the broken Buddha statue. She placed them back in their spot and lit a stick scented with lemon grass. She blew it out until the smoke filled the air and shoved the end into the holder. *Where's your balance now?*

"That's not what I asked."

"Can you just go? Marcus will be back, and we can't have whatever happened ruin everything, okay?" She placed her hands flat on the dresser and bent her head. *I can't have my choices and addiction ruin us both.*

"Get over here and talk to me." One look at his hard blue eyes tugged her toward him. "Turn around."

"What?"

He sighed. "I need to make sure I didn't hurt you."

She stretched and could feel the faint, satisfying bruises on her back. He lifted her camisole then touched where it ached. The warmth of his delicate strokes seized her insides.

"Is it sore?"

"A little. It's fine. Really."

The sweetness should've tickled her toes, but it annoyed her. Why was he acting different? Where was the tension? She stiffened and his hands wrapped around her middle, pulling her closer.

"Are you sure? I lost my shit. It won't happen again. I'm sorry."

Her heart sank. She loved what he did to her, the way he held her as they fucked made her feel wanted, desired, and cherished all at the same time. And for whatever messed up reason, the sweet Gavin didn't.

"I've had worse than a couple of bruises." She stepped away, and he snatched her hand.

"Like your scars? Did someone hurt you?"

She yanked her hand back. "I told you *I* did it. My drug addiction did. I meant..." *What did she mean?* Zane never hurt her and neither did the other men she'd been with, not physically at least. "Never mind."

"Was it your mom?"

"What? That's ridiculous." She crossed her arms.

He swung his feet to the floor and his thumbs swirled along her skin, igniting warmth below the surface. "Not what I meant. Did you start using drugs because she died, which ultimately led to hurting yourself?"

Her hands slapped her thighs as they fell. What was he doing? Why the caring look on his face? She didn't want this guy. She yearned for the fierce dominant.

"Just because we fucked doesn't give you free rein to pry into my personal life. This isn't normal. You were supposed to get off and leave, and now you're still here...and..." She covered her face. *Goddamned tears again.* "This is too complicated. I had a long day and need some sleep."

The bed shifted, and his smell invaded her nose. The safety of his scent wrapped around her. He moved the hair from her shoulder, and his hand dragged along her scars.

"I get it, Jo. Your past is yours to own and not give away to anyone. I know what it's like when someone tries to pull shit out of you when you're not ready. My boss did the same thing and look where it left me."

Her hands fell, and he swiped the wetness from her cheek, the tension from days prior missing in his soft features. His eyes were clear and honest. Why did he want to share this with her?

"When Shane pried into my life, I pushed her away. Omega went down because of me, forcing her to start a new life. She tried to love me, and I protected myself too much to change the course of what happened."

"And that's why you protected her after." Her chest fell heavy. "Why are you telling me this?"

"It's time, I guess." A finger tugged her face to meet his. "I'll never hurt you, Jo. You okay?"

No, Gavin. I'm not okay. Where are you? She searched his eyes. They were as cool as an ocean breeze. He appeared freed from his past, or at least one step in the right direction.

"Yeah. Are you okay?"

A wailing siren passed outside as his face went to stone. He didn't answer. He straightened, and the shielded version of Gavin reappeared, calming her. *Good. We can proceed.* The way she preferred. With distance.

"It was a mistake...what happened." He flicked his hand toward the dresser. She followed it, seeing them fucking on her furniture. The feeling of his will and power over her had flooded the euphoric sensors in her brain and now, the word *mistake* filled the cracks to strengthen her version of normalcy. She was the mistake and hidden secret for men to use, a place she could rely on.

"Yeah, a mistake."

But hearing it from his lips hurt more than the bruise on her back and the agonizing way he fucked her the night before. Things would have been easier if he'd stuck to the protocol: Fuck her, then leave. Instead, he altered her state of usual hook-ups.

She stood and started toward the bathroom. A safe place to let go of the fast approaching tears stinging her eyes.

"Jo, wait." The bed creaked, and she pressed her forehead against the worn wood. "You know I'm right. This can't happen again. Not like—"

"Totally. I need to be famous and you need a job, for your friend. Trust me, I'm used to it." She pulled the knob and the door halted from his hand on the door jam. "Let me go."

"Fuck, Jo. I shouldn't have come back here with you, shouldn't have hurt you or said those things..."

Lines crisscrossed all over, writing the word *wrong, wrong, wrong*, all over her heart to match the mangled scars on her body. When the fuck would it ever be right? She was pissed at herself for not allowing it to be what it was. She lured him, got what she craved and now they could work together. Well, *almost* everything she craved.

"Open the door, Gavin."

"Jo." His hand wrapped around her waist and her gut tightened.

"Now!" She dug deep and swallowed the self-inflicted rejection away, like she used to. He pushed off the door and she opened it. "You have nothing to worry about. Our secret is safe with me."

She was a glutton for punishment and torture, and Gavin wouldn't give that to a damaged girl, repeatedly.

She'd have to find it another way.

THIRTEEN

Gavin sped through the streets of Brooklyn with a shitty unease rolling through him. After he left Jolene, he tossed and turned in his own bed, trying to come to grips with how quickly things went south.

Jolene had stripped his resolve with everything she gave. From her body to her mind to the word she used to describe herself and the ones he chose to throw back in a lust-filled sexual rage.

Used.

Dirty.

Fucking whore.

How the fuck did she know his main kink? The names he'd used to address willing subs at the club were confidential by contract. How did she know? And why did he push it?

She'd swept him up into the dark world he tried to leave behind. Jolene turned it on its side, shedding the dark veil of prior masks he'd worn with a bright light piercing his bared soul. He ached to run toward it and have the light heat him like the sun, but a cloud halted his sprint in the haze of an incoming storm when she shut down.

For once, he desired to care for someone beyond the required aftercare and the clear-cut rules of an arrangement between a Dominant and a submissive. The sated feeling he had with her next to him filled his heart. He couldn't wait to caress her soft skin, kiss her bow lips, and taste her semi-sweet darkness, willing her to know he'd be there. But she'd made it clear her boundaries had been tested, and he'd pushed too hard physically and maybe emotionally. He was unsure until a moment of relief passed over her beautiful features when he clammed up. She preferred the stony version of him. It meant she felt safe with distance. A trend he'd maintained during his own life when things made him feel too vulnerable.

Or was it a setup? If it was, he'd fallen for it hook, line, and sinker. He played right into her hands, tossing out all logical sense. And for what? A hot night in her bed...*on her dresser*...and a morning of awkward conversation and backpedaling. Hadn't the last year taught him anything? Shutting down on a sub—not that Jolene was a submissive—before understanding their feelings could mean the worst. *Newsflash, asshole: Blair Grayson exploits sex tape of Gavin Mayne and Shane Vaughn.*

He pulled up at the light in front of a diner on the corner of Broadway and Berry Street. Green cloth awnings spanned the front, seemingly as old as Brooklyn with ratty edges and faded color. The port-holed door had been propped open to allow the breakfast crowd to shuffle in and let the stench of overused fryer oil to escape. Inside the large window sat Corrine, chatting up the waitress.

As the light flickered green, he sped around the back of the restaurant. His gut spun in a soupy fusion of bile and guilt. *When are you going to start fucking thinking?* He had to nip this in the bud now, come clean with Corrine and go away silently. Jolene deserved to have her career, and he wouldn't taint it any more than he already had.

When he exited the car, the cracked sidewalk led the charge to the unemployment line. As he crossed the threshold of the diner, the smell of stale coffee filled the area. He walked over the grime-smeared floor toward Corrine, who waved with the enthusiasm of a girl on a first date. He unbuttoned his jacket before he sat. *Save the energy for writing the pink slip, Corrine.*

"What's with the suit?" She sipped her coffee. Dressed in a white and blue striped tank top and jean shorts, her baby doll blue eyes in her plain Jane face blinked up at him with optimism and charm.

He scanned the menu and pushed it aside. As the waitress flipped his cup and poured the steaming coffee into it, he ordered. Egg whites with toast. Anything light to settle the rolling tide in his stomach.

"It's business."

She laughed. "Yeah. A start-up. It's casual, you know that, right?"

He flicked two sugars and ripped the packets. The granular crystals spilled into his cup. "To be taken seriously by the acts coming through, you need to dress the part."

His alpha stance didn't faze her. Being around Liam for part of her life probably gave her some legs. Her coffee cup clanged on the saucer when she set it down.

"Cool. Thought you should know. *Again.* But whatever. I hired you to make moves and that's your choice."

He tilted his head. *Make moves on your talent.* "Corrine there is—"

"How are things with J&M?"

"Kyle said they're pushing forward."

"Good. Just checking."

"On what?" A light sheen of perspiration misted his forehead.

"Kyle mentioned you offered Jo a ride home." Her young face suddenly hardened like an old hand at running a business. "It's my company, and even though my uncle gave you the green light, I still have concerns."

Her sudden girlish charm stiffened into business savvy. She straightened, and her gaze narrowed a touch, waiting for the invisible ink to appear across his face in dark bold lettering. *I fucked the talent.*

"I did take her home to make sure she got there safely. They wrapped up recording late, and I didn't want her getting back to Manhattan alone. Has Jo mentioned something to you?"

"No mention. I'd prefer you refrain from putting yourself in situations where questions may arise. I have a business to run and investors to impress. Eco Recordz is my dream, and I want everything to be on the up and up. I won't hesitate to let you go or take Jolene off the roster if there are issues."

"You would let your flagship duo go?" His hand spun the coffee cup in circles.

"If I had to, yes. I can't have unnecessary distractions and roadblocks in the way of Eco surviving. Understand?"

He sipped his coffee and envisioned the burning reality of hell he'd surely be living in if she found out. Once again faced with a devil's bargain, his heart shattered for Jolene while his head screamed to tell the truth. *Protect her.* Jolene's entire life hung in the balance over one night of lust. He had no option.

"Understood."

The waiter set down a towering plate of Belgian waffles in front of Corrine and her toothy grin came back as if they weren't having a serious conversation revolving around his secret violation. The sticky strawberry mixture dripped onto the plate. It brought him back to the predicament he'd found himself in. Corrine slid over her opened laptop.

"What's this?"

A revenue forecast and production schedule were displayed.

"Our new projection." She cut into a large piece of waffle and shoved it into her mouth, chewed twice, and said with a muffled sound, "We need them up and running by the end of the month to make the Q3 and Q4 revenues."

"That's less than three weeks away." Gavin swallowed a slice of egg and chased it with the burnt toast, which scratched his throat all the way to his stomach.

"The shareholders, one being Uncle Liam, are looking for a quick return." She turned her eyes to the syrupy concoction on her plate.

"Impossible. Marcus and Jolene would be working 'round the clock and could put strain on their vocals. Besides, marketing only started the branding cycle. This can't be rushed."

Visions of Halst came to mind. The rush to release their sophomore album dulled their muse from exhaustion thus busting the tour and sending them packing. He wouldn't have another disaster on his hands. Especially one that prevented Jolene's brilliant musicianship from becoming one every music lover should experience.

"It has to be. We hired you to push the talent, get them recorded, and out onto the airwaves. After that, you can start with a new act and so on. J&M will be proof why other acts should come to Eco instead of a huge record company. It's a loss on their time to get their sound out."

Maybe this could work. A quick release would mean less time with Jolene and less time for what happened last night to come out in the open. Any lingering desires would cease the constant thrumming through his veins when he thought about her beautiful body aching to be called debased names and begging to orgasm.

It took all he had to stop the shimmy of his ass in the booth to ease the lusty discomfort threatening to make him hard. Jolene had been right: Getting it out of their systems was good. With an accelerated plan staring at him in calendar form, he felt every muscle disengage from the ball of tension.

He clicked the laptop closed. "Do they know? Marcus and Jo?"

"That's what you're for." The metal of the fork scraped her teeth.

"It won't be easy. We need to be careful not to affect the quality."

She nodded in excitement and wiped her mouth with a syrup-stained napkin. "Agreed. Whatever you need to do. I trust you." She raised a hand and held it across the table. "High five. Seal the deal."

He slowly raised his hand and slapped it. "I prefer a handshake."

"Says the man in a suit." She giggled and went back to her breakfast.

The man in the suit and the guy who achieved great things because he kept his feelings in a lockbox. The proverbial mask slipped onto his face and he attempted to block the memory of Jo from his mind.

FOURTEEN

"WHAT ARE YOU DOING, JO?" MARCUS SHOVED THE LAST BITE OF the burger into his mouth as Zane walked inside to use the bathroom.

Jolene shifted her feet from under her and let them fall to the cement patio. They were tucked in the corner table on the courtyard outside the Eco Recordz studio.

She tapped on her phone screen, and it lit up the time. Nearly one in the afternoon and Gavin remained MIA. Had she been too hard on him? To be considered a mere a lapse of judgment shocked her heart and tore it to bits. Had he not felt what she did? And why did she care? After he tried being cozy and warm she'd made him stop, turning him back into the harsh closed-in man she desired.

"Zane needed me. It's not the worst thing."

"You know he's not good for you."

"He's fine."

"I thought you told him you didn't want anything."

She didn't think she did. It woke up too many silhouettes of her prior self. But in some fucked up way, when he texted, it filled the rejection.

"I did. But he needs me. And it feels good to be needed."

"*I* need you. How about that? And so do your father and Elliot. This *album* needs you. There are people counting on you and bringing back that asshole isn't helping."

The plastic straw from her drink nearly shredded along the hole in the lid when she pushed it down. "I'm sick of people telling me what I need and who I am, okay? What do you have against Zane anyway? You don't even know him. He disappeared long before you and I met."

Flashes of the hospital room and the *beep, beep* of machines flooded back. The smell of lemon disinfectant still turned her stomach. The last day she saw Zane, he'd left her to "get better" and it killed her. Why not heal together? In her self-made hell she needed more than her father and a crowded room of past addicts at the rehab center to tell her to: *"Stand on your own two feet. Get a good support system. Be strong."* She needed love.

Marcus shifted his tongue around to clean his teeth or maybe to hold back the *but I know you.* "You're different around him, and you're already showing up late to work."

"I was a few minutes late. No big deal. You were still tuning the drum set. He came to find me—*like he promised*—and I owe it to him."

Zane was a lost man, and she found a purpose living with him. Anything he asked, she did. And everyone *assumed* her addiction and overdose had been caused by him.

Zane approached the table. His white one-pocket tee hung on him, and his pants practically fell off his hips if not for the belt holding them up. His gaunt eyes looked tired. "Jo, I gotta head out."

"Where you off to, Zane?" She glanced at Marcus who casually leaned back in his chair. He knew about Zane's drug-selling history from what she'd told him.

A flash of anger from Zane met Marcus' smirk. "To let you get back to work. Jo?"

He crooked a thumb behind him, with the other shoved in his pocket. As his body vibrated with disdain, Zane's tendons rippled into tight masses down his arms. The tattoo of Mary screamed as it flexed. He hated being tested. A normal reaction used to be gripping a guy's shirt and lifting him up, warning them to keep the questions to themselves. At least he was trying.

"Come on." She tilted her head and gave a *please don't do this* look to Marcus.

After they exited the courtyard through the vine-covered gate, Zane took her hand. "You sounded great today. Thank you for inviting me."

She laced her fingers with his. Slight warmth ran up her arm, but cooled before it hit her heart. "Sorry you're alone up here. How long are you staying?"

He shrugged. "Not sure. Thanks for the handout. Glad you kept the money I left."

"Thank you for telling me you needed it. I guess I was saving it for you." A small burst of warmth unfurled in her heart. She'd done something right. The money he'd left kept her afloat, and she used it sparingly, never wanting to take the gift for granted.

"I wanted *you* to have it. To keep you surviving until I came back."

His promise to find her jolted the dark areas she'd pushed away. "You never did that before, ya know?"

"What?"

"Made me feel needed. I mean, in *that* way. You are a proud man, Zane Pearce, who never asks for support."

He stopped when they reached the front and turned to her. "I'm learning. It took us being apart to understand how to change and give you what you need." His eyes pleaded. A ghostly gloom glazed over his harsh gaze. "Come home with me. Back to North Carolina or even better, our trailer. You can pick out the furniture, our bedding…" He squeezed her hands. "It's yours to decorate how you like."

She swallowed against the rising tide of guilt against his sweet desperation. "I can't. My life is here."

"But I need you."

I need you. I need you. I need you. The echoes were like Pavlov's bell to a starving dog. Her mouth moistened, yearning to kiss him and make him feel alive. A deep pang pierced her chest, chasing away the buzz of acceptance from moments ago.

"I can't give you what we had, Zane. Not yet. Not right now."

His top lip curled for a beat, and he rubbed a hand over his shaved head. "You think I put those scars on you, don't you?"

Her hand shot to her shoulder, covered by a long-sleeve sweater in the summer heat. "N-no. I did it."

"Then what's the problem?"

Her knees wobbled at the indignation in his voice. She cast her eyes to the cement as a trail of ants marched in line, falling into place and obeying their instincts. "Nothing, I—"

A ripple of electricity ran up her neck when the shuffling of feet alerted her. Before she turned, a magnificent undertow of lust heated her stomach and raced to her skin. She spun on her booted foot, and the sheer ferocity in Gavin's eyes threatened to swallow her whole. She dropped Zane's hand.

"Ready to work?" he barked. His gaze flicked over Zane's form.

Her eyes darted away. "Zane, this is my manager, Gavin Mayne. Gavin, this is my friend from North Carolina, Zane Pearce."

Zane whispered in her ear. "Friend? We're more than friends, Jo." He straightened. "So, you're the guy. Surprised someone let you back into the industry and around young girls too."

Gavin crossed his arms. His muscles tightened in his shiny gray suit, bulging under the jacket sleeves. "This isn't time for play. We're on a tight schedule. Say goodbye to your *friend*."

She moved away from Zane and stood straight, meeting

Gavin's gaze. Rage took over the guilt from moments ago. "Says the manager who blew off his responsibilities."

"It's cool, Jo. I'll call you later." He pecked her forehead and walked to the street. "And Gavin? Take care of my girl. She's gonna be a star. We can't have your reputation tarnishing that, now can we?" He turned and strolled down the sidewalk.

"Get inside."

She remained stock-still, shaking in her boots. Her heart pulled toward Zane strutting away, but her feet remained glued to the cement in front of the double door entrance to the studio. "Where've you been?"

"We'll discuss it later. Are you seeing him?"

"None of your concern."

He shoved his hands in his pockets as a few Eco employees exited the main doors to the street. Through clenched teeth and in a rumbling whisper, he said, "It is my concern. I'm your manager. There's no time for distraction."

"Is that it? Or are you jealous?" A powerful rush of defiance possessed her as she fed off the god in front of her. He was back. The demanding ball of fire and energy wafting from his stance penetrated her, pulling her in like a planet into a black hole of desire. She aimed to push and push, until maybe he'd react like he did the night before.

"This isn't the place for this conversation. There's business to tend to." He reached for the door and ushered her inside. When they reached the studio, Marcus came out.

"There you are, I was coming to get—" He looked at Gavin and narrowed his eyes. "What's up?"

"Our recording schedule has been moved up." Gavin grabbed the knob and pulled the door wider. "Let's talk."

They went inside and sat on the couch. "Moved up? How?" she asked.

"Your album and launch party are set for three weeks out. We need to push hard in order to make the accelerated schedule.

Recording will be finished by week's end, then Kyle will edit the tracks. In the meantime, marketing will kick off your branding."

Marcus put his hands up. "Whoa, I thought we had a month."

"Not anymore." Gavin looked at Jolene. Was he speeding up the process to get rid of her? Marcus would have a shit fit when he found out what had transpired. She faded into the leather couch and buried her face in her hands. "Corrine and the investors need you to jumpstart the business. And first things first, record your debut single."

"Which one?" Marcus asked.

" 'Mother'."

Jolene froze. Her mother's song? No way. She hadn't perfected it. It wasn't ready. If she recorded it before she's ready, her mother's spirit would leave her for good. She shot up. "Absolutely not."

"You don't call the shots, Jolene. I'm your manager."

She looked at her guitar sitting in the corner. It was the vessel to tell Lily's story. She had written the song only a few weeks ago but her heart had orchestrated it twenty years ago.

"It's not ready. It'll be forced."

"You're an artist now, and your muse can't afford to be picky," Gavin interjected.

A burning ball of fire sank into her gut and rolled around. "You don't have a say in this."

"I do, and this song will be completed today."

His coldness chilled her to the bone while her mother's memory kicked against her rib cage. She ambled to the guitar and stroked the smooth wood.

Marcus came up behind her. "You can do this. I'll be here."

She found his hazel eyes and immediately softened. "Okay."

"You can go for the day, Marcus. Less distraction."

"What?" He walked toward Gavin. "Can't you see she needs a little support?"

"She needs to be pushed, and having you here won't help."

The door creaked open and they spun to find Kyle walking in with a bounce in his step. "You guys ready?" He noted Gavin's expression and chuckled. "I guess so. Boss is here."

"You have the schedule, Kyle?" Gavin growled.

"Yes, sir." He shuffled into the recording area behind the glass and returned with his tablet. "We are on track. We finished the backup vocals and will start on their next duet. The photo shoot is scheduled for Thursday."

"Change of plans. Her single is being completed today and Marcus was leaving."

Kyle's expression dropped, and he looked at Gavin then to Jo and Marcus. "Let me set it up." He shuffled around the room, pulling out a single microphone and stool. He perched them in the center of the studio.

"Marcus…" Jo's chin quivered.

He hugged her and whispered, "Fuck this guy. Show him who you are."

"Jo, let's go!" Gavin boomed.

She glared over Marcus' shoulder as Gavin crossed his arms. A glimmer of the bossy man she yearned for shimmered in his blue eyes. A challenge. So be it.

"You're right. See you later?"

"I have a gig tonight, I'll be home late. Okay?"

She nodded, and Marcus kissed her forehead before leaving. She strutted to the mic stand, then sat and picked up her guitar and cranked the tuning pegs.

Kyle gritted his teeth behind a nervous smile. The small vinyl records printed on his shirt seemed to spin as he disappeared into the booth. Gavin remained perched like a god in front of her, testing her emotions. She threw him a smug look and nodded to Kyle behind the glass.

He gave her a three-two-one count silently with his nubby fingers and she started strumming. The strings bit into her sore fingertips, and pain flooded her soul.

She closed her eyes as she sang.

Whenever you were near,
With Tiny Dancer in my ear,
We were together...

Strum, strum.

She opened her eyes to meet Gavin's searing gaze, causing her to hit a wrong chord. *Fucker.*

"Start again," Kyle said kindly.

The immediate release into the zone typically came easily. She could focus on a particular part of the microphone and off she would go, but seeing Gavin's roiling angst had her in knots. Conflicting messages from his eyes to his body to the tone of his voice made her feel alone in a room with many, while trying to channel the purest love she'd ever known. *Mother.*

"Okay, sorry." She cleared her throat and sang the first line of lyrics.

"Again," Gavin gritted.

"I have been. All damn day." She adjusted the strap as it fell from her shoulder. Her fingers shook from his coldness. This was the Gavin people knew. The front he put up when he demanded things go his way.

Gavin shot Kyle a glare. "Play it back."

Kyle's hands flew across the deck and her voice came through the overhead speakers. She loathed listening to herself. The fleeting moment when it hit the audience's ears and burned into memory was enough for her, but not this song.

"Stop," Gavin called out. He flicked a wrist to the speaker imbedded in the corner of the room. "*That* is mediocre."

A shock of disappointment rippled through her, taking her to the dark place. She needed to push Gavin away on her own terms but the dissatisfaction in his voice muddled her into a pile of gritty sorrow and torrid fury, all because of the hot *mistake* they made last night.

"Sorry to have wasted your time and the company's money," she muttered.

His jaw noticeably tightened. Maybe she should refrain from poking the bear, but she refused to roll over.

"Again." He pointed to her guitar.

She reluctantly straightened her spine to play, not because he told her too, but to prove to him she was serious and would work. Hard.

She started again. Half a phrase in, and he waved his hands in the air. "This isn't working. Again." She bit the array of petulant responses back and started again only to hear, "Stop. Again."

"Jesus!" she yelled. "What's with you?"

"Me? You're the musician; act like it."

She unstrapped her guitar and slid it to the floor.

"Hey, Gavin. Maybe she needs a break." Kyle peeked around the booth door. His curly hair plopping over his forehead.

"Give us a minute, will ya?" From the corner of her eye she saw Kyle leave the room and click the door shut. Gavin's arms dropped, his voice softer than before. "Sit down."

"No." She crossed her arms.

"I need more, Jo."

"I'm giving you all I have on this." She flung her arm out wide and it slapped her thigh when it fell.

He pursed his lips and grunted, "It sounds as though your mother didn't die."

Tears instantly blurred her vision. "Fuck you."

"Do you want to make this album? Do you really want this? Because you're not giving me enough to make this count."

"Of course I want this!"

"Then show me how you feel about her being gone!" Every fiber of his control snapped in half. His body shook and his ruddy complexion brightened with each second. He appeared to be unraveling as quickly as she.

A single tear moved down her cheek. "That's none of your business."

"It is my business. *You* are my business."

"Only if your business is fucking the women you work with. I'm so stupid." She slung her purse over her chest.

His arms swiftly wrapped around her and the room spun. His barrel chest heaved along her back. Hot energy rippled through her flesh and seeped into her blood. The heat from his touch attempted to snuff out the clawing turbulence of anger inside her body.

"I know you didn't mean that." The twitch in his Adam's apple bounced along her nape.

"Let me go." She jerked to fight him off.

"Not until you tell me about your mother, Jo," he pushed.

"I am, Gavin! You're not listening. Everything in this song is her." She broke away and snatched her guitar to lay it in the opened case.

"Where the hell do you think you're going?"

"Why are you doing this?" She didn't appreciate him prying into her life since she became an apparent sexual blunder in his eyes. "Can we record this and move on?"

"You would be okay with laying a mediocre track on your debut album?"

Snapping the locks on the case, she gripped the handle. "The song is not mediocre. You said it could be my first single."

"I did, but I meant when you put some feeling behind it. Don't you see? That is music. That vulnerability grabs an audience." He sighed. "You showed it to me the other day."

Her eyes met his. "What do you know about that, huh? You're guarded and aloof to anything around you. You have no idea what it's like to lose someone." She stomped out of the studio.

On the cab ride to her apartment, Jolene picked up her phone and dialed her brother. He would know what to do.

"Hello?" A lady's voice came through the receiver. Jolene removed the device from her ear. *Home* displayed on the screen. "Hello?" the woman asked again.

"Ah, is this the Harrison residence?

"It is. Who's this?"

"Jolene Harrison."

"Oh! Jolene!" she squealed as if they'd known each other for ages. "Hold on, let me get Jim for you." She shuffled through the house and the television got louder. "It's Jolene."

"Hello?" her father's gruff voice clipped through the phone.

"Dad, who was that?"

"You know Cheryl Kline."

The Rolodex inside Jolene's brain flipped to the "K" section and pointedly stopped. Cheryl Kline, the sweet woman who owned the café in their small town. She'd given Jolene a shot at performing live in front of her patrons.

"Yep, Dad. I know her." She narrowed her eyes as traffic crawled slowly back to Manhattan. "Why is she answering *our* phone?"

"I assumed Elliot told you."

"Told me what?"

"Cheryl and I are..."

"Together?" She sucked in a breath. Elliot's suspicions were right. He'd moved on. It was as if her father couldn't wait for her to move out to allow his new girlfriend to move in. "As in living together? How long has this been going on?"

The screen door squeaked and clacked as her father went to the front porch for privacy. "Yes, living together and a year."

She straightened in the back seat of the cab. "A fucking year?"

"Jo, settle down. You don't need to get worked up."

"So tell me, Dad, did you keep me a secret from her because you were too ashamed to let her know your daughter was a junkie?"

Jim insisted on keeping family affairs private due to his clients and business associates. At the time she didn't mind because seeing the pitiful glances on the hometown residents made her skin crawl. It was best to keep her past locked away and let them assume what they wanted. *He protected you.*

"Jolene, watch yourself. I'm still your father even if you did pick up and move."

She laughed. "Don't act like this wasn't a blessing in disguise. I mean, she's *living* there and I haven't even been gone a month."

"I'm really happy," he admitted. "I need you to understand: This didn't happen overnight. Cheryl has been there for me and things progressed. This wasn't an easy decision. I'll never forget your mother as long as I live. She's not being replaced."

"Been there for you. Like I wasn't. I was the constant reminder of Mom, and the reason I went off the deep end was because she wasn't there, right? Well, shout it from the rooftop, Dad. I'm out of your life."

"Jolene," he stressed enunciating the *N* in her name. "Settle down."

The cab crawled a few blocks from her apartment. She shuffled cash from her purse and tossed it to the cab driver. "I'm getting out here." Flinging the door open and snatching her guitar, she propped the phone between her ear and shoulder. A walk would do her good.

"Don't tell me to settle down. This is *shit*. This day is shit. I can't wrap my mind around why in the world you chose to keep me separated from your life and why you wouldn't tell me about Cheryl. Maybe I could've been a part of it with you..." She trailed off as tears bubbled from her eyes. "Fuck! I'm doing this all for you!"

Shouts and laughter from passing New York tourists

drowned out the silence from the phone.

"You shouldn't. You should be—"

"Should what? Do this for *me*? Well, here's news for you. I can't. All of this is hinged on you and Elliot and for fucking Mom who I can't even touch or see or remember loving." She crumbled onto a stoop, her head landing in her free hand.

"I can't either," he admitted.

"Wh-what?" Her breath hitched as she rubbed the falling snot on her sleeve.

"I can't remember either. I remember the love, but with each passing year, the feeling gets farther away."

"Really?" Hearing her father confess any emotions came as a shock. With Elliot being too young to remember Lily, Jolene assumed she was the only one fighting to keep her mother's soul alive.

"Yes," he sighed. "I've learned hanging on so tight only set my life back. Cheryl stepped in and something new started to grow. I should've told you."

She focused on a crack in the sidewalk to avoid pitiful glances from passing tourists.

"Jo? Are you okay?" His fatherly voice suddenly sounded different. The condescending tone he normally had and the defensive nature she used to protect herself flooded onto the street with her tears.

"No. But yes."

"Where's Marcus?" he asked.

"At a gig. I'm on my way to the apartment now."

"I'm going to call him when we hang up."

"Don't. I'm fine."

He exhaled into the receiver. An air of trust she could hear and feel.

"I should go, pumpkin."

He hadn't called her that since…since before she left home at seventeen.

127

"Okay. I'll call you later."

"And, Jolene?"

"Yeah, Dad?"

"I love you."

She sobbed gut-wrenching tears as her chest spasmed uncontrollably. It meant so much to hear him say those rarely used words. This was living, like Marcus said. The pain and forgiveness tore down her walls, and she felt something good could come out of it.

"I love you, too. I want to make you proud."

"I know." He paused. "And you are. I'm scared and worried, but I know you're doing your best."

"Will you and Elliot come to my release party?" she asked, hopeful.

"I wouldn't miss it, pumpkin. Be safe up there, and don't get into trouble. Promise me you'll check in with Marcus."

"I will."

They hung up. She stared at her phone, stroking the glass with her thumb to clear the wetness that had touched it. Years of resentment had passed and for what? The whole time they both harbored the same fears and captured the same love. She pushed a sobering sigh from her lungs.

Ping!

A text came through from Gavin.

G: Don't ever leave in the middle of a session. Where are you?

"Fuck you." She shoved the phone in her purse and grabbed her guitar. He wouldn't take this moment away. In the sticky heat, she strolled the few blocks to her apartment.

Once up five flights, she crashed onto her bed, sleep taking her away.

FIFTEEN

ANGER ALWAYS REVOLVED AROUND GAVIN'S ROULETTE WHEEL OF emotions. When there was fear, anger showed up. When he needed control over a situation, there it stood. A long relationship with the emotion ensured anger became automatic.

As a child, his brother and father made him feel small and insignificant. He was a loser of any game they pushed him into. When he'd go for love, they taunted him, saying he was weak. When scared, especially after losing his mother's love, they kicked him when he was down. That was the start of bottling up emotions. If, even for a second, that bottle of forgotten feelings fizzed open from the inertia of someone clambering to get in, he'd coat it with a thick layer of fury. Normally, it provided satisfaction, but not today.

He stood at his kitchen island and read his angry text.

G: Don't ever leave in the middle of a session. Where are you?

It spoke volumes about the way he pushed blame on Jolene. After a long day and a hot shower, it sank in that his outburst was his problem, and not only did his "job" run out the door, his desires went with it. Two opposite ideals never to be merged, and still he attempted to blur lines when his dick did the talking and all logic flew out the window.

What a fucking asshole. Jolene didn't deserve the wrath he resorted to when things got too close.

He wouldn't be surprised if she ran to Corrine, told her everything and got him fired. He fucking deserved it. Maybe he wanted that. Maybe if she did, he could have her. Unless that Zane character was something. Maybe she wanted him. Why else would he show up, barking about "taking care of his girl?"

Zane didn't sit well with him. He didn't like his threats, and why was Gavin drawn to protect her? So what, they fucked and got it out of the way, but their night together made him feel he had the right to shield her from danger. But his friend, anger, had other ideas. *She could never love you, and you aren't capable of it.*

The front door creaked open, and Ethan came around the corner with a shit-eating grin on his face.

"Please, come in," Gavin said with a grunt.

"I thought you skipped town on me." He laughed.

"Not yet. The house closes in two weeks; you're still stuck with me."

"There are worse things."

Ethan opened a bottle of beer from the fridge and leaned back on the counter. He was dressed to impress in a navy suit. The track lighting glinted off his gold watch as he sipped his beer.

"You look like shit. Work getting the best of you?"

Gavin waved him off. "You'll have your money sooner than expected."

"Really holding up on that promise." He could see the anticipation on Ethan's face.

"We have till the end of the week to finish the album." At least he hoped.

He whistled. "Didn't think it was possible."

It still might not be. "There is no other option."

"You know I don't want the money."

He shrugged and toggled through his phone, hoping Jolene would fucking answer him.

G: Where are you? Answer me. We have a schedule to meet.

"How about an, 'Are you okay? I'm sorry for being a dick'," a voice chirped in his brain.

"It really says a lot about how much you're trying and think it's what I want."

Gavin looked up from his phone as the light faded to dark. "It's not enough."

Ethan tilted his head and released a deep breath through his nose. He understood Gavin's determination when his mind was made up. "So what's next?"

Thankful for the reprieve from the sappy bromance, he answered, "We fine tune the album and it should be set. I will know more details later."

"Cool. And what's *really* up? You sound exhausted."

"I'm fine. Can you do me a favor?"

"Depends." He took a swig of the long neck.

"The lieutenant from the Bronx, is he still a member of The Resort?"

"Yeeaahhh." He elongated the word suspiciously.

"Do you think he could look up a Zane Pearce for me? Tell him it's for your girlfriend."

"One, I don't have a girlfriend, and Brad will see right through that shit. And two, not until you tell me what's going on."

He paced to the windows overlooking his back yard. His

brain fought over telling the truth or letting it go. But he owed Ethan honesty after everything he'd done to him.

"It's Jolene. This guy's lurking around, and I get a weird feeling." He tried to make his tone even and distant. "Tell Brad it's for a friend, he'll understand."

"Are you checking up on her? What do you care anyway?"

"I'm her employer."

"Does she know you're doing this?"

"No, and I need to keep it between us. He's a threat, and I want to rule anything out." He went for a beer and stopped. *Something stronger.* He shooed Ethan from his stance to reach for a rocks glass and bourbon. The wax seal cracked, and he poured the smooth liquid into the glass.

"What did you do?" A slight chuckle came out.

Gavin took a swig hoping to burn his admission to dust, but when he slammed the glass down, his chest tightened and the truth rose up out of his esophagus and pushed out of his mouth. "I slept with her."

"Oh. Fuuuck."

He poured another and threw it back. "I don't know what happened. It's over though. No more."

"What's over? Her or your job?"

"Her. The job? Who knows? Can you do this for me?" He sat on the stool next to the island to catch himself from falling into the defeat of honesty.

"Gavin, you need to ask her yourself. Remember how secrets got in the way last time?"

"This is different. I'm protecting her, not me."

The sound of a sigh escaped Ethan. "What do you hope to find?"

"I don't know. Ask Brad to run a background check, past phone numbers, addresses, and track his phone and next of kin."

"Geez, Gav. What's this guy into?"

He twirled the glass hoping the remaining drops of liquid would show him. "Not sure."

"You could *ask* her."

He rubbed his face, flashbacks of hiding truths and digging for information flew through his mind. Ethan was right, but he refused to alarm Jolene. *Or lead her on.*

"I need to rule him out. Precaution."

"What did he do to her?"

Jolene's scars sickened him to think a human could cause that level of harm to her. Was it her, or did Zane do it? "Not important."

"Secrets, man. I'll tell, ya. But I can't expect you to change everything overnight. This is fucked up, but your head's in the right place."

"She's our way to helping me reestablish your business, and if something happens to her, this won't work." As he made the bland business statement, it felt as cheap as a knock-off brand of suits.

"Don't put this on me, and don't trick yourself into thinking she's a fake pawn in your grand plan to make my life better. I'm flattered..." He chuckled in his egotistical way. "...but this is more than I could've ever asked for."

"What is?" Gavin glared at his friend's know-it-all face. It never penetrated him in the past, but now he saw things he used to avoid.

"You're willing to clean up your mistakes, *and* you might be falling for this girl."

"I'm not..." he trailed off, seeing Jolene soft and pliable the evening before. Her smell and taste as he brought her to orgasm, sent a heat wave hotter than the July sun straight through him.

"Dude, you should see your face right now." He laughed.

Gavin grumbled. "Can you get me the damn information?"

"Nope. Sorry. Good or bad, she deserves to know you're prying into her life. I would know. The agency held a file of my entire life, and people pried all the time, judging me as to whether I was an acceptable child to adopt. And once they read about my"—he air quoted—"issues, it was over. No forever family for this guy." He crooked his thumbs to his chest, and Gavin's heart sank. While he had run far away from his family, Ethan wanted nothing more than to run toward one.

"This is different."

"Give her a chance to tell you. Remember your own file, Gavin? The one where you spent time in jail after the accident with Nicolette?"

He almost hurled his drink. "Please don't mention her."

Ethan put a hand on his shoulder. "You need to listen, man. For once. Your daughter died in an accident, and regretting what happened is natural, but you need to forgive yourself. And don't judge Jolene for something on paper like everyone did you. Digging into people's lives without consent is as bad as dominating someone under false pretenses."

He didn't want that, no dubious consent, or anything for that matter. Not like with his past boss, Shane. Virtue ate away his insides like acid or perhaps it was stripping the outer layer of rusted protection he wore.

"Not sure when you became all wise, but thanks."

"I've always been this way; you never listened."

He lifted his glass and swallowed the remaining contents. "Why are you here anyway?"

"Glad you asked." Ethan bent to the side perusing Gavin's attire. "I'm not sure basketball shorts and a tee shirt are appropriate for a Fourth of July party."

"What party?"

His face went deadpan. "The Silk Road is playing at Webster Hall. Swanky afterparty. Hot ladies. VIP lounge." He pulled two tickets from inside his jacket.

"No, thanks."

"Do you know what I had to do to get these? They sold out months ago."

The Silk Road was a heavy punk band on the rise, and Ethan claimed he'd discovered them years ago when he met the bass player at The Resort.

"Let me guess, Tanya had a hard time forgetting you the last time they came through?"

"Well, of course." Ethan smiled, and his uniquely placed dimple appeared along with a glint in his mismatched eyes. "She felt bad for the club going under and thought she'd make it up to me."

"It's on hiatus. It will be back."

"Yeah, well, this would make me feel better, especially after imparting my wisdom to you." He waved the tickets back and forth. "Besides, you're kinda my bitch now, and I need to take advantage of me calling the shots."

"Fuck you."

He shrugged. "All the ladies do."

Gavin touched his phone one more time. No answer from Jolene and sitting at home obsessing over her wouldn't change anything. "Twenty minutes."

Several hours and a migraine later, Gavin saddled up to the bar with Ethan.

"Well?" Ethan gnawed on his cocktail straw.

"Punk's not my thing." He waved down the bartender. "Two beers." She nodded and quickly pulled a few bottles from the cooler.

"Doesn't mean it wasn't great. Tanya can rock."

"Sure."

"Are we going to address the hotness that is Jolene?" He smiled wide.

"It's complicated." He swigged the beer left on the bar as the bartender rushed to the mob of thirsty concertgoers.

"You like this broad."

"She's not a broad, and yes, I like her. And...never mind." His jaw clamped shut. Admitting how Jolene tapped into his dominant side—the one he tried to keep locked tight—would only hurt matters more.

"Whoa. Hold on." He swiped his phone from his jacket pocket and held it up. "Can I get that on Snapchat?" His thumb tapped the screen. "Attention everyone. Gavin Mayne *likes* a woman."

Gavin slapped his hand away. "No. It's not like that. I care about her. Wait..."

Ethan's laughter cut through the crowd banter and ambient club music. "Cool, man." He tucked his phone away. "What's so complicated about that?"

"I went off on her because she couldn't get a song right. Now she's not responding to my texts, and I have no clue if she's going to ride out this contract."

"Let me see." He held out a hand and flicked his fingers toward him. Gavin's brows rose. "Your phone. Give it to me."

He reluctantly unlocked the device, and Ethan grabbed it, opening up the text chain with a few clicks. "Seriously? This is *not* how you get a girl to answer." The *tick, tick* of Ethan tapping the keyboard ratcheted his nerves like a bomb counting down to detonation. Then the bomb exploded with a *swoosh*. Gavin snatched his phone and read the sent text.

G: I like you. Please call me. I'm sorry.

"What the fuck!" It was out there in the universe, and now Gavin couldn't hide it. His fingers shook around the device. "Fuck you, Ethan."

He shrugged. "Admitting it is the first step."

"This is about my job. Your money."

"Fuck the money. This is about you following through with this. Stop playing the brooding Alpha card. It's old. I saw the way she looked at you at her show."

"Nothing happened then," he lied.

"*Ah*…but it did. I know you better than anyone, and she's interested."

Gavin's gut rolled over, and he rubbed his temples. He'd made a mistake. He'd hurt her, called her names and for what? A first place trophy engraved with: *Douchebag*.

"Man, are you okay?" He touched Gavin's shoulder and yelled for two shots to the passing bartender. "Is something else going on?"

"Mom's dying." Saying it out loud smacked him in the chest. Time worked against him to get the answers he'd secretly pined for over the years. Why did she let him go? Why didn't she call?

"Oh, shit. I'm sorry." They raised their shots.

"Such is life. All the way to her dying day, she never came to get me." He threw it back hoping the sting would calm the anxiety he held.

Ethan slammed the shot glass on the bar as a spunky girl bounced in between them.

"Hi!" she squealed, throwing her arms around Ethan. Gavin hitched to the side, nearly sliding off the stool.

"Hey, darling! Great show. Tanya, this is Gavin Mayne."

She spun around; her heavy-lidded, small eyes were smothered in blue glitter. Her sable bangs had been highlighted in red, white and blue with two long ponytails drifting over her front with colored tips to match. The romper she wore displayed a burning American flag with the anarchy symbol emblazoned in black ink over her chest. A somewhat punk Hester Prynne came to mind.

"Gavin Mayne?" Her eyebrows went up. "Are you…?"

"Yes, I'm *that* guy," he grunted. Would the fact that everyone knew of his scandal ever stop hurting?

"He's a talent director and manager," Ethan said trying to sway her from blurting out his past.

"Oh." She giggled holding her small hand to her mouth. "I thought you were someone else."

"Who?" Gavin asked.

She pointed to a door. "Some girl in the back mentioned you earlier. I assumed you were her boyfriend."

"Boyfriend?" Ethan coughed.

"Some hippy chick with long blonde hair. Can't remember her name."

"Jolene?" Gavin asked anxiously.

She put an arm around Ethan and he cinched her waist to pull her between his legs. "I think, so? She's pretty smashed, so it was hard to make out what she said."

"She's drunk?" Gavin shot to his feet.

"It *is* a party, and we put on a great show."

Before Gavin heard another word, he shuffled through the jungle of people to get to the door. What was she thinking? *You drove her off the wagon. Fuck.* Another woman caught in the shit storm that was him.

The bodyguard at the door halted him. "VIP only. Private party."

"I am VIP, move."

"Are you on the list?" He met Gavin, eye to eye.

"Yeah, I'm on the fucking list. Gavin Mayne." He wiped his mouth impatiently waiting for the guy to move or be moved.

"I suggest you cool off, man."

"Let me through!"

He tapped his clipboard. "Sorry. Not on here."

"You didn't even—"

"He's on the list," Ethan interrupted.

Tanya patted the bouncer on the cheek. "It's all good, Andre."

The bouncer clenched his jaw and opened the door. Tanya bounced through the opening, and Ethan snagged Gavin's arm. "Go easy on her."

He cut past the doorway and searched as incense and pot ransacked his nose. The low vibe of trance music beat in the background as the fog of vapor stuck to the ceiling.

Jolene's laugh caught his ear, and his eyes darted to the back of the room. She was nestled on a sofa with Zane. He whispered in her ear.

Red, red, red.

He marched over and swiped Zane's hand from her cheek. "Hands off, pal."

He peered up and sat back in sleazy confidence. "Look who's here."

Jolene followed his gaze and her eyes attempted to go wide, failing from obvious intoxication. "Oh hey. It's my manager."

Zane took a drag off his cigarette. "The one that said she was mediocre. You might be careful, Mayne. My girl is no ordinary musician."

"See. I'm awe—some." She hiccuped and a slow grin appeared on her face.

"Get up. We're leaving." He swooped under her arm.

"I'm not leaving with you," she said.

Zane stood, pushing her back into a seated position. "Watch it. I'll have the media all over your shit." He pushed two fingers into his chest.

Jolene stumbled to a stance. "See, Gavin. He apper...apper... gets me."

If the floor opened up and swallowed him whole, he might be happy. But his dark seeded friend, rage, spurred him on. "You shouldn't be drinking. Where the fuck is Marcus?" Gavin's eyes darted around the room, hoping to find him.

She shrugged. "Don't know."

"Jesus Christ." He bent to sling her over his shoulder, and she backed away.

Her red lip curled and her nose ring caught the light. "Fuck you." A whiff of two-dollar liquor invaded his nose.

"I would think twice about touching her. She's mine." Zane pushed forward and Gavin's hand wrapped around his thin white T-shirt.

"Sit the fuck down, asshole. She's my responsibility, and as I see it, you don't give two shits about her."

He puffed his cigarette and blew out a plume of smoke. "Says the manager who got her to this point." Gavin's eyes stung as he fought to keep them open.

"Fuck you, Mayne. I can get down. I used to *always* get down." She pushed him away from Zane. Not hard enough for it to be forced, but Gavin dropped his hand anyway.

"You're in recov—"

Her green eyes flared. "Fuck recovery! Overrated bullshit. It's easier when you give up. Why fight? All this…" Her arm flailed in a circle. "It's too hard. I'm not good enough for you, my family, all of it." She tugged Zane's arm and wobbled around Gavin's body. "Let's go."

His heart fell. He'd pushed her toward her lowest point all because he had a shitty day and wanted to pull out her saddest emotions to feel the song. He had to push her out of his life to save their careers and for what? To align their comparable aches so he could understand what it's like to lose a mother? To lose his job? To lose…her.

"Is that it then, Jo?" he barked back, as the VIP lounge quieted to whispers and prowling eyes.

"What?" She spun.

"Are you throwing it all away?"

She teetered on her booted foot, and Zane wrapped his bony arms around her waist. He glared while whispering in her ear. She nodded.

"What do you care?"

"Because I do." *I care about everything, about your music, your life, and your mystery.*

"I don't, at least not with you. I deserve more in a manager and a…whatever. Zane, take me out of here."

Gavin leapt forward, and Zane put his hands up. "I wouldn't if I were you."

"You're not seriously leaving with this guy?" he grunted glaring at her *friend.*

Her glassy eyes shifted to Zane. A glimmer of hope swept her gaze, the color of her eyes now a mossy concoction of yellows and blues. "He's not just some guy. I love him."

SIXTEEN

ALCOHOL SPREAD THROUGH JOLENE'S VEINS, TURNING HER emotions from a guilty haze into a pumping rage. Seeing Gavin heightened her emotional roller coaster into overdrive. From what she could make out through the alcohol-fueled dizziness, his savage eyes held worry. They'd always managed to cut through her, but the liquor coursing through her blood weakened her ability to make the right decision. The one where she should go to her apartment, sleep off her mistakes, and start a new day. Instead, she became the woman built to make men jealous.

And why? All because she was hurt? So she left with Zane who embraced the woman she'd always been. A place where she knew acceptance.

The cab rolled up in front of a dingy motel off the highway in New Jersey. Rusting rails lined the two story sea-green building along the pathways to each room. A place where people entered to get high or to fuck out their aggression with whoever would have them for the evening.

It both welcomed and terrified her as she stepped out of the cab. The sticky summer heat pursed her skin, and Zane scooped up her hand to press it against his lips.

"This is where you're staying?"

"All I can afford right now. Come on." He led her to the second floor.

Soiled and frayed vinyl blinds shaded the window next to the gray door labeled: *Room 218*. He pulled a key card from his pocket and inserted it into the slot. The light beeped and she froze as the liquor settled into the familiar headache of pre-sobriety.

"You coming, Jo?" He turned as he crossed the threshold and his eyes dipped slightly, the usual color smothered into dullness. She shuddered a breath as his look pulled her toward him.

Stale cigarettes and bad choices seized her senses, flinging her back in time. She placed her purse on the round table by the window. Newport butts spilled over the edges of an overstuffed ashtray. The burns and watermarks permanently marring the surface told a story of the lost souls who had battled their demons here.

"Go ahead and get comfortable. I'll be right back." He made his way to the bathroom. The lights tinged as he flicked the switch, prickling every nerve ending until the door clicked behind him.

The room housed double beds covered in blue polyester bedding. She brushed the stiff fabric. She was here to fuck, like the last time when she fucked Trip for Zane's plan to steal his stash and his money. She sat on the bed, and the worn out springs squealed their welcome. She put her head in her hands.

Go home! You don't need him or anyone.

Her heart knocked a sad beat. She didn't have a home. Staying with Marcus meant a brief stint of comfort until she could fix the missing piece in her heart. Maybe Zane could fill that spot again.

"Pull yourself together. Be the girl you remember. The one without fear." She pushed a quick breath from her lungs and stood, pacing the room.

A faint sniff followed by a cough came from the bathroom. The instant the noise reached her ears, all of her nerve endings awakened. *Was Zane doing drugs? What did he have?* The pang of need shot through her veins. Her stomach cramped as her hands shook. She found herself stepping toward the bathroom before her mind could catch up with reality. The door opened, and she jumped back with a yelp.

He smiled. "You okay?"

She balled her fists at her sides. "Maybe this is a bad idea. I shouldn't be here."

"Sweetheart..." His pupils were pinpoints. "You came because I need you."

"I know. And I want to be here for you."

"Then show me."

The hollow and desperate command slithered along pebbled flesh. Where Gavin's commands had been in control and desirable, Zane's weren't. *It can't be; Zane desires you too.*

Her gaze wandered down to the patriotic shirt she wore. All she wanted was to feel whole again and not by some sober version she tried to fake or battle daily; she wanted to give in for a change.

He moved the hair behind her back and kissed her neck. She closed her eyes to feel his familiar touch. It always took her away from the fear and disappointment she held in her heart from her family and herself.

"Oh my God, Jo." He sucked in a breath. "You smell amazing. I've missed you."

Her head fell against his chest and tears welled in her eyes. *Let it go. Give in to him and you'll be fine.*

"Show me how much," she whispered. The acquiescence scratched past her throat as she forced it out. She wrapped her arms around his middle and pressed her cheek against his pectorals. Drugstore cologne of the spicy sea enveloped her in the bubble of security she remembered.

He bent forward and took her mouth, hard and possessively. They'd always shared an animalistic need to fuck with no tenderness or apologies. She opened and his tongue, laced with the taste of Mountain Dew and cigarettes, invaded her mouth as he backed her against the bed. Her legs touched the edge and she whimpered. His fierce control did nothing, not in the way Gavin's had. Instead of hot warmth flooding her system, a coiled gut and frigid sadness triumphed.

She took each button of her high-waisted jean shorts and pushed it through each hole before the alcohol completely simmered away. The fabric dropped to her ankles, and she started on his. His cock flexed against her hands as she fumbled with his belt.

"Agh…" he rumbled when her hand made contact with his flesh. "Fuck…Jolene."

Something in his growl spurred her on. His lips covered hers as she played with the long column of heat and velvet under his pants. His hands wrapped around her long hair and pulled. Aggression and pain tipped the scales of her worried mind, and she aligned with her past. To be missed meant the world. To know he'd thought about her meant their love never died.

"Then show me. Fuck me like you used to."

He stripped her blouse and tugged her bra down to her waist. His face flinched for a minute at her scars. A sudden vulgar shame arose in her chest as he turned away from the sight of her outward ugliness. *Rejection.* For the first time, she felt naked and stripped.

In the dim yellow light of the table lamps her scars leapt from her skin. Pitted and ridged forms spread from her shoulder to her wrist, running over her chest. Her nipple, or what was left, was now tattooed with a flower symbolizing hope and salvation. Even in an attempt at hiding shame, she failed. No matter how beautiful the flowers, they only masked the repulsive reminder of her choices and the ugliness on the inside.

She went to lift her bra to cover her breasts and stopped. The need to know he still desired her ran her heart. She unclasped the back and let the garment fall to the floor.

She went to touch his elbow, and he jerked away as he shuffled through a duffel on the bed.

"Face down, then," she said, answering his silent command. Heat traveled up her spine and spread to her face. The abhorrence from his sudden repulsion ran so deep she wondered if she'd live through another rejection.

She slid off her panties and crawled onto the bed on all fours. A small burst of confidence flickered as she looked back at the stony edge sliding over his face. The chocolate brown glint in his eyes pierced her. The obsession still remained. As anxiety and sadness shook her limbs, she sank her face into the mattress and cried.

She didn't know how much time had passed...after. She lay there in the darkened room until Zane passed out. His shallow, vibrating snores racked the space, ticking up her nerves as her mind relived the evening over and over.

"I never got over not needing to wear a condom with you. Still a dirty whore who enjoys fucking men."

Her body had betrayed her, giving herself over to Zane. She hadn't been turned on, rather, disgraced as the evening washed her in regret. She had no way out except to live the fantasy of Gavin inside her. His voice calling her filthy beautiful names. His touch revving her body to the highest cliff while his own groaned for orgasm. It took her out of the room and into a safe place to push through until an unplanned orgasm swept over her. Zane had been pleased, assuming her pleasure was his. He showered her with expletives: *slut, stupid cunt, dirty whore*, and all she could do was weep. It wasn't Gavin.

Would she ever stop being her former self?

Would she ever be loved…even by her own heart?

She forced herself out of bed. Gathering her clothes, she crawled on the brown carpet as if wandering through a swamp of desolation. She pulled herself across the doorway to the bathroom, and the cool linoleum floor welcomed her. She clicked the door in time to empty the remnants of alcohol and bad life choices into the porcelain god in repentance. Her body ached as she sat. She noticed Zane's fingertips had left purple bruises on her hips.

"How could you?" she whispered as tears racked her body. In an attempt to be quiet, she snapped a towel from the rack and covered her face until the crying jag ceased.

She tossed the towel and curled her fingers along the basin of the sink to hoist her body up. She went to turn on the water and found a perfectly laid out line of powder on the sink's edge. She knew what it was since Zane only sold her favorite. *Heroin.*

Zane *was* using. The tears resurfaced as her heart plummeted to the floor. She caused him to use by refusing to go with him. She'd taken down the sole man who loved her.

A rolled up one hundred dollar bill invited her to partake. It would be easier than dealing with the pain. The "womb" called to her to join him in the grave she'd dug for them both. Every cell awakened in her flesh and her stomach cramped. A familiar rush of drug fever permeated her body. The anticipation of floating on a warm cloud to quiet the screeching demons spurred her on. She picked up the dirty bill and tightened the coil of paper.

It would be easy. Take the road she knew.

She glanced at her reflection and sobbed.

Time to give up, Jolene.

SEVENTEEN

BANG, BANG, BANG.

Gavin's fist throbbed as the door swung open.

"Do you have any idea what time it is?" A man in his boxers stood there with a scowl.

"Sorry, wrong room."

The door slammed in his face, and he turned toward the faint line of dawn peeking over the horizon. Where was she?

Up and down the exit off the highway, Gavin searched each motel within ten miles. Several doors opened with no Zane and no Jolene. This was the last stop, the last door, and the last shot at helping her.

His feet slithered down the stairs as his palm scraped the rusty guardrail. His body sank in a pool of exhaustion and anger when he reached the bottom. He gripped his hair when he sat. "Fuck...*FUCK!*"

Why would she leave with that asshole? Were they still together? And how could she say she loved him? And why the fuck should he care? She stated loud and clear she couldn't be around him. This was his fault. He'd pushed too hard to connect with her about losing a mother while attempting to quash his insane compulsion to have her. "Fucking asshole…"

"G-Gavin?"

The wilted voice shook him and his head shot up. Jolene leaned limply against the railing. Her face was smeared with mascara under her eyes, the streaks meeting a quivering lip. Her hair was in disarray, wild and beautiful, even given her state. He stepped forward and she cringed. He stopped himself from scooping her up and taking her away from this hellhole.

"You're here," he said in disbelief.

A watery sheen overtook her cloudy and bloodshot eyes. "W-why are you…?"

"To make sure you're all right. Are you?" She stepped down, and his arms caught her as her body gave out.

Sobs flowed from her exhausted body. The smell of her hair strengthened his muscles and mind to care for her, no matter what.

"I'm not. I'll never be all right."

"Let's get you home."

"No!" She tried to push away. "I can't, not like this. Marcus… he'll…"

"Okay…okay, Jo. I got you."

Her chilled arms encircled his neck, and he carried her through the soupy air and across the dark pavement to his SUV. Her cries were a call for help passed the girl who fought to protect her emotions.

His chest bloomed with fire and desire. He beeped his fob and clicked the door to open, then gently sat her in the passenger seat and buckled her in. Her hand touched his.

"Gavin? I'm scared. I'm so scared." Tears streamed rivulets from her cheeks, dropping to her shirt.

"I know. Me too."

He held her, and for the first time, he had no plan in place for anything other than getting her to safety. There were no weapons to use on the dark specters shrouding her soul. Powerlessness sucked him into a drowning pool of fear with no way out.

But he needed to try.

He set Jolene on her feet in his bathroom. "Sit," he said softly, pointing to the toilet. She did, looking misplaced. He opened the glass doors of his shower and turned on the hot water. As the billowing steam filled the room, he crouched in front of her.

"Jolene, look at me." She did, rather, through him. "I don't know what happened tonight or today, for that matter. I'm so sorry I drove you to him."

"You didn't. I did it to myself." She forced a half smile. "I'm good at that, you know? Whoring is my number one talent."

He gritted his teeth. "You're not a—"

"You said it yourself, Gavin. Fuck, I *told* you to say it."

Heat radiated out from his chest. How could he call her those names and allow his preferred kink to overcome his control? All because lust broke him, flooding his mind with Dominance, and once again, he used it the wrong way.

"It was a mistake." He collapsed against the wall. "That night was a mistake; I should have controlled myself."

"*Mistakes* are the consolation prize for all of the sluts in the world."

He shot up on his knees and cupped her face where defiance replaced her earlier sadness. "Listen to me. *You* are not a mistake. How I treated you was. You deserve someone who will honor you, Jolene. Treat you like the queen you are, and all I did was take my own pile of issues and toss it on you."

"What do you know? Huh? I'm the girl who sleeps with men for a warm bed or a high. I'm the one who, to this day, can't stand to leave the house without a spare change of clothes because I don't know where I'll end up or choose to escape to."

Spit sputtered from her mouth as tears caught her throat in a panic.

"I only know the Jolene who came to New York to become a musician and have a better life. So much so, she stalked the guy she wanted to lead her there." He forced a half-smile, but her face remained tortured.

The shower spouted water like a rainforest, and the steam created a sauna he swore would suffocate them from their truths.

"And what about you, Gavin? Who's the guy I know? Are you my manager right now or the guy who fucked me over the moon and held me as I crashed to Earth? Because I need to understand. I need..." She swallowed. "I need to know so I can move on."

He stood and leaned on the basin. How was she so honest all the time? He brought her here to allow her to sleep off the night and they could go back to...what?

"I don't know," he whispered.

"C-can you give me a minute? I need to..." She plucked her wrinkled shirt then glanced to the shower. "Forget this night ever happened."

The urge to scoop her up and wash away the evening almost became too much. He went for the door. "Jolene, I'm sorry. I'm just the guy who's fucked up without a plan."

"And I'm the girl without the will to move forward."

EIGHTEEN

The mirror squeaked as Jolene wiped the fogged glass with her palm. A lost girl stared back at her—sunken eyes, pale skin, and contrition. It was one thing to be addicted to drugs, but her reflection pushed her to hide from reality. She breathed out a thankful sigh she didn't snort the welcome wagon on Zane's bathroom sink. A disastrous night with a bright spot. *At least one step in the right direction.*

The medicine cabinet squealed its lesson on intoxication as she opened it, reminding her why she strived for sobriety. She swiped the mouthwash and took a few pain relievers from a bottle on the shelf. After spitting her regrets down the drain, she swallowed the pills and stepped out of the bathroom through Gavin's walk-in closet and toward his room. Embarrassment still thrummed in her veins, but the faint smell of fabric softener and cologne relaxed her.

As she stepped into his room, a man's T-shirt and shorts had been laid out on the bed. *His clothes.* She couldn't help her smile. She looked down at her body covered in a tank top, sweater wrap, and yoga pants. A girl always on the run, with a change of clothes in her bag, suddenly uncomfortable. She pulled her phone out to check for any messages from Marcus and saw one from Gavin. She clicked it open.

G: I like you. Please call me. I'm sorry.

A wave of confusion and heat knocked the wind from her lungs.

"Oh, hey…" Gavin said.

She dropped her hands to find him in gray jersey shorts and matching V-neck shirt. The fabric caressed all the right places. His chest and a hint of a washboard abs flirted with the fabric. A tribal tattoo peeked past the sleeve on his right arm and flexed as he set down water and a bottle of medicine next to the night-stand. *Good, Lord.*

"I see you already had clothes."

She bit her lip, watching him move about the room in bare feet, toned legs, and an ass the Roman gods would ache for. "I tend to travel with emergency items."

"There's some aspirin and water for you." He gathered his clothing items and put them away.

"I took some." She crooked her thumb toward the bathroom.

"Figured you would have. You seem to poke your nose into things."

She smiled. Even though his muscles flexed, the aura he gave off let her know it was okay.

"What's this?" She held out the device, and he read the text.

He turned toward the bed and folded down the pillowy duvet. "Ethan sent it."

"Why?"

"Because he pokes his nose into things too. I've surrounded myself with people like that." A small smile crept on his wide lips.

"So you didn't mean it?" She tossed the phone on top of her purse.

He peered over his shoulder. The dawn light filtered through the shaded windows and illuminated him in a halo of light. "Maybe I did," he mumbled. "You've had a long night and need rest."

She twisted her hands together. "You want me to sleep in your bed?"

"I have a guest room but this is more comfortable. And feel free to sleep as long as you need, the office is closed for the holiday. We can hit it hard on Thursday."

"You're giving the talent the day off?" she called before he closed the door.

"Whatever you need, Jo." His blue eyes revealed a dichotomy of emotions. They were the gateway to his soul, holding the truth behind the strong man he conveyed.

"Stay," she whispered. "Just until I fall asleep."

"Jo, I can't."

"Please? I normally don't ask anyone for help, but the thought of being alone scares me."

In a rush of words she admitted her deepest fear. Loneliness. But the repetitive lessons from rehab countered her thoughts: *If you think you'll use again, tell a friend you can trust.* Was he a friend? It didn't matter. She trusted him.

The knob rattled under his slipping hand. He approached the bed and sat at its foot opposite her. So close, yet a world away.

"How do you feel?" he asked.

"Like a punk band playing the same ratchet song on repeat in my head."

His lips fell serious. "You could have put yourself in real danger tonight."

"I know," she sighed, trying to figure out when things went south. She'd crawled into bed after talking with her dad, then woke up needing someone. The next thing she knew, she was half a bottle deep with a man she should've never called.

"What were you thinking?"

"I wasn't. That was the point. Besides, it's not my D-O-C anyway." His eyebrows furrowed in obvious confusion. "Drug of choice. The real shit is heroin." She waited for the look of disgust, but nothing. Not even a single flinch, only a caring sigh.

"Needles?"

She stripped her sweater and moved the pillow flat from the headboard, then curled into a ball, pulling the soft blanket over her. His presence swaddled her in comfort more than the blanket provided. She slipped a hand under the pillow and grasped the sheets to relieve the building tension.

"No. They give me the heebies. When my mom got sick, seeing her in the chemo facilities did me over." She laughed, fixating on the pale green stitching of the duvet. "Doesn't make it any better."

"You need to be careful. Alcohol or otherwise can—"

"Lead me back to it. I've heard it all. Every NA meeting, my family, Marcus."

"Why did this happen? I can't help thinking I'm to blame after what I said to you yesterday."

The hard edges of his expression blurred into kind lines. He was here, vulnerable without the walls guarding him.

"You're not to blame. Why were you at the motel, anyway?"

"That's my job. I'm your manager."

"Thanks but I don't need my manager cleaning up my vomit and micro managing everything I do."

He leaned over, placed a hand on her leg, and tucked her closer.

"You fucking scared me. All I need is another woman on the road to hell with my ticket. I saw what my actions did before, and I needed to make sure you were okay."

"You did a bang-up job. I'm safe." The defensive attitude took the reins knowing she should stop resorting to such lengths. The guy did find her and gave her a place to stay.

He squeezed her calf and a moment of desire zipped up her

leg. "We need to talk about yesterday. I can't have you shutting down on me."

She sat up and pointed to her chest. "Me? You're the one shutting down all the time. What the hell was that?"

She half expected him to give her an excuse, but he didn't. "It was a lot of things. Work, your boyfriend, and when you started singing, I lost my shit. I know how important 'Mother' is to you, and I wanted to know how it felt to lose a mother, the anguish and pain you went through and the powerlessness to stop it."

Her gut rolled over, threatening to spew the contents of her drinking binge. "Zane is not my boyfriend."

"You said you loved him."

"I did once, but I don't anymore."

"Why? Did he hurt you?"

She rested her head against the distressed headboard with a thump. "No. Not in the way you might think. I hurt myself. And I don't want to be that girl anymore."

"What girl?"

She snorted. "The whore."

The word circled the room like a three-ton weight looking for a place to fall. If Gavin had ever seen her differently than other men, that moment was gone. Or so she thought.

He scooted up the bed and leaned against the headboard, crossed his ankles, and clasped his hands. The energy pulsating off his body matched her heartbeat in a *thump, thump* of fear and shame.

"You're not a whore. I'm sorry I ever said that to you."

"But I wanted you to. That's the fucked up part. When Zane said it to me..." She looked up. "I fucked him, Gavin. I let him touch me, because I needed to feel something again. And it wasn't the same as when you called me those names. With you I felt... I'm sorry."

The sound of his knuckles cracking broke her. "If he ever touches you again, I'll kill him."

The disgruntled intensity of his body became the antithesis of his environment. His body unfurled and he lay down next to her. She scooted under the blankets to face him. His blue eyes met hers, which made her want to let go of the hopelessness attached to her.

"I know what you must think."

"You have no idea what I think, Jo. Fuck, I'm not sure what I think anymore. You've turned any plan upside down, and lately, I'm trying to keep up. But what I do know is Zane will never touch you again."

He tucked himself next to her, exuding what felt like a steely protectiveness and vulnerability. With caring in his eyes, she knew he'd be there for her. It was the spark she'd missed with other men.

"You slept with him," he finally whispered as if he needed to process things.

"I did." She lifted her eyes, and he didn't speak. "You and I— we made a mistake and aren't together."

"No, we're not," he said, cupping her hand. The warmth of his touch froze her in place. "And for the record, what happened tonight doesn't change the fact I'm here for you."

"As my manager?"

"I don't know. Maybe more." His fingers shook as he laced them with hers.

She retreated her hand, gripping the seam under the pillow to work up the nerve to grab him and kiss him senseless.

The desire for sex ran her body and her mind. It had become a means to an end in the past. The zap in Gavin's touch meant more, and she couldn't put him through what he was suggesting. Moreover, she was damned sure, after sleep and a clear head, she'd run again.

"Why did you make me sing that song?" A classic diversion helped her to deflect her heart.

"It's twofold. Corrine pushed up the launch, and I saw it as a way to push you away because I couldn't work with you and not *want* you."

"You still want me?"

"Yes," he breathed.

"And the second?"

"I miss her. My mom." Tears glistened in his eyes. "I've missed her for sixteen years, and I'm not sure what to do with it. I didn't think I would ever feel anything."

Her hand snaked out from under her pillow and touched his shoulder. "Where's this coming from?"

"My brother called while you were in the shower. It's not good. A few days, tops."

She remembered when her father told her, *"It's time Jo-Jo. Are you ready, pumpkin?"* He'd placed her on the bed dressed in a yellow tutu until she was brave enough to snuggle in her mother's nook. She'd always smelled of lilies, which matched her name, but on that day, the room reeked of death and broken hearts.

"You'll always feel something. She's your mother. I still feel mine even though she slips farther away every day. Why don't you and your mother speak?"

"She chose my father's way of living over me."

This man was alone. No wonder he'd kept everyone at bay. He was a survivor, like her, guessing his way at life.

"You need to talk to her. The hurt never goes away but saying goodbye will ease it."

"She never tried contacting me, and I assumed she finally saw what he saw in me."

"What?"

"I was nothing to them. Now I feel officially lost." His smile rang with heartbreak. "At least before, I had this *thing* to attach to. The false dominance at the club, my job, and going through the motions compensated for my emptiness. Now I have no fucking clue what I'm doing. It's like I have nothing and everything to lose at the same time."

"Purgatory."

Their eyes met, and the quick understanding passing between them was paramount in its weight. "And every decision I make comes with questions on motives. Right. Wrong. Unsure. Why am I telling you all this? I'm supposed to make you feel confident about laying your life's work in my hands when I have no fucking clue."

Her breath caught as she touched his cheek. The stubble scratched her palm as it fell to take his hand. Electricity charged through her body, pushing the disquiet aside.

"Maybe we'll find ourselves together."

"The blind leading the blind?"

She smiled. "Yeah, 'cause Lord knows I've been searching for a long time. Together it doesn't seem so scary."

"It's fucking frightening."

"Why?" Her heart beat a mile a minute as his thumb stroked back and forth over her hand. He was devastating when relaxed and present. Had another woman ever seen him this way?

"Because of what I want to do to you."

"Tell me, please?"

He rolled onto his back and stared at the ceiling. "You saw the video, right?"

A flush of desire awakened parts that surprised her given her state of mind.

"I did."

"Then you know what I'm capable of. You saw a piece of it when we fucked."

"Did you love her? Your boss? You never answered me before."

"I thought I did," he admitted, and her heart sank. "But, now? I'm not sure if I know the meaning of the word."

She sucked in air to bypass the surfacing misaligned jealousy. "What do you mean?"

"I can't give you what you want. I'll hurt you if we do this together."

"Together? Are you...? Wait, isn't that the point with dominance?" Her face flushed red, imagining him wielding a paddle with desire in his eyes. She would jump in with both feet to get it.

"It isn't always about pain. It's about control. Giving pleasure and receiving it in return. And you know what my lack of true respect for the craft did to Shane. It ruined her career and everything I'd ever worked for."

"The dominance didn't, the false control did. Listen..." She took his hand and he tried to pull away. "You are what you are, Gavin. That will never change, but what can is the reason behind it."

"What do you mean? I'm a monster."

"Then so am I."

"That's ridiculous." He flew out of bed and paced the room.

"Is it?" She sat up. "I stalked you, letting my obsession take me to an unhealthy place, and now I've had a taste and can't let go. I'm a fucked up masochist. My history proves it. The drugs, addiction, and being with Zane hurt me. But wanting you to hurt me is different. I'm not seeking the emotional pain. I want the physical. I know the outcome. Because—"

"Maybe it will help you heal." He leaned against his dresser, dipping his head below his tight shoulders.

His words hit her like a key finding its lock. She gripped her ball chain necklace and contemplated the *Music Heals* inscription. Maybe the music brought her this far, and fate brought her and Gavin together to heal completely.

"It's fucked up I know, but..."

"It's not. It's a *need*, an unexplainable desire deep inside somewhere. I feel it all the time and have never captured it. At The Resort, I'd search for subs without limits, or minimal ones. The more they welcomed the pain, I'd think: *Okay, she'll help me heal.* Then nothing. With Shane, it became about the challenge. It spurred my need to take her down, but she provided a connection I'd never had. And I *still* put her through shit." He faced her. "Don't you get it? I'm messed up, and there's nothing I can do about it."

"I get it more than you know."

Gavin sat on the bed and folded himself in half to hide his shame by threading his fingers into the roots of his hair. He was fighting what he thought were demons, when she saw it as beauty.

She shuffled out of bed and stood between his thighs. "Tell me what you want, Gavin."

She saw the answer in his gaze and in the way he flexed his fists at his sides. "I want to stay away from you. I want to hurt you. I want to care for you, but…"

He assumed he'd do more damage, but for the first time, she believed his sadism would heal her. Something about it sang to her soul, and she trusted him to allow her to let go of responsibility as he took her to the edge and back.

"There's too much at stake."

Panic and doubt laced his eyes. She'd led him down reluctant territory so she took his cues to lead him the rest of the way.

"I don't care about the stakes." The timid, careful dance they'd swayed to in his room over the last moments made her want to capture his dark desires.

"Touch me," she begged.

NINETEEN

GAVIN GRIPPED THE BED'S EDGE, FEELING HIS RESOLVE NOT TO TAKE her by the hips as she kissed him. He'd waited days to feel it again. Agony twisted his mind, telling him to stay away, but he couldn't. His brow twitched as the wetness of her tongue rimmed his mouth, causing his lips to shake.

Living off fumes from no sleep, he was delirious with the truth of wanting to command her, spank her, and bring her to orgasm. A sadist finding a masochist was like finding the Garden of Eden. She gave him free rein to feast on the forbidden apple in hopes it would cure him of the hell he'd lived in for thirty-three years. But there was no way he'd take advantage.

His hand slid up her sides and to her cheeks, gently pushing her away. Driving into a wall at sixty miles an hour would have been better than the brutal torture tugging his libido.

He may have thought he loved Shane, but it never felt like this. He'd fought to control every aspect of that relationship until he suffocated it. With Jolene, control evaporated. She stood over him as his flesh bled out his sorry life for her to see. Maybe life had to die in order to come alive.

His chest heaved. The emerald-green sparkle in her eyes pushed him forward.

"Tell me why you want to feel physical pain."

She rubbed her shoulder. "It's the purest human emotion. All of us feel it without choice. To feel the pain of the deepest scars—especially the ones you can't see—lets you know you're alive. I find myself chasing pain to feel the pleasure. Maybe that's why all my songs are about painful experiences and not happy ones."

He would gladly help her chase the suffering to find ultimate pleasure and to release her demons, but Jolene was raw. And he wasn't sure if he could give it to her. Dominance had always been a mask of protection, and it scared him to the bone to offer it a different way. The *right* way.

His finger traced her mangled skin, swirling around two circular indentations. "Is that all you want?

"What do you mean?"

His fingers continued to follow the deep pathways of her scars to her wrist. All the hurt and past travelled to the one thing he searched. He opened her palm and traced her love line.

"After the other night, I wanted to care for you, but you shut down. Then I retreated because I assumed you only saw me as the man in the video."

Her fingers curled around his ministrations on her palm. "The sweetness surprised me. I'd never had that before."

"So you didn't want that part of me?"

"I-I don't know."

"Jolene, I think I need more now. I'm done with the old me. And…" His voice faded as his forehead fell against her breasts. His arms curled around her waist. Never had he admitted his needs to a woman. He'd collected their needs, their desires, and acted on them. Subs were only privy to what he wanted, not to what he *needed*.

Her soft body trembled. "Okay."

"What?" His head shot up.

"I want you, Gavin." She placed his hand on her heart. "In here, no matter what it looks like. Because, if I leave, I'll never find whatever this is again. And for the first time, I don't want to run away."

Acceptance. The unknown hormone coursing through his body had never been tapped into before. She wanted him *for him.* Not for his successes, not for his looks, not for his ability at consensual violence. She wanted it all, even his failures and mistakes. He wanted to ride the wave, but not yet.

"Jolene, we should get some rest."

She followed his gaze to her scars and backed away. "This must disgust you too."

He snatched her hand. "What? No. Did Zane say that to you?"

"Yes."

"Look at me. You're beautiful." She rolled her eyes and he pinched her chin. "I don't care what happened with Zane, tonight or before, because you will always get the sweet and the sting from me. And you will know it comes from a place of caring."

"Could you show me now?"

"Is that what you want?" All his hot buttons rebooted.

"Yes, please."

"Are you sure? This will change everything."

"Promise?"

All the blood in his body left his face and went south. He made no attempt to hide the erection in his shorts. He wanted to be inside her despite her having been with another man. Tonight, he'd baptize her into pleasure so strong she would feel the euphoria vibrate through her body and his. Together.

He took off his shirt and watched as her gaze seemed to trace the outline of his muscles and desire percolated in the green depths.

"Gavin...I..."

"Do you trust me?"

"I do, very much."

He kissed her. The way their tongues danced in anticipation rippled down his spine. "Let me show you how to chase the high. Undress and bend over the bed," he said, rising.

Jolene's eyes widened. Curiosity created a ring of yellow sunbursts around her expanding pupils. If he could bottle up the emotions resonating from her pliable body, he would never feel alone again. His erection agreed and expanded before her eyes when she shifted her gaze to his shorts.

The whisper of fabric slipping from her curvy hips sparked the flame. Her yoga pants plummeted to the floor and she kicked out of them. Her hands went to her pink and yellow striped briefs.

"Leave them," he ordered. She was fucking sexy.

She looked down at the cotton underwear. "But…"

"I said, leave them. Turn around."

She obeyed, swallowing hard and dropping her hands to her sides. Her round ass filled the cotton, creating shadows and planes to her crease. *Jesus.*

"The shirt too."

He tugged the hem and she gripped his hands. "No. Not yet. Just hurt me…here." She placed his palm on her ass. His hand smoothed the area, then gripped. "Yes. That's good."

His gaze burned over her shoulder line to where scars disappeared below the tank top. This wasn't the time to push her. "Bend over for me."

She folded over the edge of the bed. He tapped her feet to widen her stance and pushed her shoulders flush with the mattress, her fine ass on display. He slid a finger under the hem of her underwear along her soft flesh, from hip to thigh.

"Tell me what you want, Jo."

"I want you to show me pain." She sniffled.

"Are you sure?" Could he do this? He retracted his hand. She wasn't ready. He wasn't ready.

"Yes," she whispered. "Please." Her legs went taut, raising her ass an inch. He closed his eyes to channel the inner Dom. The one who could read a woman's body language. The one who deciphered trepidation from fear. He gazed at her crotch area, weeping through the cotton fibers. The scent of her arousal permeated the air.

"I've hardly touched you and you're wet." She groaned as his finger petted the area. "Jolene…"

"I can't help it. It's you…"

He continued to toy with her sex over the soft cotton. "When did you get wet?"

"Spank me, please."

"Not until you answer."

"When you came into the room." She squeaked as he moved the fabric over her crotch to the side.

"Always watching, aren't you?" Rubbing his knuckles along her seam, he clamped them around her swollen clit.

"Shit…" Her knees wobbled. "Yes…you are gorgeous to watch."

That made him smile as his dick expanded beyond comfort. "Just like you."

He knelt and licked her pussy. *Sweet fucking Christ.* Her scent was captured by the coarse hairs along her sex. She didn't shave, and for some fucking reason, he loved it. This was Jolene. Her free spirit and her unashamed nonconformity. With a deep inhale of her pussy scent, all his doubts disappeared. "Your cunt is…" He rolled his tongue around her soaked, swollen flesh. "Beautiful, Jolene."

She squirmed. "Gavin…if you don't…"

He gripped her hips and pushed his tongue into her sex, feasting on her arousal. She tasted so good he didn't want to stop. He bit her clit.

"Stop! Stop!"

He backed away from his haze-clouded lust. Her muscles

clenched and glistening arousal seeped from her opening. "What's wrong?"

"I don't want to come...not yet. *Jesus*. I...need a minute."

He'd never stopped a scene because a sub didn't want to come. He owned their bodies and called the shots. But Jolene wasn't a sub...and he was no fucking Dominant.

"Did you think this would all be pain?"

"Yes...no...I don't know."

Pulling her panties to her knees, he said, "Not all BDSM is about pain, Jolene. It's about the pleasure most of all. You're new at this, and you need to be ready."

A pause.

He kissed the small of her back, and she sniffled into the duvet.

"Are you with me?"

"Yes. I'm..."

"What?"

"Falling."

He swallowed. Fuck if he wasn't too. "Let me take care of you. All you have to say is stop. Do you understand?"

"Yes. I understand. Thank you."

His heart melted at her appreciation. "I will start out slow." He pinched and massaged her right cheek. She backed into his hand. *There's my girl.*

"Fuck, you're amazing like this. So willing, so brave." His hand met flesh. The loud crack was like a long-lost song, unheard for ages, sending a nostalgic sting from his hand to his brain.

"Harder," she grunted.

There it was. Her consent. The message he needed in order to gauge her tolerance. His handprint left a beet-red mark. He hadn't been kind. But she asked for more, and his hand twitched to send her there.

"Five. Count with me." The commands came confident and natural, and he found himself again on the same plane as before, only now it was cultivated with promise. He swatted once and rubbed the spot until the warmth spread.

"One," she gritted.

He hissed as he fingered her slit. "You like this. Your cunt is so fucking wet."

She sputtered through a slight sob. "Yes. Please."

Slap, slap.

"Two, three." She turned her face to the side, tears shimmering in the dawn light creeping in the windows. Another slap met a fresh area of skin on the back of her thigh and she screamed. The pain sent her weeping into the bedspread.

"Are you with me, Jolene?"

She gasped for air. "Four. Yes. Keep going." His hand met her ass one more time as she grunted the number. "More. I need more."

"Jo…" The welts on her thighs and ass rose to the surface. His palm stung, conveying a need to use more than his hand.

She looked back seeing the concerned look on his face. "I need it."

Need it. Rising desire and his instinct for dominance crept up his spine and down his arm. He got it. She needed pain as much as he needed to inflict it. A fucked up normalcy he'd captured a long time ago, but now, it took a new shape.

What was at the end of this scene? Another session? Another sub? A flashing moment of top space roared through his blood. Would he fly high only to crash into an emptiness ten times the size when this ended?

He brushed the stray hairs from her eyes, overflowing with tears as a sputter expelled from her mouth, "Please…"

His heart swelled and a blooming rightness filled his gut. This would never compare to before.

"You don't need to count."

His hand met flesh so many times he deliriously tasted sweet pleasure in place of bitterness. Each time she sobbed, he could swear the emptiness escaped her body. With each strike to her raw ass, the shackles on his heart broke to be replaced with something else. Something he'd never felt.

"Are you with me?" No answer. Her body remained limp until he rubbed her clit, spreading her juices along her opening. "Jo, answer me."

She shook her head and squeezed her eyes closed as tears continued to bubble outward. The last of her inner struggles seemed to splash on the bed to their death. "Yes...I'm here."

"I need you, baby. I...god damn. You're so beautiful."

"Yes, please. Take it."

He tore his clothing off, opened the bedside drawer, and snagged a condom. His hand shook as he ripped the foil and sheathed his cock.

"Rough or slow?" The strain in his voice matched his throbbing need to be inside her.

"Rough. Give me you."

He slammed home to the hilt. She gasped as his force knocked the wind from her lungs.

"Fuck..." he groaned.

His fingers wound tightly over her already bruised hips. Marks surely left by Zane. And as he impaled her over and over, he promised himself his marks would be the only ones she'd keep. Their moans, grunts, and words of acceptance spilled in unison from their lips. His hand crept up her back and tangled in her hair, and he yanked her head up. She tried to yelp but appeared too exhausted and in the moment. She was flying high, and he soared in the clouds with her. His thrusts met tender raw flesh, igniting his core. His balls lurched up, and a lightning storm raced down his spine.

"Going...to..." she muttered.

"Yes, come for me." He slapped her ass, and she tipped.

She uttered his name, over and over, as tears rolled down her cheeks. Her muscles clamped around his invasion as he continued to find his release.

"Fuck..." His body went rigid and muscles spasmed around his cock as he finished. Shock waves rippled up his back and through his neck. His mind buzzed as he opened his mouth and moaned, "Sweet Jolene."

Finally his sweaty body collapsed over her. His hips flexed once more, his cock hitting the delectable spot inside her. She was amazing, beautiful, and haunting. A small spark of completeness rolled through his veins.

She sobbed through her orgasm, and he felt her core constrict and relax as he remained inside her. He shifted to the side and pulled her against his chest. She continued crying as he held her and soothed her with murmurs while trailing his fingers over her back. And suddenly he didn't feel weighted down. A deeper emotion burst through his chest. What was it? Happiness? Comfort? No, it was more.

"Gavin..."

"Yes. I'm here."

"Thank you..."

He smoothed her hair behind her shoulder, and she looked at him through dewy lashes. "You okay?"

She laughed out loud. A pleasant and wonderful sound. He chuckled with her, taken by the moment. "Obviously a ridiculous question."

His head sank back into the mattress, and they lay there listening to each other's breathing. It was nice.

"Maybe doing this together isn't a bad idea."

"Did you just make a joke?" She rolled off him, and he sat up to remove the condom. He tied it and tossed it in the wastebasket.

"You're rubbing off on me." He lay on top of her, swaddling her in a blanket of compassion. He didn't want to let her go. She nuzzled against his chest and fingered the tattooed name.

"Who's Nicolette?" she asked.

"My daughter." The muscles of his back tensed.

"Is she the one in the picture?"

He kissed her. Long and deep. He didn't want the moment to fade. "Is that what you were snooping for? Information?"

"Not initially."

"Yes, that was her." He kissed her lips to distract from any further questions about Nicolette.

"Was?" The question was blurted out between kisses.

His head fell to her shoulder. The moment of bliss sealed up. "You've been pulling everything out of me in the last twenty-four hours."

"It's okay, you don't have to talk about it."

"No, I need to." He shifted onto his back. "She died. A long time ago. She was seven and I was driving the car."

"Oh, shit. I'm so sorry for what I said yesterday. I didn't know."

Her prior words slashed his insides. *"You don't know what it's like to lose someone."*

"You didn't know."

"How did it...?"

"It was an accident. At least that's what people tell me. Her mother and I were arguing and I took a turn too sharp. She died on impact."

The brevity of his words hit like a rehearsed explanation. Her expression flitted between empathy, compassion, even a hint of sorrow, but thankfully, no pity. She opened her mouth.

"What?" he asked.

"Nothing. I'm just sorry."

His fingers slid through her hair, and she rubbed against his palm like a kitten. Docile and trusting.

"I'm sorry too, Jo. For everything. I want you to be the best musician you've ever dreamed you could be, and I shouldn't have pushed so hard."

"It's fine." Her hand smoothed along his chest and abdomen. With her touch creeping to his cock, the tightness of desire lurched in his stomach. "Thank you for being here. Thank you for finding me."

He wrapped her in his protection. No one would ever touch her again. No one would ever hurt her. Not even himself.

"Thank you for finding *me*," he whispered.

In more ways than one, you found me, Jolene.

"Let's get you to bed."

TWENTY

A phone rang the tune of "Comfortably Numb" somewhere in the room. Jolene blinked as the sun pierced the slats of the blinds. Gavin's body was slung over her like a hot blanket. A balmy tranquility surged from her insides to her skin's surface. This was the sweetness he'd offered, the calm after the rising sting of pain. And she allowed it to permeate her mind as the phone droned on.

She would never escape to be numb again. She would escape to *feel*...with him.

"Tell them to go away," he murmured against her neck as his hand and leg tugged her closer.

A smile broke on her face. *Comfort.* "It's Marcus. I should get it."

"Be quick. I want you right here the rest of the day." He let go, and everything they'd experienced slipped away as the chilled air bit her half naked body.

She gathered the ball of underwear from the floor and pulled them up. "I won't object." She snagged the phone from her purse. "Marcus? Hey."

Gavin sat up with a lazy smirk on his wide lips. Dark and

dangerous with a soft side. Her toes curled against the hardwood.

"Where the hell are you, Jo?"

"Are you okay?" A heightening awareness straightened her spine.

"No, I'm not fucking okay. You need to get here, now. The door to our apartment was beaten in and our shit is everywhere.

"What?"

"It's not good."

"I'll be there soon." She hung up the phone and stared at the screen.

"Everything all right?"

"No." She rubbed the last of sexy time and sleep from her eyes trying to keep her panic to a minimum. "He's upset. Something happened at the apartment." She slung her purse over her head and dashed to snatch her pants. "I gotta go. What time is it?"

The post-coital haze stripped completely from his face. "What is it, Jo?"

"Someone broke in. It's not a big deal. This is New York. Happens all the time, right?" Her bottom lip started to quiver.

"Fuck..." He went for the dresser and yanked out a pair of jeans.

"No. You stay. I'll call you later."

He turned. "I'm going, Jolene."

"You can't. This is...shit, I don't know what this is. We can't have anyone finding out."

"Do you trust Marcus?"

Her head jerked back. "Well, yes..."

"I'm going."

When Jolene reached the top of the landing, she found the apartment door opened and the locks shredded to pieces. Murmurs escaped into the hallway as she turned the corner.

"We'll do a preliminary inspection of the damages and let you know what we find. There's been a string of robberies in the area and this might be connected," a man in uniform said to Marcus.

"Thanks, officer." Marcus ran a hand through his hair and his eyes met Jolene's as she stepped across the threshold.

"What happened?" she asked, scanning the area. Her heart lurched to her throat as she took three steps and knelt. She picked up the splintered pieces of her prized guitar. "Who did this?"

"I don't know." He hugged her. "We'll find out."

"But…it's gone. Lily's gone." The guitar held the last connection she had to her mother. The floorboards squeaked.

"What's he doing here?" Marcus spat.

She gripped his T-shirt. "He's helping."

He narrowed his eyes. "Is this who you were with?"

"We're going to need a statement, Ms. Harrison," the cop interrupted.

She looked at the man in uniform with a buzz cut and back to Marcus. Gavin moved about the room, inspecting the area.

"Okay, sir," she acknowledged. "Marcus. Please."

"Jesus fucking Christ, Jo." He left her in a pile of rubble of her past and fragments of a future she wasn't sure she could reach. *Purgatory.* She collected the remains of her guitar, gripping the pieces tightly to her chest.

"Okay, I'm ready." The officer led her to the kitchen to discuss the last few days and weeks. Who'd entered and left the apartment. Her whereabouts. Anything that could help them. She gave a statement while Marcus and Gavin talked.

"Tell me about Zane Pearce," the officer said, scribbling the statement in his notepad.

"What?" Her eyes met his.

"Your roommate said he's been coming around."

"He hasn't been here. He doesn't know where I live." She set the wood on the counter and covered her face. "He's my ex. I…"

Guilt for pushing Zane into drug use, combined with the fear of what he was capable of, tightened her throat. "I don't know where he is," she lied.

He took out a card from his pocket. "Call me if you think of anything else."

She took it. "Sure." Her gaze found Marcus again, and the men were having a heated, but low, conversation. She marched over to them.

"Are you taking advantage, Mayne?"

She stepped between them. "Marcus."

"This doesn't bode well for you. I knew we couldn't trust you."

"It's not what you think, Marcus." Her hands locked onto his chest.

Gavin straightened to show his height over him.

"You're a no-good piece of shit who preys on the women he works with." Spit flew from his mouth as he lurched forward.

"Marcus! Listen to me. Please. Let's talk, okay?" She motioned to her room. "Alone." Marcus didn't move even though she tugged him toward the back of the apartment. "Come. On."

Finally, he backed down and followed her. She looked back at Gavin who was whipping his phone to his ear. She stepped over broken glass from a frame knocked from the wall and entered her room. She slapped her hand over her mouth. Overturned drawers and a flipped mattress littered the area.

"Oh my God." A sick feeling overcame her as she knelt to pick up Floyd from the floor. The cactus' pot was broken, its soft center exposed to air, like her heart. "Marcus, is your room touched?"

"I don't know. I didn't—"

"Go look."

He disappeared as she took in the destruction. The faint smell of convenience store cologne moved through the area. She held her head. How could she be so stupid? Of course he'd find her.

Marcus returned. "It's fine. Nothing moved."

The lump in her chest shifted to her stomach, and she made a beeline for the closet. The rustling of her duffel filled her ears as she frantically scoured the bag. It was empty. Her money and plan B to flee New York if she needed to, gone. The girl, always prepared for a getaway, was now lost in a large city with no way out.

Marcus crouched next to her. "What the hell is going on? You look like you've seen a ghost, and that asshole out there isn't helping the situation."

She hugged her knees to her chest, the pressure inside her body too much to take. The panic bells in her head rang like a five-alarm fire. It was *him*. She swallowed back the fear that Zane would stop at nothing to have her.

"I need to tell you something. Please don't get mad."

"A little late for that."

"It...was...him."

"Him who?"

"Zane. He did this. I'm sorry. You were right about him."

His eyebrows shot up and his hands curled into fists. "How do you know?"

"I saw him last night, and we went back to his motel and..."

Marcus rolled his lips. "What the fuck, Jo. Why?"

"I needed someone. He was available, and I ran to what made me feel wanted. And now look what I did." She flicked her hand toward the empty bag.

He peeled the latch open. "What was in here?"

"My back-up. Zane's money. And with my guitar smashed, he's making sure I go with him, Marcus." The blocks fell into place, one by one. Zane needed her like an addict needing a drug. And she was the object of his obsession, his addiction.

Her memory floated back to the day she tried to leave him. She'd packed her things and he took them and burned them on the lawn, leaving her with nothing but a few clothes in the house. He'd said it was her fault for making him crazy. That was his game. Tear her down, push the blame, and the guilt to fix him became her motivation to stay. She tried to do everything right. Did whatever he asked. She quit trusting her own beliefs and believed what he'd said.

"You're co-dependent, Jolene. And he was preying on that side of you," her therapist once said.

But she couldn't comprehend it, and now, with time away and seeing the destruction head on, the veil had been removed. He took the money to send a warning, knowing an escape plan was imperative in her way of thinking. He'd taken all she had to make sure she wouldn't make it out of the final leg of hell without him.

"Were you planning on leaving town? What is it with you?"

She cringed. "I always have a getaway planned in case things go sour. Things like this don't happen to people like me." She gestured to the apartment as if to capture all the good things she'd worked for. Her sobriety, this apartment, her dreams.

He wrapped an arm around her. "You stopped running away a long time ago and started walking toward your fears."

"I used to pack a bag, no matter where I went. Extra clothes, money, anything I would need to survive." She wiped her tears. "I never told you how bad things got sometimes."

"That's not going to happen anymore. You're safe with me."

"I can't stay here. He knows where I am."

"We'll figure it out."

"Yes, today…" The floorboards in the hall creaked under each of Gavin's footsteps.

Marcus turned to her again. "What are you two doing?"

"I am so good at ruining a good thing."

"Did our manager touch you?" Marcus went to get up and she placed a hand on his knee.

"Stop. I asked for it. Like I always do."

His eyebrows shot up. "It doesn't mean he *should*. We have to tell Corrine."

"No way! We need him, Marcus."

"Stop playing with fire, Jo. He's a predator. You know he does this."

"And so do I. I'm a predator as much as he may seem to be." The fire to protect their secret burned in her chest.

"I don't ever want to hear you compare yourself to him."

"Then don't judge him. He saved me last night. Found me at Zane's fleabag motel and took me to his place."

He pushed his tear ducts with his fingers. "You haven't done this…in a long time. It worries me. Are we moving too fast?"

"Maybe it's not a bad thing. Gavin's a good guy."

"There's that look." He blushed in the way only a friend with past benefits could.

"We are attracted to one another. That's it, Marcus."

"And you think this is a good idea, given he has a history with this shit?"

"With one person for all we know. And she was his boss, not some twenty-something intern. That doesn't give him a long history book of deceit."

"I went along with accepting Gavin as our manager for you, against my better judgment."

"We all have history and should find out the truth. You took a chance on me, right?" She flipped her hair to the side. Her mind drifted to the morning and a hot shiver went south. *Man.* "Besides, he's been nothing but a gentleman with me. It felt good for a change." She smiled, feeling the burn on her ass as she rocked from side to side.

"Oh, for Christ's sake. I don't need to know what he's treating you like… Never mind." Flustered would be the word to describe her friend right now.

She rolled her eyes. "You act like an older brother sometimes."

"Siblings don't sleep together."

"Slept. Past tense."

He stood and held out his hand to pull her to her feet.

"Sorry to interrupt." They found Gavin in the doorway. "We should go."

Just like a manager, keeping them on task. He flipped the phone round and round in his hand.

"We need to clean this place up," Marcus clipped.

"It's taken care of. I have a crew coming over in an hour to get your apartment in order, including a new door. Marcus, you are more than welcome to stay with us at my place for now."

His thoughtfulness touched her, and suddenly, he went from long distant god to attainable mortal.

Marcus shoved his hands in his pockets and looked at Jolene. "*Us.* Are you two living together now?"

"She can't stay here anymore," Gavin said bluntly.

"Fine. I'll come along. But it's to make sure you know your boundaries. She's not someone to toy with."

Jolene snatched his arm. "Marcus, it's only for a little while until we figure things out."

Gavin didn't move as they sized each other up.

Marcus sighed. "Thanks." He stuck out his hand.

Gavin nodded and shook. "Jo, you ready?"

"Can you two give me a minute? I need to grab a few things."

Marcus glared at Gavin as he left. Gavin stepped closer and grabbed her hand. The feeling of warmth shot up her arm.

"Nothing will happen to you. Not on my watch."

"Which watch? The King of Kink or the manager?" She smiled.

"All of them." He tugged her closer.

"All of them?"

"There's still more *time* to discover, Jolene."

His wide lips caressed hers, and she floated, moving to her tiptoes. The rubble of her world fell away as his arms wrapped her up in his embrace. He was hers right now. And she would follow wherever it took her without the shadows of lost time haunting her. She'd make sure of it.

TWENTY-ONE

Jolene watched her reflection in the bathroom mirror as she flipped her hair. A claw foot tub surrounded by a white shower curtain reflected behind her. Due to the budget of the shoot, the hairdresser doubled as a makeup artist, making her face soft and natural with her hair wavy along her back. She felt like herself. A person she'd ignored for years. She smiled as her cheeks pinked, and she placed the wide rimmed fedora hat on her head. "You are worth it."

The door creaked when she yanked it open to what would be the bedroom of the Victorian style home, smack dab in the middle of Brooklyn. A perfect location for their photo shoot.

Marcus stood on a riser surrounded by floor length mirrors. The designer of their clothing, Ardyce Jones, buttoned the collar of Marcus' flannel shirt. He smiled and laughed. It was the laugh he used when he was interested in someone.

Ardyce's neatly twined dreads flowed down her back. Smooth mocha skin covered an angular jaw, and her brown eyes shifted to Jolene. A feeling of tranquility swept over her.

"Girl. That dress was made for you." She appeared to float

across the room with ease and grace. Her mystical eyes held the wonders of the world, scanning Jolene's cream boho dress.

Jolene tugged at the hem. "Seems a little short."

"It's made to show off those fabulous legs." Her sight drifted to her worn combat ankle boots. "It's perfect. Come up here and let me see."

"I'll see you out there, Jo," Marcus said leaving the room.

" 'Kay." She stepped up on the circular riser and gazed in the mirror. Ardyce cinched and tugged in the appropriate places, the garment flowing over her form. Jolene felt beautiful for the first time.

"Yep. Perfect fit. I knew it would be." Ardyce snatched a clipboard and wrote something.

"Thanks for hiding my scars." Jolene smoothed her hands along her shoulder and flicked out the bell sleeve.

"Whatever the talent requests, I can handle. What happened?"

Jolene glanced at the hashtag mess of skin peeking from the scooped collar. "A roadmap to present life and the future."

"Sorry for prying. Occupational hazard. I love digging into my clients' history. It helps me express who they are."

"It's okay. Have you been designing long?"

"Five years. This is my first big break, and I have Eco Recordz to thank for going out on a limb on a nobody." She set the clipboard down.

"Congratulations. It's ours too."

Ardyce's wide white smile gleamed. "They're good for that. Being a start-up and all."

"What do you mean?"

"They tend to look out for us small business folk. I'm doing this for free, and your album cover will get the word out on my designs."

Jolene ran her fingers through the delicate fabric of the dress. "I hope the music does it justice."

"I'm sure it will." Ardyce paused. "What's your partner's deal?"

Jolene could decipher the female question. "You like him?"

She shrugged. "He's sweet and, damn girl, totally handsome. Not sure how you keep it platonic." She waved a hand in front of Jolene's body.

"We weren't always…" Jolene bit her lip.

"Oh, crap. I'm sorry."

"No. It's good. We're better as friends. I think you should totally ask him out."

A manicured brow rose and she half smiled. "Really?"

Jolene laughed. "Oh my God, yes. He's interested."

"And you don't care?"

"Not one bit." Someone knocked on the door, and Jolene yelled, "Come in."

It creaked open, and Gavin stood in his tailored slacks, a green button down shirt, and a smile that awakened her insides in a rush of heat.

"Hey…" Jolene said.

"Almost ready?" She couldn't miss the way his blue eyes undressed her.

"Ah…" Ardyce mumbled. "I get it. Thanks for the tip." She looked at Gavin. "She's all yours."

In the few minutes Jolene had known Ardyce, the female acceptance card had been exchanged. She gathered her items and left them alone, the door clicking behind her.

Gavin leaned against the wall, every inch of her skin mapped out by his savagely gorgeous eyes. She sighed and shifted the hat. "Are you just gonna stand there?"

"If I come near you, I'll fuck you, and hair and make-up will have to start over." He looked at his watch. "And we're cutting it close."

She spun on her combat booted heel. "Ah, manager time today. Always on schedule."

He pushed off the wall and sat in the chair by the window and crossed an ankle over the opposite knee. He leaned back like a predator assessing his prey. Her knees weakened. "Fifteen minutes is all we could spare, and it wouldn't be enough."

Wasn't that the truth. After arriving back at his place yesterday, he didn't let her out of his sight till morning.

"Are you always this sexy?"

The tremor of his muted laugh could have been as loud as a foghorn to her senses. "Not sure what you mean."

She stepped off the dressing stage and tapped his foot. It dropped to the floor, and she straddled him. "You walk in here looking like you do and dropping remarks about sex."

"If that makes me sexy then, yes." He pulled her in for a kiss. "You smell like me."

"I always need you near."

"God, what"—his lips danced down her neck—"did I do to deserve you?" Her heart skipped a million beats.

"Nothing in particular. Just being you and everything I'd fantasized about was enough." She set a long kiss on his warm lips.

He growled, lowered the scoop neck collar of her dress, and pulled out her right breast. "You look beautiful." His hot mouth covered her nipple, and she writhed against his growing length beneath his slacks.

"We have t-time," she stuttered. Her body went from ready to conquer the world to submission kitten. He bit down on her nipple and she muffled a yelp.

"So needy. You wanna know what this…" He rolled her nipple between his teeth. The sting shot to her pussy and the wetness pooled in the area. "…makes me want to do?"

"Tell me."

"Use nipple clamps during the shoot. No one would know. Our secret."

"That would be difficult."

She heard a pop as he pulled away. "You don't know me well enough."

She swallowed and gazed into the stormy blue of his irises. Should she ruin the moment or let it pass?

"What?" he asked with a peck to her lips.

"Clamps, plural."

"Yes. They come in pairs."

"Right. Two." She leaned in. "I only have one."

He hadn't seen her completely topless. After Zane's response at the motel she couldn't bear to see Gavin's face the same way. Disgusted. Could she ever show him all of her?

"One what?" His face contorted. As if reading his mind, she watched the list of possibilities float past his eyes.

She took his palm and smoothed it over the clothing covering her left breast. With no bra, he should be able to make out the flatness where a nipple once belonged.

"One nipple." She forced a smile to alleviate the urge to wrap up sexy time.

He smirked. "Then clamp, singular."

She sucked in air, her chest rising to his palm as he cupped the area. No judgment. No question. He landed his mouth on her exposed nipple and sucked again, continuing with his mission. *Sexy time, go.*

"You really are the King of Kink," she murmured.

He winked and then closed his eyes to enjoy the feeling of her flesh in his mouth. His hand shifted under her dress and found wet pussy. "Where's your underwear?"

"In my bag." She lifted her dress, exposing her bared sex. His finger brushed through the wiry curls and tugged. "Ow!"

"This is mine, Jolene. No one else's." His eyes flared and turned her body into jelly. "I never thought I'd have to tell a woman to put her panties *on.* Go do it, now."

"Maybe those women weren't slutty enough." She kissed his neck and watched a vein pop. Rivulets of muscle tensed when he pushed her away. *Had they been slutty?* "I'm sorry. I didn't mean to bring up past stuff."

"It's fine."

"No, it isn't. I don't want to know about what you did—"

"It's fine," he said sternly.

She blinked. Sexy time flew out the window. Reading men's desires had been a skill she prided herself on. Pinpointing the most abhorrent or sweet things turning men on provided a thrill, accompanied with relief she'd have at least one night with a roof over her head. Gavin proved to be an enigma, even though she thought she'd pegged him from the first time they fucked. She went to shift off him, and he held her hips in place.

"How the hell do you know about that?" he asked.

"What?"

"That I enjoy slut shaming? I'm not putting it past you that you've done your homework. But no one would know unless they *knew* me."

"Knew the way you were at The Resort, you mean?" He nodded. "I didn't."

He snorted in disbelief. "Right."

"I'm serious. When we fucked at my apartment you asked me some questions, and I responded. Naturally, I guess. And when you called me a whore, I melted." Shame upon embarrassment layered with confusion produced red splotches on her skin. *Why did that turn you on?*

When Zane had called her those names, they'd sickened her into a cyclone of anger toward her inner self. *Slut. Dirty whore. Tramp.* But the effect flipped when Gavin said the same thing. The velvety timbre of his voice spurred her on.

"Do you enjoy it?"

"You couldn't tell?" She laughed.

"I need to hear you say it, Jolene. Because you need to understand something. You are *not* a whore. Or a slut. You are"—he ran a hand along her face—"beautiful."

She swallowed. "Okay."

"Do you believe my words, right now?"

"I've never heard anyone say that to me and mean it."

"I do. You. Are. Beautiful. Those other words? They're ugly and demeaning if used the wrong way."

"Is there a right way?" Hope flared in her chest to hear him name call her again and ease the mind-splitting definitions in her head.

"Yes. When it's consented to. I've called women names—with their permission—and it turned them on. They got off, while I did. But I would *never* call someone a whore just because."

"That's a very clinical BDSM rehearsed response, *Sir*. You despise such things." She smiled.

"This conversation calls for clinical because you need to understand there can be deep-seated shit that can arise from it. I want to be clear because I can't have you misunderstanding the context of my using them when we were together. There should have been a discussion before, but I was wrapped up in the moment."

She grabbed his chin. "We are not in a contractual arrangement, Gavin. We wouldn't have known to have a *discussion* about it. It was natural and something we both obviously crave. When you said those things to me, they washed away all the ugliness like you called me beautiful in another context. You do realize not everything needs a pen, paper, and two signatures to make something happen? We are human, and our genuine response to things is organic."

As Gavin sank back in the chair, she straightened in power. How she put it all so simply, an admission and understanding laid out on the table, made her feel like they were unstoppable. But with his eyes turned away, she felt his conflict.

"Gavin?" He raised his eyes. "I'm not sure what this is, but I like it. Please be who you are, and I promise to do the same. What happened wasn't a mistake. If it was, I'd tell you."

As if his hands had taken on a life of their own, he stroked her middle until they reached her face. "Okay."

His lips pressed against hers, and even though he didn't call her names, he showed his ability to be caring through kisses and strokes along her body, taking her to unchartered ecstasy in the last five minutes they had to spare.

"You're beautiful, Jo..."

TWENTY-TWO

SITTING ON AN OLD WOODEN STAIRCASE OF THE RENTED VICTORIAN house, Jolene brought new life to the space, a flare of new meets an old soul, paired perfectly in an otherwise dissimilar environment.

Was it possible Gavin had met his match? From her beauty to their shared kink intertwined with broken memories of a life gone by, they fit.

Watching her smile brighten with a flash of her green eyes into the camera sent an orchestra of feelings coursing through his blood. She was the melody to his harmony. The beat to his heart. He could never let her go.

She moved one foot on the step and the other on the next down. Marcus sat across from her, in a flannel and skinny jeans, looking rugged and charming. He had to admit—even though the guy irked him—he had the look every female fan would love.

"So, Jolene…" Kyle interrupted his thoughts.

He cleared his throat. "She's doing great. She and Marcus are going places."

"Sure will. Unless…"

"What?"

"I know you're my boss and all, but I feel we bonded over cat mugs and kazoos…"

He crossed his arms, facing Kyle head on. "Spit it out."

"What's going on with you and her?"

Was it that obvious? He twitched a brow. "I'm sorry?"

"I've seen the way you look at her, and I'm not trying to overstep, but we need you. Eco does. And we need them." He pointed to the twosome moving down the steps and disappearing down the hall.

"How much do you know?"

"Enough."

"Who else?"

"No one. I'm an observer-type, made to home in on the things people don't see. The music is in the air, so to speak."

The longer he and Jolene spent time together, the more he wanted to tell Corrine of their relationship. *If that's what you'd call it.* He couldn't even admit he loved her even though he was sure he did.

"Kyle—"

His hands went up. "Your secret's safe with me, boss, and Corrine will understand if you tell her."

"Right," he breathed out.

"You've got love, and Jolene's last few tracks have been spot on. Her heart is singing with renewed purpose rather than going through the motions. You're her muse. And she's yours."

"I don't need a muse. I'm not an artist."

"Well, your attitude has been tolerable." He laughed. "I'd say that's something."

"Why are you protecting us?"

He rocked on his heels. "I'm a sucker for love. Many musicians write about it, so you start believing in it. The progression is amazing. Anyway, Corrine is a woman who respects the truth. Tell her before it ruins your employment."

Could the truth set him free from the chains of agendas he'd been accustomed to? Maybe. But how could he trust anyone to believe what he felt?

The throaty laugh from Jolene echoed through the open space and her footfalls came around the corner.

"Right there, Jo," the photographer said, crouching on the floor as she leaned against the pocket doorway. Her crooked tooth made an appearance as her bow lips curled up on the sides. *Fucking gorgeous.*

"Thanks, Kyle."

"See. She's your muse."

"I'll figure this out." Gavin's phone rang; he dug it from his pocket and removed himself from the shoot into the other room.

"Liam," he said.

"Still making it work at Eco Recordz, I hear."

"What's up? I'm sure you didn't call to check on your investment."

"Hospice is here. You need to come and say goodbye."

He turned toward the bay windows of the Victorian house. A woman hop-scotched between chalked lines and laughed as she hugged a child he assumed was her son.

Love exuded from the woman and the boy looked at her like she was his world. Like Gavin used to with his mother. His heart sank to his knees. *Jolene is fighting to keep her mother's soul alive while you are throwing your own mother's away.*

He turned to see Jolene's ambition radiate with each click of the camera. She appeared to love life. She laughed at something the photographer said. She was happy, probably because her mother probably let her know how loved she was. If Gavin had given his mother the chance, would he feel differently? He'd never know unless he said goodbye.

"I'll be there today." He hit the end button on his phone.

The photographer walked over. "We got it. Give me some time and I'll have the edits to you."

"By the end of the week," Gavin barked a little too hard.

"I'll make it work."

Jolene sauntered over. The cream boho dress swayed around her toned legs.

"You were great today," the photographer cooed, placing his hand on her lower back. An innocent gesture but Gavin's alert signals rose. It took all he had to keep his hands to himself and not alert anyone else to their secret.

"Thanks. What's next?" she asked Gavin.

"Thank you for your time," he said to the photographer.

"Oh, right." He shook Gavin's hand and disappeared.

"I have to run, but your necessities have been moved to my house."

She grabbed her middle. "What necessities?"

"Your clothes and toiletries. Whatever you need. You'll be staying with me indefinitely until we can figure things out."

Jolene's back straightened as Marcus walked over. "Are we free the rest of the day?"

"Yes," Gavin said, spinning a key from the ring. "Meet me back at the house."

"Cool. I'll get my things." Marcus took it and left.

"Where are you going?" Jolene asked.

"I have some things to take care of. Family shit."

"I'd like to go with you." She toyed with the aqua stone ring on her finger.

"Not a good idea."

"My mom died from cancer; I know what to expect. The smell of sterile hospital, shuffling of nurses and stuff, even the tension between the family."

She stopped him with her hand on his bicep. Her touch could bust through the thickest walls. The exhaustion of holding up his reputation and constant guard crumbled his body. He needed someone to help take the load. "Get your things."

Her smile could have lit up the city of New York.

With a hand on the steering wheel and an elbow on the console, Gavin lifted their linked fingers and kissed them.

"You're awfully sweet today," she joked.

"You make me this way." He switched lanes onto the highway and hit the gas toward the Mayne mansion.

She pulled their joined hands into her lap and opened his palm. Her fingers danced along the indentations of a worn past he refused to relive. "My dad changed after my mom died. He bottled up any affection because it's what he knew. Taking care of two kids alone, he went into fight mode."

They were similar in so many ways. Love hadn't been poured freely from a spout. The spigot was sealed up tight to never let a single drop release.

"Do you remember what it felt like?"

"What?"

"Love. From your parents."

She gazed out the window as the trees sped past. "Sometimes."

"Can you tell me what you remember?" He breathed out.

"It was freeing. It felt full and safe. I never remember having to try so hard to feel it. Why do you ask?"

He shifted in his seat and flicked on the radio. "Forget it."

She tapped the button to silence the distraction. "Have you never…?"

His hand twisted the gearshift until the rubber heated his palm.

"Talk to me. Have you never felt love from your parents?"

"Not my father. *Ever.* My mom showed it when Charles wasn't home. Our moments alone were wonderful."

His mother's flowery perfume still came to mind from those times he'd hugged her in her fancy clothes.

"I love you, son. I am the air under your wings. You are always safe."

"Is that why you've avoided going back?" she asked.

"Yes. Seeing her will take what I remember away." He blinked past the burn in his eyes. "It's stupid, I know."

"No, it's not."

TWENTY-THREE

An hour later, Gavin pulled through the iron gates to his family estate. When the massive peaks of the blue slate roofs came closer, the house appeared alive. Nothing about this house made him feel safe, unlike the home his family had before Charles became a self-made millionaire over some widget he'd invented.

The SUV curved up to the main doors along the wide driveway, and he slammed the car into park.

"It's okay, Gavin. I'm here," Jolene whispered as her gaze surveyed the impressive grounds.

"Look at me. Charles won't acknowledge you but you being here means everything." Her smile lit the space and he kissed the spot housing her crooked tooth. "Thank you for coming."

"I...whatever you need."

He wouldn't allow her apprehension to ruin the moment. She came because she cared. The door creaked as he opened it, and she got out of the vehicle.

He rang the bell, holding Jolene's hand while brushing invisible wrinkles from his dress shirt. He glanced down, making sure his shoes were polished to an ultimate shine. The door opened and a petite, plump Mexican woman greeted them.

"Señor Gavin?" Her round hands slapped her mouth as her brown eyes glassed over. His heart warmed.

"*Ola*, Rosa."

She shot out her arms and reeled him in. He bent to hug her, still gripping Jolene's hand.

"Oh, young boy, we've missed you." She pulled away. "*Ya estás crecido.*" She patted his face and looked behind him. "Bringing home girlfriend? *Bienvenido, hermosa chica!*"

"No, not…" Jolene's voice stalled.

"Yes, my girlfriend," Gavin finished. "This is Jolene."

Her emerald eyes widened and a smile gave way to the gateway to her heart. "Yeah, what he said."

Rosa ushered them to the kitchen. He hadn't expected such a warm welcome, nor did he even think she still worked for the Mayne family. Rosa had raised Riley, his sister, after Gavin left, according to Liam. And Gavin held fond memories of their relationship when she assisted his mother in raising him as well.

"Where's Marie?" Gavin asked, escorting Jolene to the stool at the breakfast bar.

The kitchen had been built for a master chef. A six-burner Viking stove and accessories galore. A commercial mixer, a knife rack built for a butcher, and an industrial size fridge to hold all the things a king—his father—could ever desire. She dropped his hand at the Italian marble island and patted it twice.

"Your mother's asleep. She's not well."

"I know. Liam told me."

"*Siéntate.*"

He sat and leaned toward Jolene. "She said: 'sit'. In this house, we listen to Rosa." He smiled, alleviating any anxiety he'd held on the ride over. Jolene followed his cue.

Rosa rummaged through the stainless refrigerator, coming out with creamer. She waddled over to the coffeemaker and poured the hot liquid into the empty cups, then set the items in front of him and Jolene. "Sugar?"

He waved it aside.

"I'll take some, please," Jolene said. Rosa set the sugar caddy between them and inserted a teaspoon. "Perfect. Thank you."

"*De nada.*"

"How bad is she?"

She spread her plump hands along the edge of the marble. "She's not good, señor. Why you wait so long to come home?"

He gritted his teeth. "This isn't my home, Rosa. And she could have found me."

"Still a stubborn boy."

He met her small eyes. They creased on the sides with wrinkles when she smiled. "It's something I'm working on."

"You are the reason he came?" she asked Jolene.

"I…"

"Yes, she is." The words flowed as natural as dominating business deals. Gavin squeezed her knee.

Rosa patted his hand. "You must forgive in order to move forward in life. As a mother, you make decisions you think are best for your children when perhaps they aren't. Trust me."

He turned his head to the side. "Do you have children?"

"Yes. They're now grown and married. I sent them everything for a better life." She swallowed, pulling the dishtowel from her apron to blot the welling tears.

Gavin had been too blind to see she went without her children because she had treated him with so much care. Her endless devotion to her own children showed in her sad smile, but her tears showed regrets. Did his mother feel the same thing?

"Rosa, show Gavin back to my office."

Charles Mayne. His voice boomed into the kitchen, effectively stopping their moment.

He turned, and Charles' glare still made the small child inside cower. *You are an adult now.* And a man who—against all odds—

197

had become a successful person. With Uncle Rick's help and the small voice in his head telling him to never give up, he knew this day would come.

He kissed Jolene on the forehead. "I'll be back."

"I'm with you no matter what."

Her words rang in his ears. She was his rock when the seas became too much. He stood and gave Rosa hug. Charles wouldn't steal another moment.

She laughed. "Señor, what are you doing?"

"Thank you for always being there."

Walking the halls, the echoes of childhood laughter haunted him. Laughter that was effectively stifled when his father would arrive home from business trips. He turned the corner to his father's study to find him standing over his desk.

"Have a seat, Gavin."

"I'll stand."

"Have it your way. Getting chummy with Rosa, I see. And what's with the girl?" He didn't look up from his perusal of several documents spread out across his desk.

Gavin's nails pressed crescent moons into his palms to keep from lashing out. "Not sure it concerns you."

"Rosa's a hard worker. Always at our beck and call without question or argument. She does as she's told. Quick learner, that one."

Gavin rolled his tongue to fight off an array of snarky rejoinders. He wouldn't play into his father's hand.

"The only lessons I remember were the ones teaching us to bully our way through life."

Charles walked to the large windows overlooking the inlet of the bay. "That's where you're wrong. You see, you weren't cut out to call the shots and why Liam has been poised to take my role at the family company someday. A proud successor for what I built." He pivoted to face him. "You were destined to play the middle. The doer, the weakest link between two brothers. The Omega Records disaster proved my point."

"You're unbelievable." He gripped the back of the soft leather chair in front of him. "I left. You should be happy."

Charles poured an amber-colored liquid into a snifter from the nearby wet bar. "It did make my decision easier."

"You played us against each other as a sick game of puppet master. You're quite the man, Charles, and it surprises me why my mother chose you over her children and her freedom."

Charles waved his hand to swat away his declaration. "Leave your mother out of this. And correction: You wanted her to choose you over us. A family survives by a strong leader, a provider, and a solid allegiance."

The hand would always play to the house, and the cards dealt to Gavin were all jokers. His father held the king, queen, and jack.

"This is not why I came," Gavin gritted.

"You're not seeing her until you sit and listen for once." He pointed to the seating area behind them.

The command he wielded and the abject submission Charles demanded were the only genetic traits Gavin possessed. How had he not seen it? He ran away to escape a man obsessed with controlling others. Charles' sick assertiveness could be the singular reason his mother stayed. Her way to submit perhaps? Charles' way of life aligned closer with Gavin's dominance than being a true Dominant did. He took a seat to soothe the nausea rolling in his gut.

"Thank you." His father curled a side smile. *Self-satisfied son of a bitch.* Charles moved to an Italian leather couch. "It's been a rough day as you can imagine."

"It's been a rough life, as you can imagine," Gavin quipped.

The acknowledgement waned for a moment then disappeared. "Your mother wants to see you. Not sure why."

Gavin pressed his nails into the leather armrests and spoke through his teeth. "Because I'm her son."

Charles sipped his precious scotch. Macallan, aged forty years. He babied his drink more than his own children. "It's her wish, and I will see it's granted."

"Glad to see you haven't lost control in any capacity."

His eyes snapped up. "I love your mother, and if seeing you means she goes peacefully, then so be it."

Gavin leaned forward. "You never loved her. You loved *fucking*. Those other women made you feel powerful. She deserved more than this life, and it disgusted you to know she loved me since you couldn't."

His father's lips thinned into a line of disappointment. "Still a petulant child. Your poker face and negotiation style are lacking. Might want to consider that if you're hired in the future."

"I have a job."

"Doing?"

A pro at picking any sealed scab and watching it bleed was his father's specialty.

"What does it matter?"

"It doesn't. You were never my son. Not one part of you, and you are still the biggest disappointment to this family."

Hearing him admit he was never his son, stung more than not hearing it at all.

A small whisper of defeat fell from Gavin's mouth. "You made me this way. You weren't the perfect father and you were never there. Mom was the one there for me growing up. Not you."

"Still pushing blame, I see. Do you treat the young lady in my kitchen that way?"

Every bone in Gavin's body pulsed and cracked. He needed to prevent himself from unloading physical violence on a man not worth the effort. "Leave her out of this. I've reconciled my share of guilt. You can't keep holding it over me."

Charles' posture remained relaxed with one leg crossed over the other and both hands cradling his scotch. It whittled him down more, into the small child he used to be.

"Can we please?" Gavin's voice cracked. His father had succeeded in crushing the walls Gavin had built over sixteen years in a short fifteen minutes.

"We're done here. Marie is upstairs in her room."

Gavin folded his lips to refrain from begging for scraps. Charles would never utter anything to indicate he was proud of his son.

Diminished from his father's pep talk, he approached his mother's room. The hardwood creaked under his feet with mistakes and regret. Gavin pushed on as he came to the threshold of the door.

He closed his eyes and remembered the silkiness of her long brown hair and the blue of her eyes. Features he'd stolen from her. The one thing he wished he'd taken was her love. Was love genetic? Could it be? Or was a person destined to learn how to love from their parents? If that were the case, he'd left the family with Charles' version of love, or lack thereof.

He pushed the door open and the nurse looked up from the bed.

"She's comfortable and awake. I'll give you a few minutes."

His mother lay on her side, away from him. A picture on her nightstand of the two of them came into view. It reminded him of the one he had with Nicolette on his dresser. Memories from a forgotten time.

He took a step and she whispered, "Charles...did he...come?"

Gavin knelt by the bed. Her eyes were closed, and her hands were curled under her cheek on the pillow. Her hair was gone, replaced by a soft knitted cap to keep her head protected from a chill.

A rush of tears pooled in his eyes, as the heartache threatened to pull him into the darkest pit of sadness. What had he done? Why did he wait this long?

"Mother?"

"Who...?"

"It's Gavin."

Her brows furrowed as much as her energy would allow them. "Son?"

"Yes. It's me."

Her eyes opened and the blue had faded into a silver sky gray. She blinked slowly, adjusting to what he imagined was a blurred image. She reached out a shaky hand, and he moved closer to allow her to touch his face. "My son."

The tips of her cold fingers left reality in their wake. This would be the last time he'd see her.

"I'm so sorry I didn't come sooner."

"Shhh, my baby. Let me..." Her voice faded in and out between labored breaths. "You are so grown. Don't cry. You are as stubborn as Charles, you know that?"

"Yes." He covered her frail, curled body with the comforter.

"T-tell me something wonderful."

Did she know about what the last year had brought? None of it mattered now, and he wouldn't tarnish her last days with his filth and demise.

"I've met someone. Her name is Jolene." The one glimmer of hope in his life.

"Is she good to you?"

"Yes. Very much. And she's honest and talented."

"A musician?"

He smiled. She did know his life. "I'm helping her with her career."

"That *is* wonderful..." She coughed as her lungs wheezed. "You deserve love, son. Love I wasn't able to give..."

"It's okay, Mom."

"I thought I made the right choice but now..." Her hand stretched to the nightstand. He followed her motion. "Open it."

The wooden slats scraped as he did. Cedar scent emerged as if the drawer's contents had tried to escape for years. He grabbed a sealed envelope.

She rubbed her aging fingers over the paper. "Take this and read it after I'm gone. It will explain everything. Promise me you'll wait."

He took it, feeling whatever had been written was as heavy as his heart.

"I love you, Mom. I've missed so much time." She wasn't responding, but he kept going. "Why did you stay? We could've had a life together. All of us. Liam and Riley too. You always looked at me like I mattered, and I threw it away over a grudge from some misunderstanding." He leaned into the mattress holding her hands. "Please stay."

She slept soundly, and he pushed on.

"Please do something for me? Tell Nicolette I'm sorry and I love her, please," he begged. His chest crushed inward as shudders moved through him. "Take care of her, Mom. She's all alone in the dark. Be her light. Can you do that?"

He was unsure of how long he knelt there as his legs and knees went numb. The nurse rubbed his shoulder, and he swallowed his grief. Collecting the envelope, he kissed his mother's head.

"I'm sorry for letting you down."

It was the most honest thing he'd ever said. His heart bloomed even though this was the end, because someone waited on the other side.

Jolene.

TWENTY-FOUR

Jolene flipped through her moleskin journal, every page inked with her songs over the last few years. Her journey toward survival.

She curled her hands around the coffee cup, and the warmth filled her palms. Rosa had scurried off to maintain the Mayne household, leaving her to take in Gavin's childhood home. She imagined a dark-haired, blue-eyed boy running around the kitchen as his mother cooked with Rosa. She leaned from the stool and, in the back yard, caught sight of the tire swing, which was connected to a giant weeping willow bending into the bay.

Each edge and line of the finely decorated house felt warm, with flower arrangements, and maroon and cream decor. The gold chandelier over the breakfast table seemed to fit the area with raised ceilings. Even though Gavin couldn't see it, love resided in this house.

"Taking it all in?" A man dressed in an expensive suit stood in the doorway.

"Oh, hi. Rosa said she'd be right back."

His onyx ring sparkled off the lighting when he held out his hand.

"Liam Mayne." He smiled. Liam was tall and had blondish-brown hair and brown eyes much like his father.

She took his hand. "Do I know you? Wait, weren't you Gavin's assistant?"

He laughed. "I'm sure he would love to hear you ask that, but I'm his big brother."

Nerves tingled to her toes. "I thought…Are you sure?"

"Last I checked."

The memory hit her like a punch to the face. "Wait. We met in North Carolina last year! You told me *Gavin Mayne was looking for new talent at Omega Records.* You promised he'd see us perform."

"Jolene Harrison."

"Yes! Oh my God." She touched his bicep. "You're his brother?"

"I am. And why are you here now?" His brown eyes seemed to be calculating. Gavin had the same look when he asked questions filled with weighty assessment.

"Um…Gavin and I are…" She shook her head, feeling silly, but wanting to admit it to the world. "We are together."

"I see. How did you meet? I clearly failed at getting him to see you perform when all that shit went down at his last job. You heard about that, right?"

"I did. But once I had it in my mind to work with him, I had to make it happen."

"Even though he took down a record company? Trust me, I know he got my message to 'discover' you, but it was obvious he was dealing with his boss." He winked.

She shrunk in her chair. *His boss.* "Why did you tell me you were his assistant?"

"It might sound juvenile."

"Try me."

He crossed the kitchen and filled a steaming cup of coffee. "Not sure how much he's told you but we haven't been close for a long time. Seems the death of our mother is the one thing that could get him here." He sipped. "I wanted to be a part of his life in some way, and he cared about his job. I thought finding him talent would help."

"Very kind of you."

"Not sure he would see it that way, but he's changing."

"How?"

He set the cup on the island, and his brown eyes smiled. "He's here now, with you no less. I'd say he might actually have a heart in that cold exterior of his. Do you love him?"

Love him? She wasn't capable of love but hearing it sprouted a foreign feeling in her blood. "Not sure it's your place to ask."

"I think you might feel something for my brother." Did all the men of the Mayne family give off the elusive vibe?

"Sorry about your mother," she said trying to change the subject.

"Thank you. It's been rough caring for her these last few months. She'll be in a better place soon."

"You seem like a saint. Taking care of your ailing mother and looking out for Gavin. Why has he never brought you around?"

"There are things Gavin doesn't want to know, so I tend to be a little more behind the scenes."

"What does that mean?"

"Eco Recordz."

She gasped, all comfort flying out the window. He *did* know. "You...um...got him a job there?"

"I'm a shareholder for the start-up. Corrine's my niece, and Gavin needed a job."

Her breaths came quicker. "You're his boss's boss." If Corrine found out, they would be over and all would be lost. His career, her dream...their relationship. "This is soooo bad."

He covered her shaking hand. "It's okay, Jolene."

"Wh-what?"

"Gavin will never admit to needing help, nor will he ever listen to his brother's advice on talent."

"I don't understand."

"You were special and I couldn't let you go, even if Gavin wouldn't find you himself. But Jane Popper…she was a music director with no clue. All I had to do was nudge her in the right direction to find you."

"You did this? You sought us out?"

"I knew the board would be terminating Jane and an opening would happen. I signed you and hired Gavin." He laughed. "This probably sounds creepy."

She shifted her hand back into her lap. "Ya think?"

"Trust me, it's all out of love." He went for the door. "Jolene?"

"Yes?"

"For the record, I never thought when I found you he'd fall in love with you. Thank you. I mean it. You're good for him."

She smiled as he disappeared around the corner. For once everything would be okay.

"Jo?"

She found Gavin in the doorway. Still strong, but his eyes gave him away. Upset and exhausted. His hair was disheveled as though he'd run his fingers through it.

She walked to him and held him close, hoping to suffocate the pain. She buried her face in his chest and smelled anise, clove and Gavin.

Air expelled from his mouth in a guttural sigh. He kissed the crown of her head, and they swayed side to side as if a song about goodbye and regrets played around them.

"I couldn't have done this without you."

She ran her hands up and down his back, the tight muscles shifting and softening as he relaxed.

"I'm so sorry."

"Are you ready to go home?"

Home. A word rarely used in her vocabulary. A girl on the run, finding somewhere to hang her hat and now it seemed she had.

"Yes." She went to pick up her journal. "Can we stop at Duane Reade on the way?"

TWENTY-FIVE

THE SODA BOTTLE HISSED WITH THE RELEASE OF THE CAP. GAVIN poured Jolene a seltzer and lime in a wine glass as "California Dreamin'" piped through the open area into the kitchen.

He grabbed their drinks and found his way to the living room. Jolene was on her belly, wearing tight black yoga pants and a baggy shirt. Her bare feet kicked in the air to the beat as the pen curly queued against the pages of her journal.

She was so sexy. *Are you dreaming? Never, you didn't deserve someone like her before.* He smiled despite himself.

"I know you're watching."

"I can't help it. You're too damn adorable."

She spun and placed a hand on her hip. "Adorable? That's a first."

He placed the glasses on the end table and sat on the couch. "Mamas and the Papas? Didn't know I had this record."

The pen met her lips, and she sucked the tip.

Good fucking lord, her lips were made of kryptonite. His dick flexed.

"Helps me think." She set the writing tool down. "My mom and dad used to play this all the time. We'd dance in the living room. It's tied to many memories. Elliot, my brother, was named after the lead singer."

"Who, Cass?"

"Yep. This band was Lily's favorite." She turned onto her back to stare at the ceiling. "I'll never forget it. Mom was ready to pop and they hadn't picked a name. Since my dad chose mine, I suggested she pick Elliot's. We were on the floor and she was so beautiful lying there. Bright green eyes, long platinum hair. And then it hit her." She rose up on her elbows. "I could tell because her dimples created little caverns in her cheeks. And then she said, *'Elliot,'* as if she'd known his name before he grew in her belly."

Her eyes misted a shimmer of emerald dust. If he could get her into this vulnerable state, she would capture her mother's song.

"And you?"

"What about me?"

"Who was Jolene to your dad?"

She beamed and sat up. "Dolly Parton. He had some weird thing for her. You know, *before* all the plastic surgery. Lily was his real-life Dolly. The dimples, green eyes, blonde hair. I guess he was connected to me somehow, too."

"Do you miss him?"

"All the time. I'm realizing people change, especially with life events. I couldn't imagine being a single father with two small children." She huffed. "He's always loved me, I guess."

The record switched songs leaving the memory behind from whence it came.

"Sorry to get all deep."

"No, Jolene. It's wonderful you're seeing it now." He slid off the couch, unable to keep from touching her. "Besides, couples share things."

She laughed as her legs parted, an invitation to settle between them. He kissed her clothed abdomen and chest. She still smelled like his cologne, but with a sweet, sexy finish. He wanted to eat her alive.

"I'm not your conventional kind of"—she air quoted —"girlfriend."

"Fuck conventional." He kissed her lips; everything felt right. Her. Him. Together.

"What about Eco?" she said breathlessly.

The name of their employer hung in the air, threatening to take away the moment. What would he tell Corrine? His hand smoothed the curve of her face. "We'll figure it out when the time is right. Right now, all I want is to enjoy this moment with you, Jo."

"Me too."

"What are you writing?"

She snagged the book before he could reach it. "Nothing."

"Is that what you bought at Duane Reade?"

"Yep. My old one had been filled."

"Is it about me?" He chuckled.

"Maybe."

He held her hip with one hand and reached with the other. "Let me see."

She shook her head mischievously as he tried to rip the book away from her herculean grip. "It's not ready."

"What if I made you?" He moved to kiss the tops of her breasts peeking from the scoop neck shirt. His stubble scratched her flesh. A little bit of pain would loosen her up.

"Mmmm… Not gonna happen. This is the one time you don't get your way, *Sir.*"

"Give it to me." He tugged its edge, digging his fingers into her side.

She wiggled beneath him; her husky laugh floated to the rafters. "You'll have to wait…*stop! Don't!*"

"I have no patience." He tore the book away from her grip and caged her with his elbows on each side of her head.

"You'll think it's stupid." She no longer fought him. Maybe she wanted him to read her words. Ones she couldn't say out loud.

You are the wind beneath broken wings,
Forever there,
We will share,
I soar because of you.

He rose to his knees. "Jesus, Jo..."

She peeled the journal from his weakening grasp. "See? Stupid." She gently closed the book as if it was the most precious thing to her. "I'm sorry. I..."

He lifted her chin. "Don't be...it's a lot to—"

"I overreach and imagine things are real," she babbled on. "It helps to understand what's inside..."

Her lips moved rapidly, explaining her lyrics written within her notebook, and he couldn't comprehend them. His mother used to say similar things when love was a real, tangible thing. Something he'd thought he was incapable of feeling again. Her words sparked a stirring in his loins and swelling of his heart. They plucked a chord so deep it resonated within his entire body; he couldn't deny he was falling in love with her.

"Stop." He placed a finger on her moving mouth. "Do you mean it?"

"The pen is an extension of my heart."

His body hovered over her. He wanted to breathe the air stirred by her wings, to ingest it, but how? The magnitude of chaos this would bring to his career changed all the odds, and he didn't care. He wanted to be her wind and allow her the freedom to fly, even if it meant losing his own.

He dipped, taking her lips, and they opened. Her hands threaded behind his neck and tugged him closer, her legs splitting wider to allow him a bond no other man possessed.

Her wet mouth consumed him as his cock expanded beneath

his shorts. He ground against her cleft wanting to take her gently and with purpose. This wouldn't be a normal fuck. A lifetime of hollowness would be filled with her love.

"Gavin, wait."

She shimmied to her knees and removed her shirt. Her bare breasts hung heavy. He caressed the beautiful scars tangled along her shoulder to her chest. A flattened nub, where her nipple would have been, attempted to purse to match its mate.

She knelt proud, thrusting her chest. "I know I'm not normal, but I want you to see me."

"You're gorgeous."

"I want you to be the first man I give myself to without it being about sex and a place to stay. It's more." Her hand touched his chest. "I want to stay in here."

"You mean love?"

She shrugged. "Yes. We've both been through pain. It's time to allow something different to take us forward rather than hold us back."

"I don't know how."

"Me neither. Let's rewrite it. Our way. Allow the curve of ink to curl and bend with no end in sight."

He kissed her fully, pushing his entire body against her. She tipped back, and he gently guided her to the floor. A fierce urge to take control over her vanished, passing the initial desire to find a field of lust in her kiss.

"No pain tonight," he whispered.

"Good. I want you slow and deep."

He stroked her curved edges until he cupped her scarred breast. The rough skin heated in his palm and his thumb grazed the area of her absent nipple. She arched her back with a moan.

The music droned on in the background, enhancing his high. He pulled away, and her eyes sucked the shadows from his heart. Her color flushed red, like a rose waiting to be picked from his garden.

He undressed them in a frenzy and yanked a condom from the pocket of his shorts. Her hand covered it.

"I'm on birth control. I want to feel you, if you'll have me. I've never been with anyone that way. Not even with—"

"Shhh. I want to feel you too." The heat from her pussy caressed the sensitive skin of his dick as it notched in place. "You're shaking."

"I'm scared because I've never given my heart. Only my body. You own me, Gavin."

Jesus.

He finally breathed out. "You own me, too. I love you."

He pushed in slowly and purposefully to feel every inch of her core. Their flesh connected and both moaned in mutual pleasure. Her hot breath pushed against his ear when her body curled.

How could he ever experience sex without commands or *yes, Sir.* Feeling her softness sent him soaring higher than any dominant top space could. It permeated his bones and blood.

"Fucking Christ, you feel so good." He aligned her palm with his to meld their love lines as one.

Their bodies danced along the floor in a rhythm of passion and love. In and out. Moan to moan. Had it ever been like this? Electric and alive? *Never.*

"Love me...please," she groaned. Her eyes closed as he imagined her not searching for a high, but finally living.

Just like him.

A week later, they fell into a raging desire. The peace he felt from exerting his hand mixed with plain old vanilla sex brought worlds of pain into pleasure. And she owned him completely.

He snuck downstairs to make a few calls. The record was complete, except for the one that would make this album extraordinary. He called Kyle.

"Hey, boss. Kinda early."

"Lots of work to be done."

"And I'm already in the studio finishing the last of the edits."

Gavin saw a lot of his own work ethic in Kyle. He had a way of working hard while allowing the day to pass with ease. He liked the kid.

"Thank you."

"Right on."

"Do you have today's schedule?"

"We have Jolene at eight tweaking a few guitar layovers and recording 'Mother' and Marcus around ten for the *Indie Rox* blog interview."

"Switch Jolene to the afternoon and scratch 'Mother' from the recording block. I have other plans for it."

"Like what?"

"You'll see. And don't worry, you'll get final cuts."

He laughed. "Cool."

"I'll see you later." He clicked the phone and searched his contacts. His thumb landed on Uncle Rick's name. His body went tight, flashing back to the scene in his mother's room. It broke his heart her own brother couldn't say goodbye. He tapped the call button.

"Hello?"

"Rick. It's Gavin. You up?"

Rick laughed. "Already at the studio. You sound better than the last time we spoke."

The sealed envelope his mother gave him was perched on his desk. He stared at the black script written on the outside. *Mayne.* He was determined to rewrite his name in a new light, and her letter might add more havoc in his life than good.

She had passed a few days after he said his piece, and he couldn't bring himself to attend the funeral. Nor could he handle seeing his father. All that needed to be said had been, and he was ready to move on.

He loved Jolene, and even though she hadn't said the words, *I love you*, he knew in his heart she did. It was more love than his mother and father ever showed him, and he looked to that as a place to walk toward and leave his past behind.

Throughout his time with Jolene, she'd taught him something else. How to preserve the love of a mother after all these years. That's what he wanted to remember, not something written in a letter. He would embrace the times when his mother gave what she could. The moments they'd shared listening to Sinatra, or walking through the estate grounds during fall. The way she smelled, looked, and felt. Those were the things he would take with him into the future. That and Jolene.

"I need a favor."

Gavin nuzzled his hard body against Jolene's soft one when he slid under the covers. He immediately got hard as he moved her hair from her neck and kissed the spot behind her ear.

"Haven't you had enough?" She stretched out of sleep.

"Never." He rolled what he could of her scarred nipple through his fingers.

"I can't feel that." She yawned.

"You sure?" He dipped a finger into her opening as her legs fell wide with permission to check. "Appears you're wrong." He sucked her arousal from his finger and she blushed all over. "Did I make you shameless?"

She giggled as his mouth covered her other nipple. Once it pebbled, he bit gently as he shifted to lie between her thighs. *Fuck, she was a goddess.*

"What's it feel like when you suck that nipple?"

"Jo," he breathed.

"Is it weird for you?"

"Why would it be?" He toyed with it, circling figure eights

around the smashed nub as his fingers followed the line of flowers she'd gotten to cover it.

"Come on." She tried to push him off but he held her.

"Seriously, baby. Why would it be weird for me? I love your body."

A flicker of hope appeared in her eyes. Had no other man looked past her disfigurements? It saddened him to think no one could be drawn to the intelligent, honest and mischievous girl he'd fallen for because of it.

"I mean, look at it."

"I am and it's beautiful." He nudged it with his nose.

"Really?"

"Well, yeah." He cocked his head to the side. "It's winking and offering me a good time." They broke into laughter, and her abdomen flexed as the huffy sound overtook them.

"You're something else," she managed to say.

He shifted to spoon her and traced the tattoo on her back along her shoulder blade. Silhouettes of birds flew away from the inky truth she wore. "Only with you, Bluebird."

"Bluebird?"

The inscription entranced him as he spoke, "Do you like it?"

"Very much. But where did you come up with it?"

"This inspired it; you brought it to life. A resilient woman who'd fought her way to survival..."

It has been a beautiful fight...still is.

"...to bring me to life."

She turned in his arms and kissed him deeply. He fell to his back as she straddled him. Had anything been this complete?

She broke away. "You know those aren't bluebirds."

He shrugged running his fingers through her hair. "What are they then?"

"They're swallows." Her contagious laughter swept any last fear of loneliness into the air.

"That would make for an interesting nickname, wouldn't it?"

She shifted between his legs running a slow hand over his clothed erection. Her tone suddenly dripped with a filthy timbre. "Maybe."

"Jo…" He feigned a warning in spite of the painful hard-on.

She slipped his boxers off and tossed them on the floor. His cock jutted to his navel and she moved it, then lowered her mouth and kissed it once, twice.

"Let's see if the name suits the owner." Her lips sheathed him in a slow, agonizing descent.

His head craned toward the ceiling, and his fucking toes curled. *God damn it. That fucking mouth.*

"Let's…" He moaned as she sucked his cock, root to tip. Her eyes wickedly gleamed with desire as she tried to take him whole and back out. *Was there anything sexier?*

"Open for me. Wider."

"Like this?" Her tongue emerged from her widened mouth. Her eyes seemed to convey: *Take it*, causing sharp pressure at the base of his balls.

"Perfect." He pushed her head down and fucked her hot mouth over and over. Her eyes rolled slightly. *A goddess of submission when tamed.* His balls tightened. "Ready? *Fuck*…I'm coming…"

Milky jets darted into her mouth and her eyes closed. She didn't crinkle her face. She loved taking him as much as he liked giving himself to her. He jerked his cock to allow the last of his semen to escape and wiped a pearly bead on her lip. She sucked it into her mouth.

"Fuck, that's hot." His head hit the pillow as his orgasm rolled through his spine and sent a chill through his body.

She fell into his arms. "So, swallows then?"

He laughed. When did he get so lucky? Beautiful, sexy, and funny as hell.

TWENTY-SIX

A̠N̠ ̠H̠O̠U̠R̠ ̠L̠A̠T̠E̠R̠, J̠O̠L̠E̠N̠E̠ ̠F̠I̠N̠I̠S̠H̠E̠D̠ ̠H̠E̠R̠ ̠C̠O̠F̠F̠E̠E̠ ̠W̠H̠I̠L̠E̠ ̠F̠L̠I̠P̠P̠I̠N̠G̠ through online reviews from a small show she and Marcus performed to drum up interest.

"Ground Breaking! A Sexy New Duo Takes Manhattan By Storm!"

"What are you reading?" Marcus asked with a yawn.

She looked up as he scratched his abs under his T-shirt, hair knotted and wild as he strutted in wearing navy sweats. His feet dragged along the floor to the coffee maker, and he poured a cup.

"Our reviews."

"Shouldn't read that shit." He tipped his cup and drank. "It's a rabbit hole of false confidence."

She laughed. Marcus knew the music business inside and out. A drummer for multiple bands, he'd had his run with bad and good reviews. "It says here we are taking Manhattan by storm."

His eyebrows popped up. "Really?"

"*And* we are a sexy duo." She held up the tablet.

"That I agree with." His boyish smile appeared, making him Marcus the Musician.

"How've you been sleeping? You know you don't need to be here. The apartment has been ready."

"Not bad." He glanced around the space. "And true, but he's got a nice pad and thick walls, thank god."

She blushed into her cup of coffee. "Sorry, we...um...try to keep it down."

"Look, I get it. A good-looking man with money can sweep a girl off her feet, but what are you doing, Jo? When Eco finds out—"

"They won't. We're careful and keep it here. I want to tell everyone we are together, but the timing isn't right."

"*Togeth*...as in more than sleeping together?"

She'd dodged any conversation with him regarding Gavin's and her relationship because she thought admitting it to her best friend would make it real.

"Yes." Her heart felt as though it was pounding out of her chest.

"Shit."

"I am capable of more, Marcus."

He walked around the island, and she spun on the stool to face him. "I never said you weren't. I've been your guardian for a long time, and now it looks like it's time to let someone else take the lead."

"What? No lecture?" She sputtered a laugh.

"Remember when I told you all the good things would come in time when you let the pain go?" She nodded. "As much as I hate to admit it, Gavin reached you more than I was able to."

"I...I'm sorry." Regret spilled with the tears rolling down her cheeks. Deep down, she had wanted Marcus to be that man, but in her heart, she knew he wouldn't be. "You're not being replaced."

"I know. We are friends and no one can take *that* place. But if Gavin can get you to smile and get you to glow on stage, then I couldn't be happier."

Her body relaxed at his blessing. Years of wondering what was wrong with her for not being with Marcus fell to the hardwood floor. She wrapped her arms around his waist.

"Thank you, Marcus."

"I love you, Jo. Just be careful, okay?"

"I will." The sound of creaking stairs alerted her, and she backed away, wiping the remaining tears from her eyes.

"Good morning." Gavin entered the kitchen dressed casually in a full suit sans the tie. He moved with precision as he grabbed a cup from the cabinet.

"My work is done here. Guess I'll be moving home." Marcus winked at her. "See you at the studio?"

"Jolene will be in later this afternoon," Gavin interjected.

She straightened. "I have an eight o'clock with Kyle to finish 'Mother.'"

Gavin's boyish smile curled his lips. "Change of plans." He looked at Marcus. "We will be back in time for your interview."

"Whatever you have planned, please spare me the details." Marcus bolted, taking two stairs at a time.

Gavin plopped the cup on the counter. "What's up with him?"

"Nothing." She laughed. "Where are we going?"

He leaned back against the counter, holding his arms out, his gaze filled with mischief and love. His sweetness soothed her, but the invisible thrum of commanding desire mixed like a sweet sundae with an actual hidden cherry inside.

"I want to show you something today."

She set her chin on his chest. "What?"

He kissed her lips with such tenderness she melted. He took her slowly. *Tongue, peck, swipe, nibble.* She nearly combusted at his dance. He grabbed her ass and squeezed. "Get dressed before we lose a whole day in this house."

"That wouldn't be so bad." She rubbed her thighs together, hoping they could take a few extra minutes.

An hour later, Gavin pulled into the spot in front of her apartment.

"Here?"

He turned off the ignition. "No. Come on."

He took her hand as she stepped onto the sidewalk and laced his fingers with hers. They walked down the street and he stopped.

"Here." Electric Lady Studios.

"W-what?" She couldn't suppress the smile plastered on her lips.

Would you like to see the inside?"

Her heart fluttered as she became dizzy from excitement. "Hell, yeah."

He ushered her in, and her feet touched the holy land of music. The greatest musicians of all time had left their melodies and stories in those halls. Gavin nodded to reception as he led Jolene into the back hallway.

"Do they let anyone wander in here?" She smirked.

"I'm not just anybody."

At the end of the hall, signs read Studio A and Studio B with arrows pointing to what she assumed would be their destination. The wide corridors were lined with space exploration portraits painted with groovy seventies designs. Her heart stopped when she encountered one of a comic-like woman floating before her.

"Jolene?" He stopped beside her.

"Yes, I'm..." Tears glazed her sight. "This..." She touched the painting. It could have been a replica of her mother in a white gown with an effervescent gleam of pink in her long blonde hair. Green eyes shone, and dimples marked in her cheeks. "She looks like my mother."

He stroked her arms. "She's beautiful."

"And adventurous." She laughed. The image floating in space reminded her of her mother's determination to try anything.

"Like her daughter. Come."

I love you, Mama. I won't let you down. She looked over her shoulder as emotions fluttered through her.

He stopped. "You are so beautiful when you let yourself see the world. Are you ready?"

"There's more?"

His bright white smile lit her heart as he opened the door to Studio A: Jimi Hendrix's home. In the center of the room on an oriental rug sat an island of promise. One microphone with a replica of her guitar

She looked up at Gavin. "Is this…?"

"This is where you need to record your mother's song." Tears leaked down her face as she stuttered a breath. "This is where you'll find the love you never thought you'd regain."

Gavin was the vehicle to finding the person she'd lost twenty years ago, but although the journey seemed to veer off path, it now connected her to the present. *Fate.*

She grabbed his face and kissed him. His hands wrapped around her waist and pulled her closer.

"Eh-um." She tensed and turned. "You must be Jolene. I'm Rick." The kind man shook their hands. His gray hair hung long over his ears and brushed the collar of his shirt. His wire-framed glasses shielded his blue eyes.

"Thanks for setting this up," Gavin said.

"Don't tell Charles. He'll have me on a stake."

Jolene looked at Gavin, tilting her head. "He's my uncle and got me involved with the industry. He saved me when I had nowhere to go. He took me in. No questions."

She hugged Rick with all her strength. "Thank you."

He tensed, stock-still. "Ah, sure. And thank you for what you've done for him."

She moved back. "What do you mean?"

"He's never gone to such lengths for a girl."

"Is that so?" Gavin rubbed the back of his neck and she smiled.

"He broke the silence between his family to do something he knew you would appreciate."

"Can we move this along?" Gavin looked at his watch. "The clock is ticking."

"Manager time." Jolene crooked a thumb in Gavin's direction.

"Right," Rick said winking at Jolene. "There's your stage and I'll be behind this glass. Let's take it as it comes, okay?"

She nodded, walking to the guitar and picking it up.

"It's not the original, but I found something close to it," Gavin remarked as she took the new instrument in her hands.

"You are"—she swallowed—"making it really hard to sing."

The energy thrumming through the room inspired her. The blood, sweat, and tears famous artists must have spilled and imprinted on tape and digital media gave her the strength to sing to her mother. She propped up on the stool and cradled the guitar in her lap.

"I will leave you to it," he said.

"No. Stay."

He sat on the couch along the wall, his presence meaning more than it had before. This was the right time and place to make it happen.

"You ready, Jolene?" Rick's voice sounded over the speakers.

"Yes."

She set her fingers on the bridge. They floated over the strings, and the melody glided from her throat without conscious thought. She closed her eyes and saw her mother's smile, felt her arms around her, smelled the lilies from her skin. With each verse, the spirit of her mother enveloped her through the song. Jolene had never experienced such a powerful reaction to her music. It was as if she'd become possessed. Lily was there, in that room, smiling and laughing with her little girl.

She didn't even realize the song had ended until the tears dropped from her eyes as the final chord reverberated in the room.

"Perfect, Jolene." She jolted back to reality at the sound of Rick's voice. Gavin leaned forward on the couch with a single tear falling from his eye.

"Did I...?" Her bottom lip quivered as she relaxed over the guitar.

He stood and in two strides caught her to his chest. "Yes, baby. You did. I love you so much." He kissed the crown of her head, and she melted further into him.

"I love you, too."

Jolene's leg twitched like it used to when the heroin high became too much. Meeting Zane alone made her old alert signals rise and jones for him...or rather what he used to bring her. He brought out the past dormant addiction reflex. Cold skin, hyperawareness, biting lips, and paranoia. It appeared everyone in the café stared with judgmental glances, assuming she awaited a drug exchange.

Underneath it all, she'd lied to Gavin. She'd told him she needed air and change of scenery to write. With her new confidence in her relationship with him, the impulse to squash any drama flooded her nerves. Her fingers had taken on a life of their own, texting Zane to meet her. And for what? To prove she wasn't scared anymore?

She closed her eyes to remember why her impulses led her here. It was time to separate the shadow dragging along the concrete and walk toward the sun, with the wind in her hair and the breeze on her face.

"Here ya go." She blinked to find the barista setting her coffee in front of her.

"Thanks."

"Hey, aren't you Jolene from The Dive?"

She nodded, acknowledging the show from the prior night. Well, as dive as New York City in Manhattan could get. It really only held the name. "Yep."

"Great set last night. I'm Dee." She gave a small wave.

She was petite with long faded pink tresses held back by a matching bandana. Her gray eyes were sunken slightly. Jolene's gaze drifted to Dee scratching her arm. There were marks. *Poor girl.*

"Nice to meet you, Dee."

"Where did you learn to play like that?" She bit her chipped fingernails.

"Back home, a long time ago." When her father bought her a guitar, he'd wanted her to learn "Tiny Dancer" for her mother. Now she and Marcus sang it as the first song to kick off a performance.

"Oh, yeah. Like, that's cool. Where's that?"

She blinked, taken back by the girl's inquisitive nature. "Doesn't matter. Are you from here?"

"Yeah. Sure." She shrugged looking around the room.

The unclear answer told Jolene she wasn't. She shook it off; most people were transplants from other cities.

"Dee." The girl looked over her shoulder at the manager behind the coffee counter.

"I better go. Nice to meet you, Jolene."

The bell of the café rang, taking her from Dee's face to the one she'd come to see. "You too."

Zane took up the space as he dusted off the first droplets of rain from an impending summer storm. He went to the counter and Dee took his order.

As he approached, she had to fight the desire to hug him. *I'm sorry* and *I'll do better*, rested on her tongue.

"Baby..." he breathed, wrapping his arms around her. Stale cigarettes and cologne beat her nose in disgust. "I'm glad you called."

"I'm not your baby."

"You always will be, Jolene."

"No, I won't. You robbed my apartment and smashed my guitar to scare me. It's not going to work anymore." The small girl she used to numb with opiates shook inside.

"You had my money, and your guitar kept us apart. You always had one eye on leaving me. Either come with me or I'll have to resort to things I'm trying to leave behind."

Dee walked over with her head down and placed a paper cup of coffee in front of Zane. He leaned back and his eyebrow twitched. She visibly swallowed and scurried away. *What was that?*

"I never planned on leaving you. You left me, remember?" She was falling into his trap as his voice wrapped around her insecurities and her voice lost its gusto.

"I love you, Jolene. Come home with me, please."

Home. Home. Home. A place where hell existed. "I don't love you, Zane. You need to understand that."

"I should have left you at that apartment."

She jerked back when his hand landed on her shoulder and she met his brown eyes coated with distaste. The flooding memory of her last night with him back in North Carolina swept her mind. Were there candles? *Yes.* Could the wicks make the circular marks marring her skin?

Her mind searched her old room. A mattress on the floor. A dresser. Clothes strewn about. An ironing board in the corner.

The smell.

Burning flesh taking her out of her dope high.

Zane on top of her.

The singeing of skin and a metal sting.

A finger found the circular divots. *Iron marks.*

"You did this." Her eyes weld up with tears.

"After you fucked Trip, I had no choice. No other man would touch you again, and I had to make sure of it."

The room spun, and all she could see were his eyes as the focal point. Gavin would never do such a thing. She was precious to him. His to use and to cherish.

The chair screeched across the floor and fell with a crash. "You *made* me sleep with him and for what?"

"To get us out of there. To start a new life." Suddenly his eyes went slack, pleading as his control slipped away. "I *need* you."

For the first time, his words fell on deaf ears. She didn't want to be needed. She wanted to be desired and cherished. Zane held a mountain of lies and manipulation over her. She was *his* drug, and without her, he'd resorted to a synthetic substance to settle the ache. A life of survival. She didn't want to survive; she wanted to *live.*

"Save your *needs* for someone else."

"Has Gavin even shared your little secret with the label?"

"Shut up," she whispered, meeting the eyes of several patrons.

"That's a no. Anything not to ruin his reputation, again. I know the score. He's using you, and if you go, I will find you both." He patted his waistband, the outline of a gun evident.

Threats or the truth? She understood the depth of his violence, but would he take it as far as killing her or harming Gavin? The one perfect thing she called her own? She had to break the cycle. Falling into his trap would hold her back. She was a survivor with the will to live a life of love and freedom.

"You will not take away anything anymore. Not my pride, my success, and not my love."

She dashed to the door, and the bell rang as she hit the street. She stomped down the sidewalk as raindrops splashed along the cement. *He manipulated and mutilated you.* Love and obsession were a fine line, and she could never tell the difference, until now.

As tears ran down her face, a hand wrapped around her bicep, dragging her into an alleyway.

"Never walk away from me." Zane slammed her against the wall and her head ricocheted off the bricks.

She spit in his face, pushing past the stars scanning her vision. His arm clamped her neck. "Does he know what a fucking slut you are?"

Slut. Coming from Gavin's lips, it held power and sexual desire. He didn't *need* her. He *wanted* all of her.

The tears tracked down the sides of her face. The Holy Mother tattoo on Zane's arm screamed in agony. She whispered, *"Give in"* as each of the souls, being dragged into hell, represented all the things Zane had taken from her. Freedom. Confidence. Power.

His hand moved below her skirt, and a rush of strength filled her bones. Her thumbs pushed into his eyes. He screamed releasing her and her swift knee met his groin.

She stood over him, tall and proud, her former keeper and the man meant to hold her down now curled up in pain.

"He does know what I am, and when I give it to him, he makes me feel like a fucking goddess."

She kicked him in the ribs and swiped the gun from his waistband. Her trembling hand aimed. One shot and he would never hurt her again. He'd never control her mind.

"Go ahead and do it, Jo."

"Hey!"

Her eyes shot up as a man exited the alleyway to pitch a bag of garbage into the dumpster. He stalked toward the scene while her past was laid out with an invisible chalk line to death. She dropped the gun with a thud.

"You made me feel like a whore not worth a shit. And these

scars? Proof you held low regard for the things you found precious."

"Are you okay?" The man pinned Zane down.

"Better than okay." She wrapped her arms around her middle as the rain pelted her. Each drop washed away any belief she wasn't good enough. Although frightened, the heavy rain bathed her in a baptism of personal acceptance.

TWENTY-SEVEN

GAVIN CLICKED OPEN THE LOCK OF HIS HOME. WOULD JOLENE BE at the breakfast bar strumming out her next creation? A completely natural, expectant response to what life had given him. *What. The. Fuck.* She turned his world sideways and the immediate comfort took him to a new level of power. A power not to be mistaken for contractual Dom/sub, but rather an organic feeling he belonged.

His keys clanked against the hardwood foyer table.

"Hey."

Jolene. His previous bright light faded. Her blonde hair was clumped in wet waves around her face and her shirt and skirt were soaked from the earlier summer rain.

"Why the hell are you wet? What's wrong?"

She curled into a ball on the couch. "A little rain never hurt."

He pulled her into his lap. Fresh rain and Jolene tickled his senses, stripping the darkness to gray.

"What happened today?"

"Nothing. Just tired."

"You're lying." He moved her hair behind her shoulder.

"Hold me, please."

Even though her body attempted to go limp in his arms, a trembling tension rippled her chilled muscles. How long had she been there?

"Look at me." Her dull, mossy green irises bordered dilated pupils with bloodshot whites and a far off look. "Did someone find out about us?"

"No. I'm tired and need to rest."

"Bullshit!" All patience fled his controlled thoughts. She flinched. "I'm trying to help. Please tell me, Jo, so I can fix it."

When the world came after him, he lashed out, but with his girl, she withered in shamefulness.

"Will you hurt me?"

His hands shook as they stroked her back, twitching at the invitation to exert force. Normally, he'd jump at a chance to inflict pain, but she held too many emotions.

"No."

"Please!" she shrilled.

Pain coated her gaze, and he wanted nothing more than to take it away, but not in the way she asked. "Why?"

"Because I need it."

He'd seen *need* before with subs looking for release but he'd never crossed this particular boundary. The club Dom was his job, of sorts, and this was real.

"I'm going to ask you a series of questions, Jo. I need you to answer honestly." She nodded. "Are you okay?"

"No."

He grimaced, wanting to coddle her and kiss the physical pain away, but he knew it would hole her up longer.

"I love you. You know that, right?"

"Yes," she whispered through shaking lips.

"Why do you need pain right now?"

"To help me talk. I feel nothing."

Her path to submission and discovery was new for him. Subs had lined up ready and waiting to be punished because they understood *need*. Working through a dynamic with an unsure Jolene was uncharted territory.

"Because of what happened today?"

"I-I don't know. Yes?"

"Do you want me to get you to your space to bring you to center?" he asked without expecting anything in return.

"Yes. I do."

He kissed her gently. She was hesitant at first, then opened wider, allowing him to love her while dominating the kiss. He helped her stand and patted his lap, fighting off the desire that was causing his cock to harden. "Bend over, love." She splayed her body over his leg.

"Over or under the skirt?"

"Under." He lifted it to find a purple thong with the V disappearing into her crevice. He rubbed it and sucked in a breath. *This is about her.*

"Count with me."

"Go until I say stop. Please."

In the past, no sub told him how to scene. *Jolene isn't your sub.* They weren't in a D/s relationship and he was still exploring her limits.

"Okay. Ready?"

"Yes."

Slap!

A grunt left her mouth. His hand mark quickly reddened in a perfect outline on her cheek.

Slap, slap, slap!

His erection pulsed with each hit to her flesh and sweat dotted his forehead. She squirmed as tears pushed out. *There she is.*

"Harder, please."

He slapped her twice on each cheek, his hand stinging from impact.

"Harder." She sniffled as he wondered how much he could

give her. "Do you have anything you can use?"

He pinched her reddened bottom. "Like what?"

"A paddle? I need more, please." Her hands squeezed his calf as she fought through something. *Is this why she numbed herself through drugs?*

"Jolene, we haven't…"

"Just do it, Gavin!" she yelled.

He pulled her up to straddle his lap. Her green eyes went vacant and the sobs stopped completely.

"Okay, Bluebird." He kissed her head and moved her to the cushions. He walked to the closet inside his office and opened it. Three boxes from The Resort occupied the space. The tape snapped as he opened the box labeled *implements.*

A black leather-spanking paddle caught his eye. An oval head and short grip would hurt like hell but it was better than a wooden paddle against her virgin skin. Having it in his hand, he wiped his brow. *Is this what you will always be?* A man getting off on hurting women consensually? He wished Jolene didn't invite it.

He walked back to Jolene. Knees to chest, she rubbed her cheek against the fabric of her flowered skirt. The vibrant woman he loved was in there somewhere.

Holding out the paddle, he showed it to her. She made no response to it, only nodded.

"Your knees on the couch and bend."

She did, but not before she stripped. Her clothes landed in a puddle on the floor. "Don't hold back."

Fuck. He needed to get his shit straight before they both ended up hurt.

"I will give what I think you can take. Now quiet." A visible shiver ran down her spine and goosebumps followed. Her scent from her glistening pussy floated through the air. He touched her slit, and she cringed forward.

"Jo," he warned. She'd never backed away from his touch.

"Not there." She reset her posture.

"Here, then." *Thwack!*

She screamed and reset, her body begging for more. *Thwack, Thwack!*

He wanted to touch her, but her reaction halted his need to push for it. Sex wasn't what she needed. She wanted his force.

"Are you with me?"

"Y-yes…" Still no tears. "Break me."

His arm went numb from reality, and his body transcended into a space he hadn't explored in a year. He felt like a protector, not a mere vehicle for release. She wanted him to take her over the edge to find whatever she needed to come back to him. A gift he'd forever cherish. "Just say stop."

Five more swings on each cheek and down her thighs. She sobbed as her skin turned past redness into a blueish tint.

"More," she cried.

Thwack!

"Fuck…" She shifted up then back.

Two quicker slaps followed hysterical shudders from her body.

"Up, Jolene. I need you present."

She pushed her ass out toward him, like the brave goddess she was. Wetness spilled from her cunt. Overly sensitized and aroused, she was coming back.

He swung and as the paddle met skin she screamed through tears. "F-fuck …God please! One more!"

He put his back into it as the leather met her bruising flesh. The paddle hit the hardwood and he draped her body over his lap.

"I'm s-s-sorry, Gavin," she wailed.

"Shhh. Lay still." He slid out from under her and grabbed a jar of soothing cream from the closet. He moved back under her and rubbed her sensitive skin with balm as her tears slowed. A swell of pride and protectiveness bloomed in his chest. She trusted him to take her to a new level of pain. He hadn't felt this way. Ever.

"Gavin..."

"Yes?" *Pat, pat.*

"I can feel it when you do that, ya know?"

He put the cap on the container and set it aside. "I would hope so."

"I mean the love. I've never *felt* it before. I thought I had, but with you, it's different." She turned her body and winced.

"Careful." He smoothed her damp hair back. God, she was striking. The sparkle in her eyes lit up like emeralds. His girl was back.

"I feel you pulling me out of this hell I live in."

"I feel you coming toward me. You're so beautiful when you release."

"Release? But I didn't finish."

"Not all release means an orgasm. It's a chemical thing. Up here." He lightly touched her furrowing forehead.

"I feel spent." She stretched slightly until the pain on her backside appeared to be too much.

"I'm sure you do."

"What about you? Do you get a mental release even though we didn't have sex?"

His dick still throbbed as he thought about taking her as she flew. "Yes. Very much. I've had subs I'd punish only for their pleasure."

"Really?" Her look of surprised warmed him.

"BDSM isn't always about sex. Does it arouse me? Sure. But it's all about the mindset going in. Some subs need punishment to feel free, which the turn-on wasn't an end game to sex, it was the astonishment of how they felt after. And the fact that I brought them there."

Looking back, he did have a swell of pride with those women. *God damn it, he was a son of a bitch.* Why hadn't those memories hit him before? Blinded by his power and will, it never registered. He twirled Jolene's hair in his fingers.

"Makes sense. It was a gradual lift to the light, then the last blow pushed me over. But..." She touched the button on his shirt. "I was still aroused. It confused me. Why the pain makes me want you inside me."

"Some people react differently. And I will admit, seeing you like that...so ready..." he groaned. "I wanted to take you, but this wasn't about me."

"I'm still trying to understand why a man wouldn't take something he wanted."

"I did for a long time."

"Do you hold back?"

"Only until I can assess and find cues from you. A red line for me is crossing into a false state of control. It doesn't have anything to do with you. You are perfect."

She rested her head against his chest. "I lied to you. I went to meet Zane at the cafe."

"What aren't you telling me?" His knuckles popped.

"He...he..."

Anger rippled through his body. "Did he fucking touch you, Jolene?"

Tears spewed from her already bloodshot eyes. "No, but he would have, had I not stopped him. If a man hadn't helped."

A red haze tinged his vision as he tried to pop up from the couch. Jolene snagged his shirt.

"I went to the police, and they arrested him. I only want you— right now, Gavin. Please." Her beautiful face pleaded. His fists furled to dissipate the rage within. "Please..."

He shushed her and carried her upstairs, then set her on the bed. "I'll be right back."

He escaped to the bathroom down the hall to splash his face with cold water in hopes it would extinguish his desire to find Zane and kill him. *Not yet. Not right now. She needs you.*

He patted his face with the hand towel and ran a hot bath, lit some candles and found Jolene in a ball on the mattress. "Come here, Bluebird."

Her arms went up like a child, and he scooped her up. With each step, her scent wrapped around him. He was in the right place, for now. Setting her delicately on the bathroom floor, he helped her into the warm tub. She winced as she sank into the water. He undressed and joined her.

She sobbed, curled up between his legs with her face against his chest.

"I'm here." He wanted to cry with her and for her. His girl had been through so much, and seeing her stripped of her toughness not only speared his heart, but swelled it to be the one who protected her. He snatched a loofa and poured liquid soap on the edges, fluffing the suds and cleaning her back.

"Do you want to talk about it?"

"You must think I'm stupid for meeting him."

He cringed as anger threatened to surface. The constant stroking kept the anxious mood at bay. "Can't say I'm thrilled. What were you thinking?"

"I thought I could face my fears."

"No one is built to face all their fears alone. I'm here to fight with you."

"I'm used to doing it alone."

Me too.

"He did this." Her hand dripped with water as she caressed her breast and shoulder. "He'd burned me with an iron while I was unconscious. It all came back to me today."

"Why did you go there? Why didn't you tell me?"

"After the robbery, I knew it was a scare tactic because I denied him the chance to take me upstate. I thought I was strong enough to face him."

"When?"

"At Eco when you met him. He has this place off the highway, not too far north of Manhattan. A place where we dreamed of living together when we decided to flee North Carolina."

"Did you want to go?" he asked regretfully. Was this the real reason she came to New York? To meet Zane halfway? A list of recent events lined his vision.

She broke into his house, obsessed over finding him.

She was the musician at Eco.

She lured him with her body and presence.

Her willingness to move in with him.

She went to see Zane *alone*.

He swallowed, drifting between truths and agendas. It appeared, on the surface, as purposeful. Could it be? He'd lured Shane with his charm and took down her business. What was Jolene's angle? Or was there one? *Get it together, man!* He shoved the insecurity away. He had to believe he was worth it. And right now, she needed him, and god damn it, he needed her too.

"No, but I led him on, after you and I argued. After he and I were at the motel, my past showed itself to me, and suddenly everything felt wrong. Dirty."

Her arms slid under his, and she hugged him close, as if telling him the truth meant he'd leave her. Her desperation, as though she'd read his mind moments ago, was too hard to ignore. It felt sincere.

"Nothing you say would make me leave, Bluebird. Help me understand."

"The way he treated me, when we fucked and the names he called me, woke me up. And then I was in the bathroom, and he'd laid out a line of heroin. I was so close, Gavin. So close to jumping back in but something stopped me."

"What?" He smoothed her face with his hand. He didn't care that she'd made a mistake because she was in search of a comfortable past, no matter how radical. He understood the rules of life: Reverting back to a familiar place became habit. Running away from New York for a year had been his way of resetting to push people away. For Jolene, finding Zane was hers.

"You. And when I left his room, you were waiting for me. *Fate.*"

"Fate is a strong word, Jo."

Her hands ran through his stubble. The friction of her touch and understanding gaze hung him on the precipice of losing complete control over her. A familiar fear from when his mother didn't return his love swam around his gut and stabbed his heart. Would Jolene do the same? Take it away and turn her back on him?

"And one I've come to understand. You were there like a beacon of truth. I love you. I know that now. I felt it before, but now I know it to be true."

He moved her to straddle him. He felt the shockwave of what she said through his entire body. And he believed her.

"I love you, too. Zane will not survive what he's done especially in here." He touched her chest over her scars. He leaned to kiss her where it must have hurt the most. He wanted to erase all the hurt and insecurities. He wanted to leave her with his love and the love she should feel for herself.

"Make love to me, Gavin." She moved her hips, which caused his hard-on to reach full length.

He kissed her gently as her hands touched his face. He caressed her breasts and down her form until he reached her folds. He rubbed where she desired, and she whimpered into his mouth.

"I want to, Jo. More than anything." He raised her up and she slid perfectly onto his cock. Skin against skin, she felt so right. Water sloshed over the edges of the tub as she rode him gently. Her vision cleared completely as she bit her lip, her body shaking through panting breaths.

"I want you to know how this…" He shoved his hips up as she came down, water spilling over the claw foot tub. "…is what I need to do to show you how much I love you. You are my every-thing. The only person...*Fu-uck...*" He lost his breath as she clenched around him.

Her rhythm became precise, slow and meaningful, as her beauty was lost on him. The electricity they'd created cocooned them in the warm bath and inside their hearts. Nothing could take it away from him. No one would stand in his way of having her. Not even himself.

"Yes...Gavin...keep going."

"You are the only person worth living for. Say you'll always be mine, Bluebird." He groaned through her movements.

"I will always be yours. We will always be...ours."

TWENTY-EIGHT

GAVIN CLOSED THE DOOR TO THE BEDROOM AFTER JOLENE FELL asleep in his arms. Anger bubbled over in a heap of fiery protectiveness. He dialed Brad's number.

"Brad Trainer," his cop voice clipped.

"It's Gavin."

"Gavin Mayne."

He walked down the stairs and paced the kitchen. "I need your help."

"This sounds like it goes beyond the call of duty for you, Mayne."

Gavin had expected a defensive conversation. Brad had never agreed with Gavin's outlook on life but helped him at The Resort because Ethan dealt with him directly.

"You're the only one that can make this happen."

"After what you did, I'm curious as to why you think I would want to get involved with you."

"This is different."

"Humor me."

Gavin clamped his jaw shut. "This isn't the same. It's for someone else."

"Jolene? Ethan mentioned her."

"She's in trouble. Zane Pearce attacked her today. I need to make sure he stays behind bars. You have the resources—"

"Sticking my neck out for you is suicide for my career. There's nothing I can do, unless she files a report."

"She did."

The clicking of a keyboard sounded. "Looks like he's out on bail. Third degree."

"What does that mean?"

"He was charged with a misdemeanor, and the guy has no priors. Therefore, he probably won't face jail time. He walked an hour ago."

Gavin's hand shook and the helplessness sank his gut. "Please, Brad. She's in danger. Can you get me a security team?"

"Not in that business anymore."

"Remember what happened with Maggie?"

Silence drew out. Gavin knew he'd overstepped, bringing up Brad's sister. An obsessed boyfriend had killed her, and Brad blamed himself for not paying attention to the warning signs.

"Leave her out of this."

"I'm begging you."

"Why?"

"Because I love her, god damn it!" He shut his stinging eyes.

A deep sigh. "Fine. Okay. I need to make a few calls."

"Thank you."

He plopped himself onto the dining room chair. As he set the phone down and crawled into a state of relief, the device buzzed along the barn wood tabletop. The hard sound sent him into heightened anxiety. The screen flashed *Corrine.*

"Hello?"

"What the hell is going on?"

"It's late, Corrine." Her question told him one thing.

"Is she with you?" And there it was.

The truth is a peculiar thing when it's never truly been tested.

Honesty with Jolene started becoming natural. He couldn't hide from her. When he peeled away a layer of himself, the light flashed brighter while his feet moved forward, no longer weighted in cement.

But with Corrine, the truth morphed into a layer of tar, suffocating his chest and locking his throat shut. The dual hemispheres of his brain fought to cover up his relationship or tell her the reality and gravity of the situation.

What helped was the promise of having Jolene. She was his salvation even if he lost his job—rather *when* he lost his job. A career didn't help him survive. Instead, it cast a purpose to run from himself and all the things transpiring in his life. And with Jolene, it didn't matter as long as they had each other. He *was* someone. He was hers.

"Yes. She's here."

A brief second of time burst the stress he held, but as quickly as it dissipated, the tension returned screaming in his head, *"What the hell are you doing!"*

"You know what this means, right?"

Of course he did. "I'll see you in the morning to discuss everything."

"I'm incredibly disappointed."

"Corrine?"

"Yes, Gavin?"

He could tell there was no smile on the other end of the line. He'd let her down, and over the last month or so, it had begun to matter to him. Eco was her baby and he understood what that meant.

"I'm sorry."

"Hey," he said quietly. The dawn light crept through the slatted blinds, surrounding Jolene in a morning haze.

"What time is it?"

"Early." He stroked her cheek with the back of his hand. "It's a big day."

She rolled to her back and stretched. One nipple was taut under the thin fabric of her pink tank top, while the other remained smooth. Her mussed hair spread like a tidal wave of silky sunshine across his pillow.

"I know. I can't wait."

Tonight marked the rehearsal for their launch. All the hard work they'd put into it would soon be released to a small crowd chomping at the bit to hear Eco's breakout duo. At least he still had hope.

"I'm so proud of you, Jo." He kissed her, capturing her excitement, success, and love in her kiss. And when he deepened it, he tasted her recovery and confidence. Everything she'd fought for to become a successful musician sated his hunger for his own achievements. She was it for him. The one thing that mattered.

"Whoa," she breathed as her body went limp into the mattress. "Just when I thought you'd shown me all that is *Gavin*, you lay a kiss like that on me."

His lips curved sadly.

"Are you okay?" She cupped his face in her hands. Getting anything over on a professional observer proved near impossible.

"Get some rest and warm up before rehearsal. You need to save those pipes for tomorrow." He stood and her hands ran the length of his arm, sending a spike of desire to his heart.

"Are you heading to the office?"

"Yeah, Bluebird."

"But you're in jeans." Her green gaze moved from his legs to his collared shirt, then his eyes. "What's going on?"

Why was saying goodbye to a job he didn't want to begin with so difficult?

"Get some rest." He kissed her again. "I'll be back later."

A different man.

TWENTY-NINE

HOT WATER FLOWED DOWN JOLENE'S BODY AS SHE PREPARED FOR one final rehearsal toward her dream. She smiled when the race to be a star faded into the warmth of Gavin's love. Could it be possible for two damaged souls—two halves of a whole—to become one? Was it possible to have it all?

She squirted his shampoo into her palm. A manly scent of earth permeated her nose. The base of the man who hid behind several layers and she'd crawled into each one.

Without thought, her voice opened up into a hum of happiness. With each scratch of her scalp the melody took up the glass box of the shower, filling the space in wonderment and surprise.

> *Bluebirds soar...hmmm...*
> *His freedom lures.*
> *How can love be....hummm...*

A creak from the shower door caused her to jump. She turned with soap bubbles falling into her eyes. She wiped them away to see the man she loved.

Gavin Mayne stood with aching blue eyes. The normal lustiness had been replaced by vulnerability even though his magnificent energy—still palpable to a man who inherently owned the air—held steadfast.

"Jesus, Gavin. You—"

Still clothed, he pushed her against the shower wall. Fingers fisted over soaked fabric as she ripped his shirt open. The buttons dropped away followed by the *splat* of his shirt falling to the floor.

"I want you, Jo."

"I'm here."

He fumbled with his belt and removed the sopping pants and underwear as his cock sprang free. His powerful hands at her waist, he lifted her body with ease. She locked her legs securely around his hips. He growled. She knew he needed her to be whatever he wanted, and if it meant a whore or a slut or the love of his life, she'd give all of it.

She wrapped her soapy body around him. His erection pushed up for permission, notching her entrance. "Please..."

He slid her down, and she received his cock in one slick stroke.

"Oh my God..." she panted, leaving crescents in his flesh with her nails. Her core adjusted and swelled around him.

He pulled out and thrust in over and over. "You like that, Bluebird?"

"More than anything. Fuck...I'm..." Her eyes rolled back. Could she climax that quickly? Stars sprouted behind her eyes— seeing heaven, a higher power— told her she could.

"Patience, love. I need time to show you..." He grunted as her pussy dripped for him, coating his shaft with proof she could cave any moment.

"Show...me...what?"

"How much I love you. I want you to feel what you do to me. In my heart." He slowed his thrusting hips and moved the wet hair from her face. "Look at me."

She did and all the answers were there. Love. Happiness. A future. *Home.*

"You slay me, Jo." *Thrust, thrust.* "You are my family and my future."

She inhaled the admission with her mouth on his lips, sucking his soul into hers. Her throat caught with each slow push and pull of his cock inside her. Had sex ever felt this good? This right?

"Come for me."

She went over, calling his name as if to carve it in stone. He spurted his love and whole being inside her, gripping her body forcefully. Marking her as his.

They groaned in unison as one more thrust took them to the heavens. He was her man. He was her God.

As the hot shower pelted over them, she hummed the song from moments earlier.

"What are you singing about, Bluebird?"

"Our love." She blushed.

"I hope it's enough, Jolene."

"It is. Are you okay?" Her wet hands wiped the mist of the shower away from his rugged face. Stubble scratched her skin, and his lips caught her palm to kiss the love line, which grew whenever he was near.

"I've never wanted anything so much in my life and here you are believing in me. You've made my heart beat for the first time. I don't care about anything else. As long as we are together we can *live.*"

She wrapped her arms around his neck, and he took them under the hot water, washing away any last bit of soiled pasts.

To live was her purpose.

To love was her choice.

And the two together made whatever came at them possible.

Jolene took a sip of her sparkling water with lime. Vintage gold chandeliers hung from the ceiling contrasting with the deep mahogany wood décor and red walls. It held a dream-like vision, and Kyle said it was the hottest live music venue in New York.

"Marcus told the guy: 'Stop touching his girl.'" Ardyce smiled. Her eyes beamed up at him.

"You're telling it wrong." He grinned.

"No, I'm not. It was the lunch hour and crowded."

"And he was standing too close."

He kissed her, and Jolene's heart soared. Her best friend had fallen for Ardyce faster than she'd ever seen him with any girl.

Ardyce's phone rang and a huge grin appeared. "I have to get this. Jolene, your fashion debut is about to make a splash!" She floated away into the empty room.

"What's up?" Marcus pulled out a neighboring barstool and sat.

"Nothing."

"Where did Mayne run off to? Shouldn't he be back by now?"

Gavin had dropped them off at the venue and had a few things to take care of. The ride to the club had been quiet, other than Marcus and her chirping about the set list. On a dime, he'd turned icy and distant when they got in the car.

"You would think. He's not answering my texts."

"I wouldn't worry."

She hit the button on her phone. It lit up. 8:37. *Where was he?*

"J&M!" Corrine bounced over to them in a hunter green jumper and gladiator sandals with Jane Popper closely behind. Why was their old manager there?

"Jane?" Marcus asked.

She pressed her cat eyeglasses at the bridge to meet flush against her face. She looked like she'd raided Zooey Deschanel's closet. A navy fit and flare dress hit her knees and the white collar had cartoon kitties all over it.

"What's going on?" Jolene slipped from the stool, a grip of fear and nausea sinking to her stomach.

Corrine cleared her throat. "Jane will be taking over your launch."

"What? Are you crazy?" Jolene squeaked and Jane's eyes widened past her glasses. "I'm not trying to be rude, but where's Gavin?"

How was he at the house? He was fine. No, he wasn't, not when he took her in the shower.

Marcus touched her shoulder. "Settle down."

"This is our career, Marcus. He got us this far, and he will see it through." She didn't know whether to be upset with Gavin or Corrine.

"Jane, can you give us a minute?" Corrine asked.

"Absolutely. If it means anything, Jo, I'm excited to work with you again." Her ruby red lips thinned and she spun on her ballet flats toward the stage.

"Come talk to me," Corrine said.

"Not until you tell me what's going on."

Corrine's blue eyes looked at Marcus and then her. "Haven't you been online?"

"No, I've been preparing for the launch."

"I know about you and Gavin. The news broke late last night. There are pictures of you together, at Electric Lady Studios and you entering his home. Have you been living with him?"

"Oh shit," Marcus whispered.

"Um...we..."

"*We* are, but because our apartment got robbed. Jolene's ex has been lurking around and Gavin offered us a place to stay until things blew over." Marcus stepped in trying to alleviate the situation.

"It's not what you think, Corrine."

She blew out a breath. "There's more. Some source told the *Indie Rox* blog you were attacked by someone named Zane

Pearce. The article mentions your past and speculation as an artist. They'd tried to spin it into a positive in connection with your music but dug up your history and Gavin's in the process. Quote: '*Recovering Addict And Runaway Seeks Salvation With Music Predator.*'"

Her past skeletons rattled inside her chest, dancing their way to the front of her existence, again. The hurtful quote ate her alive, and the demons feasted on exposed scars she'd always have.

"I'm fine," she breathed. "Please don't tell me you're giving up on me."

"I'm not. I'm *worried* about you. As a boss, I want to protect you. You are a strong woman, Jolene; I see that. And these things should be handled with a reputable team. That's why I accepted Gavin's resignation."

Guilt and shame corkscrewed their way into Jolene's chest, and blackness crowded her vision as she backed into the stool. "He...we love each other."

"He said as much."

"Then why let him go? Why not talk to me first?"

"He'd said the decision was final, and he couldn't let the news tarnish your debut."

"We were supposed to tell you together, supposed to do this *thing*"—she waved her hand around the room—"together."

Corrine's pale complexion paled even further. "He came into the office and packed his things. He and I had had discussions that, if he crossed any lines, Eco would put a stop to the launch and all parties would part ways."

"So he..."

"Said it was his fault, and you and Marcus shouldn't suffer the consequences. Eco has a no tolerance policy for this, and he wanted to make it right."

Jolene's trembling hands covered her face. He'd quit his job and was too ashamed to tell her. *"I hope it's enough, Jolene."* A proud man without a job or a family, he wanted to make sure his love would be enough.

"I can't do this without him. Where is he?"

"Jo, listen."

Jolene snapped up her phone and purse from the bar. "I'm not performing unless *he* is here to manage us." Adrenaline poured into her muscles as she made her way to the door.

"Where are you going?" Marcus called after her.

"Gavin quit his job for *me*. Saved us from losing our record deal. He won't be solely responsible for the choices I've made —*we* made together. Tell Corrine she better reassign Jane. Gavin is our manager and he's the only one I'll work with."

Marcus cracked a smile.

"What? It's not funny." She threw the shoulder strap over her head.

"You are *alive* right now. I've never seen this level of determination in you. Do you know where he is?"

She swallowed, and her heart spoke to where she would find a man searching for his soul, even when he thought he had nothing left.

"I have a pretty good idea."

Jolene tipped the cabbie and shuffled out of the vehicle in an abandoned lot behind The Resort. She noted the white Range Rover SUV. *He was here.*

When she reached the entrance, she tugged on the handle. *Locked.* She beat on the door with her hand until it hurt. Waited. Nothing.

"Shit..." She tapped her foot until an idea coalesced in her mind. She rummaged through her purse. "The things I will do for this man. At least picking a lock is the worst of it." She jimmied it, and like magic, it turned. "Old habits die hard."

The back hallway led her past several dark rooms, which she assumed were spaces for private play sessions. At the end of the L-shaped corridor, a door called to her. She opened it and the space enlarged into a humongous dance floor with bars set on two levels.

She heard a rustling below and stepped to look over the railing. Nothing. She moved around the mezzanine and took each step leading down into the depths of The Resort. Gavin came into view, bent forward rolling a tumbler of amber liquid between his palms. His hair was flopped over his forehead and over his face, which was semi-hidden behind a black mask.

She took a step and he looked up. Had she ever seen him this way? The intensity in his dark eyes? The Resort seemed to enhance his true self. The dominance seeping from his body sent a ripple of pleasure to her core. What if he took her with the animal vibe he portrayed? This was Gavin and she wanted him to unleash his dominance on her.

"You shouldn't be here." His voice came through strong and determined.

"*You* shouldn't be here. We had rehearsal."

His lip curled. "It's not your place to tell *me*."

She moved about the space, not letting his fury curb her bravery. The mahogany leather of the booth cooled her hot skin as she ran a hand along the seat back. She craned her neck up to gaze at the massive spherical chandelier in the center of the room. It was partially lit to allow a dull light to cast shadows around the space. It looked like the heart of the place, housing sexual promises, and she imagined it spurred many desires between its members.

Gavin observed each step she made through the black mask. The one he'd apparently worn to hide his internal self and keep people at bay, now he appeared to be using it to keep his own truth at a distance.

His jaw clamped as he leaned back in the open lounge booth,

and it gave her a few moments to examine what he used to be.

A feral man who made his own rules for survival.

A Dominant who took women to sexual heights yet blocked them from his world.

The man beyond the truth.

"This is you."

"Yes."

"Why have you been hiding from me?"

He laughed darkly and drank his bourbon. "This lifestyle isn't for you, Jolene."

The tone had been meant to scare her; instead, it stirred a mysterious craving in her gut. This could be her lifestyle. She wanted to show she accepted all of him or nothing at all. The small amount he taught her had come full circle. They were bonded by pain and felt a rebirth with pleasure.

"But this lifestyle is you, Gavin."

"You need to leave before it's too late."

"It already is. I'm here in this room, and I'm inside you."

He stood and tossed his glass. It shattered against the floor beyond her stance. "No, you're not! No one is!"

She cringed as his rage hit a nerve she wasn't sure she could overcome. She closed her eyes as visions of Zane and his torment came into view. It made her cower in the corners of her heart and lose herself.

But the fear was washed away by her trust in Gavin. His anger wasn't present to create a false superiority. It was there to protect her from him.

He whispered in her ear, the smell of bourbon hitting her senses, "You can't understand, Jolene. I am poison. I hurt people, and you will suffer like all the others."

She swallowed, allowing her courage to push through. Gavin only showed love and conviction, proving time and time again he remained a safe place. She needed to make him believe it by killing any remaining self-doubts he held close.

"You believe you are nothing," she stated, seeing his dark and tired eyes through the mask he wore.

"Fuck you."

"Where's the man I fell for? He's in here." She touched his chest over his button-down.

"No, Jolene. This is me. All the time. This is who you should run from."

"It's not black and white. Your good heart and this part of you coexist. I'm not running away; rather, I'm speeding toward it."

He took her biceps. The hot warmth of his control rippled her skin. "You should run away. I'm meant to be alone. I fight to save myself. I protect, so no one sees the ugliness, and I kill..." His eyes glazed over.

"No, Gavin. What happened with Nicolette was an accident."

He pulled her to the stairs leading to the exit of the club. He tossed her and she gripped the guide rail to keep from stumbling. "This isn't for you!"

"No!" she grunted, regaining her footing. "Whatever happened with Eco doesn't matter."

He laughed. "I'm a sick man, Jolene. We got wrapped up in something that could never be real."

She choked on the constriction of tears in her throat. He didn't mean it. She closed her eyes and thought about the day he pulled her out of herself on his sofa. He found her through pain and dominance, and she needed to find him.

"You are *not* pushing me away. I'm not one of your subs you can toss aside. I am your Bluebird. I'm the one with the power to make you soar. And you"—he remained facing away—"helped me realize the world isn't out to get me. You made me see I matter."

The shackles on her heart released. Her knees hit the hardwood with a thud before she realized she was offering herself to him.

Her higher power.

The man she loved.

THIRTY

My dearest Gavin,

I will never know if you read this letter, but you must understand you are my son. You always will be. I haven't been the mother I should've been, and I've worried about what had become of you.

I thought I'd made the right choices toward a better life for my two sons and daughter by staying with Charles. But as the years passed and you never returned, the decision to let you go crushed me. I mourned the loss of my son that day, a grief no mother should ever endure and all at my choice.

I understand what you must've gone through when Nicolette died. It's a bottomless cavern. A never-ending free fall. It never gets easier, and I assume you still battle the loss daily.

Charles is a good man. He built a life for us. His money was a means to keep us going. I had no education and no strength to take my children from their father. I had nowhere to go. My family disowned me, as you know, and when I became pregnant with Liam, Charles protected me, offering us a safe place for our growing family.

You must wonder why I stayed with a cheating man. He wasn't that man in the beginning. He was a caring, thoughtful, and tireless working father. He stuck by us until my worst mistake occurred. I was the cheater, not him, and I became the reason for those other women. I pushed him into their arms, all from a moment of weakness. Then I felt helpless, wondering what would happen to my sons because of my wrongdoing, so I stayed. We conceived Riley in hopes of rekindling the love. But it was gone.

The man involved was Rick. And no, he isn't your real uncle. He was the man who stole my heart and fathered a strong and diligent son. Rick is your dad...

Gavin crumbled the note as stinging tears fell from his eyes. An empty shell hardened his hope for a normal future. Knowing the truth felt like a knife slashing open his insides in a pattern of gashes never meant to heal.

Even though he loved Rick, the betrayal and fury bubbled in his stomach as he found himself surrounded by The Resort. All he could do was reclaim who he was. It was what he knew.

The man behind the mask.

Turning at the hard thump, Jolene was on her knees in front of him. Her arms outstretched along the floor as she tried to pull him in through submission, things she didn't fully understand. How could he have brought her into this world?

His whole life was a sham. His mother's fucking letter proved it. All truths now found to be lies crawled over his skin.

"Do you even know what you're doing?" he asked.

"Finding you, Sir."

"That's not my name."

"It is in this room. It is within your dominance. You are *Sir*."

Her conviction broke him, and he paced the room to snatch

anything he could break. *Not this way. It could never be this way. Who Am I? What...am...I?*

"Get out, Jolene!" *Crash.* "Leave me!" *Boom!* "No one wants this! No one can understand this! I belong to no one!" He punched the wall, and pieces of the damaged drywall piled at his feet.

"You are mine, Sir. I am yours!" she yelled against the hardwood.

Except Jolene. Her declaration sent a sobering shockwave through his veins. He swallowed to push back the constricting tears as he leaned his head against the wall. She couldn't understand what she said. She could never want the monster living within. He stomped over to her, grabbed a handful of hair, and pulled her head up to meet his gaze. She yelped.

"I am no one's," he gritted.

Her emerald eyes were clear and present. They flicked over his face, leaving a hot trail of desire in their wake. "You. Are. Mine," she snarled. Her bow lips curled and her crooked tooth showed. Her expression threatened to melt him.

"You want to understand this side of me, Jolene? You want to see why people leave?"

"I'm not leaving."

He pulled her hair and led her to the booth then ripped her midriff shirt in half. Her tits bounced behind the blue demi lace bra she wore. Her nipple pursed as her skin glowed a fiery red.

"Do it, Gavin. Take all of it."

He stripped her skirt and found her bare underneath. His dick raged in his pants. Her disobedience ticked up his inner Dom. She desired a punishment only his hand could wield. A violent connection to what burned beneath the facades they showed the world. Here they were free to be who they really are—the sadist and masochist.

"Oh, you bad girl. What did I tell you?" He pushed her shoulders down until her forehead touched leather and her ass lifted.

Thwack, thwack, thwack.

She yelped with each strike and fell into a deeper groan. "Yes, Sir. I've been a bad girl."

Her unmistakable scent filled the air. *Slap, Thwack.* "What have I told you?"

Thwack

"To wear underwear."

Thwack

"Why?"

"Because this cunt belongs to you and no one else."

Thwack, slap, slap. Her cherry red bottom turned hot, and his dick throbbed against his zipper. He smoothed her juice along her folds and up to her anus. She tightened. "And what else belongs to me, Bluebird?"

He circled a finger around her hole wanting to claim all of her. Hoping she would consent to silence the echoes in his head.

"My...*fuck*...my ass."

He groaned as he pushed two fingers in her cunt. "You think you can take all of me, slut?"

"If it pleases you..." He thrust his fingers until her core flexed at the invasion.

"Does that feel good?" The reflexive clench and release of her tender tissues surged through his hand, up his arm and down to his groin.

"Yes...so good."

He touched her tightening anus. "We take it slow. Are you with me?"

"Yes."

Any past thoughts of isolation from the world melted away at her bravery and beauty.

"Push out." He rimmed a finger around the sensitive area. She did and his finger unhurriedly slid in to the first knuckle. "How's that?"

"Good."

"Has anyone ever taken you here?"

"No."

He slid out and in gently until his whole finger pushed to where the knuckle met his palm. "You are so beautiful."

The hot, smooth tissues opened and rippled as she relaxed. His other hand coaxed her bundle of nerves to life and her moans became shallow. He inserted a second finger then a third.

"You're doing well, Bluebird." Sweat slipped down his face behind the mask he still wore. Seeing her through the false lenses brought him pleasure and distance.

"May I come for you?"

"No." He removed his hands and undid his pants. The zipper hitched every nerve cell in his body and the belt buckle clanked as the fabric fell to the floor. He smoothed his pulsing crown through the hot wetness of her swollen pussy. He pushed in and relief sputtered from them both. To feel her skin and friction against his cock made the world right. She would be there for him. Forever.

He slapped her ass and she tightened.

"Harder," she requested.

He pummeled her until the lightning storm in his balls shot up causing a roar to escape him.

"Please, need...to...."

"No!" He emptied his seed inside her, and he gripped her corn silk strands. As her neck craned, her succulent red lips parted. "You will, Bluebird. When I find it pleases me, remember?" *Smack!*

"Oh...yes!"

She raised her ass in the air, and the breath left his body as he released his hold on her. Come seeped from her pussy. *His come. His mark. His. His. His.* He pushed his face against her ass and lapped up their juices without a care. This was them, together. A salty and sweet tinge hit his tongue. He wouldn't stop until he possessed all of her.

She moaned when he bit her clit. "Give it to me."

He smeared their fluids on his fingers and coated her anus. "This is what you want?"

"Will it hurt?"

"Do you want it to hurt?"

"Yes..."

The word tumbled from her lips like a decree of their love. She wanted him raw, unabashed, unforgiving and honest. He was hard again from her trust and power. He notched his dick to her dark back entrance.

"Push out again."

She did, without reservation, and he pushed past the initial resistance. He pulled out slowly then back until fully seated inside the soft tissues.

"Does...it hurt, Bluebird?" He clamped his jaw to suppress the need to fuck her too hard.

"Yes...it's so full," she moaned.

"Need to move," he grunted. His hips took on a life of their own as the tightness around his cock rippled up his spine. "You feel fucking amazing. I'm going to make you soar."

Curling his arm around her hip, he gathered their fluids from her opening and smeared them over her clit as he slid in and out. He smacked her ass again and fucked her like a possessed animal. She was excising all his demons. His rage. His loneliness. Had he ever gone over like this? *No. There was only one who could...Jolene.* Pulling her hips into each thrust, the succulent tension built in his balls.

"Fuck, Jo. You're fucking beautiful. Come for me."

She called his name over and over. Her body quaked from the rolling orgasm he felt through each moan and thrust. He came again with a force he'd never felt, his body soaring above the clouds with her at his side. Only her. *Sweet fucking Jesus.* He crumbled over her as he lost his legs.

He blinked. Dazed and unsure. He felt her shift under his

weight. He moved to allow her room and pulled her back against him. "Jo," he breathed out.

"Hmmm?" she asked, sated and...amused?

Not scared. Not running. Amused. His body was flayed out as his wounds remained vulnerable for her to heal. *Finally.*

She turned, and her features were soft and accepting. Her lips curled as her hand moved to outline the mask he still wore, a thing he'd always identified with, now an object holding no purpose. As she rose over him, she slid the mask off his face as a ceremonial gesture of freedom. *Rightness.*

"There you are."

He kissed her longingly. The harmonious strokes of their tongues matched their hearts. They were one. Two lonely souls who'd found light in the world through their own darkness.

"I'm here. I'm so here, Jo. Fuck, I can't hide anymore. You won't let me, and I get all twisted on what's right and what's wrong. Why do you do this to me?"

As the high from moments ago dissipated into reality, regret slipped in.

"Because I love you. I don't want you to hide. This is you."

"I don't want it to be. I want to be the other guy. The one who's sweet and tender." He brushed the damp hair from her shadowed face.

"He's in there too. The one who bathed me. The one who bought me a guitar and found a way to bring my mother's song to life. It's all there, Gavin. Just because you have this ah-fucking-mazing dark and sexy side, doesn't mean the tenderness isn't there. It's beautiful watching you unravel. And it's fucking hot that I'm the one who does it to you."

She crawled up his naked body, straddling him. They laced fingers, and she kissed him gently even though her eyes seemed to have other plans.

"What happened today?" Jolene's raspy voice coated his skin like warm honey.

"I read a letter my mother gave me. It explained why she stayed with Charles and how she was sorry for letting me go."

Jolene said nothing, but the hitch in her throat let him know she was listening.

"I'm not who I thought I was, Jo. And I don't even know what it is to be myself. I've searched and searched for answers and have come up empty."

"Keep going…"

He swallowed the lump as his shadows forced their way out. "I'm not Charles' son. It all makes sense why he and I are so different. Why he could never love me. Why my mother stayed."

"Do you think she didn't love you?"

"She didn't. She loved her life more. She loved her mistakes far more than she could ever love her children. And you know what, Jo?"

"What?" In the delicate way Jolene listened and cared through soothing strokes, he found courage.

"I forgive her. I understand what loneliness can do because I have you. The one who saved my life."

He hugged her close. They lay on the leather booth for a while, enjoying the calming silence as he stroked her hair.

"Are you coming back to Eco?"

When he was summoned to the office, he'd entered the conference room to find Corrine waiting. She'd filled him in on the news and her own suspicion that he was taking advantage of Jolene and his power again. He explained his actions and bowed out gracefully so as not to tarnish Jolene's burgeoning music career.

"No. I can't. All I want is you. Besides, you're quite a handful, requiring all my attention." He tickled her ribs.

"Stop it!" She swatted his chest. "This is serious. I need you there. We can talk to Corrine."

A rush of absolute need to be in a job surged in his body. He didn't know how to function without one. But it didn't feel right after what happened. Moreover, Jolene needed to have her own career without his help. He couldn't let her live in the shadows of his rotten reputation.

"I'll still be there." He lifted her chin. "But as your man. You need to shine on your own, baby."

"But—" He put a finger over her lips.

"You are strong enough to prove to the world you are amazing. I would dampen your success. But with me in the wings..." He smiled, thinking about being backstage. "...I can be your wind."

Gavin entered Electric Lady Studios and nodded at the receptionist as he made a beeline to Studio A. The annoying red light taunted him from outside the door. *Fuck his session.* He swung the door open and it smacked the wall. The musician yelped and jumped back, removing the headphones from her ears.

"What the hell, Gavin. We're in a recording." Rick came from around the corner.

"What the fuck is this?" He held out the note with his mother's handwriting.

The female musician set down the headset. "I'm gonna grab a coffee." She left.

"Is everything in this letter true?"

He peeled it from Gavin's fingers. "Oh, Gavin. I didn't know."

"That I was your son? That you had an affair with my mother? You were the one person in this fucked up family I trusted." He lowered his head, the anger propelling him moments ago, evaporating into nothing after seeing Rick's kind eyes.

Rick put his hands on Gavin's shoulders and squeezed, something he used to do when Gavin was younger and distraught over his mother's absence. "Of course I knew. I meant the letter. Listen, she had her reasons."

Gavin sat on the couch. "Her reasons not to own up to her mistakes. Her reasons for being a perfect socialite wife. Fuck her reasons and the fact you went along with it."

"She loved you very much. You have to know that."

Tears flooded from Gavin's eyes, emotion having become a natural thing since falling for Jolene. "How can you say that? She never once called."

Rick grimaced as he sat next to him—*his son.* "She did. Even after you went to college."

"What?"

"She made me promise not to tell you."

"How can a mother not want to talk to her son? And how could you not want to tell me?"

"Because of Charles. He forbade it. He held so much over her and she was afraid she'd lose everything. I couldn't risk her losing it all and losing you as well."

"She could have been with you."

"Tried talking her into that." He chuckled, sadly. "I wasn't good enough. A man trying to raise three children on my salary in New York would have been tough. Even after Liam moved out, she wouldn't. Said she owed it to Charles to stay, and I assumed it was her way of living with her choices."

"You would have taken in Liam and Riley, too?"

"Of course. You kids deserved a better upbringing as far as I was concerned."

"You really are something else."

"Eh…it's a man's duty for the one he loves. He must accept all things about the person, even their faults."

"Did you date after Mom?"

"Nah. Too much love for the stubborn woman."

Rick stood and gathered up cords, wrapping them around his arm. "She tried to leave once. We had it all planned, and the day I went to meet her, she never showed up, said she couldn't face her children or me if she left her life behind. I knew then I should have moved on."

"But you didn't."

"I couldn't. I loved her for so long I didn't know how to give it to anyone else. A shmuck. I know."

Gavin cracked a smile. His father—*real father*— had been with him all this time. A man with endless oceans of love to give never to have it returned. What would Gavin's life have been like if he'd known at a young age? Would he be a different man? He walked over to Rick and hugged him.

"Oh, well...now..."

"Thank you, Rick. Thank you for everything." He pulled away, and Rick's meaty hand tapped him on the cheek as he would his own son. Because he was. It warmed his chest. He was going to be all right.

"Let's not waste any more time, okay?"

Gavin nodded. "Agreed."

THIRTY-ONE

"THANKS," GAVIN SAID TO DMITRY AS THE BACK DOOR TO THE CLUB opened. He had been hired as private security along with Brad Trainer for the event. The tall man didn't smile or speak, only let him through after he'd checked the perimeter of the club.

He sidled up next to Ethan in the wings of the side stage. Jolene appeared to be having the time of her life, feeding off the roar of the crowd and a final strum of her guitar. Her too-short paisley dress floated around her long legs, and she shifted her booted ankle to the side. Her nervous tic. A normal person wouldn't have noticed with the wide smile on her lips, but he knew all her tells.

Her corn silk braid created a crown of shimmering light around her head as she tilted it to thank the crowd. She was in her element, taking what was hers, and he beamed at her bravery.

"Thank you." Jolene looked at Marcus for a beat, then back to the packed room. "I'm going to take this last one alone. I've been working on this song for what seems like my entire life. I couldn't find the right chords because the heartbeat wasn't there until someone dug it out..."

Ethan elbowed Gavin's side. "Wonder who *someone* is."

Marcus stood and left the stage. What were they doing? This wasn't on the set list. He went to move ahead like a manager on duty.

Ethan snagged his elbow. "Hold tight."

Jolene continued, "It's about something I never thought I'd find. *Love.* Do y'all have love?" The audience answered back with claps and whistles. "Good. Hold onto it and never let it go. I hope you enjoy." She shifted the guitar and tested the sound as she sat on a high stool. Then her fingers danced over the strings, making a delicate wave of notes bouncing into Gavin's soul.

> *Running away to feel a purpose,*
> *Beyond anything I think I know,*
> *Attempting to fly all on my own.*

She sang with light tenderness as her eyes clamped shut. She swayed back and forth, overtaken by the melody. Gavin peered over the crowd. They appeared to be holding their breath.

> *But something altered, I changed for you,*
> *You did the same, our bodies entwined in two.*
> *You helped me fly, into the sky of blue,*
> *And I can't explain it, so I fly away with you,*
> *I soar because of you...*

As the song drifted into possibilities, Gavin's heart melted. He'd found his *one.*

She set her guitar down and bowed. She looked over her shoulder, and her beautiful smile, meant only for him, beamed with love and adoration. As the crowd roared, she spoke into the mic, "Let's hear it for Marcus Smith!"

Marcus hopped on stage and clapped, motioning toward Jolene, sending another tidal wave of cheers.

"Thank you all for coming, and thank you to Eco Recordz for

believing in us. There is one more person I'd like to thank. Without him, I would have never had the strength to make it this far." She turned again and Gavin's knees weakened. "Our manager and the man who stole my heart: Gavin Mayne."

Gavin had expected a silencing of the crowd at his name, but they cheered him forward, and he gathered Jolene up in his arms.

"I love you," she said.

He kissed her, unashamed to show his love to everyone in the world.

THIRTY-TWO

Marcus handed Jolene a lime spritzer. "Great show, Jo."

"You think it went well?" She twisted her ankle until the side of her boot touched the floor.

"I thought you were crazy going on your own there with a song I'd never heard, but it worked."

"It did…and thank you for everything." Jolene scanned the area as her nape prickled. Love intertwined with apprehension flooding her veins. She found Gavin's blue eyes watching her.

"Jo!" she heard her brother call as he came toward her.

"Go mingle and enjoy yourself." Marcus kissed her forehead and disappeared into the crowd.

"Elliot!" She leapt into her brother's outstretched arms. "Nice beard."

He scratched it. "Trying something different."

"Jo-Jo?" she heard behind him. Elliot side-stepped, and her father appeared.

"Hey, Dad." She wrapped her arms around him.

"You were amazing, pumpkin."

"Glad you could make it." He went to let go, but she tugged

back. The smell of country air and a woody scent drew her back to her childhood. "I love you."

"I love you, too."

"Where's Cheryl?" she asked, wanting to include her as well. It still stung her heart to consider her father dating, but tonight offered a new chapter in the history of the Harrisons. Her dad deserved happiness as much as she.

"At the merch table buying up everything she can." Jim laughed. "She's your number one fan, aside from me and Elliot."

She glanced over to the table as Cheryl held up a T-shirt. Everything would be okay. Her gaze shifted as Gavin approached with a sexy smile on his face.

"Mr. Harrison." Gavin held out a hand.

"Dad, this is Gavin, my boyfriend."

He shook. "Wonderful to meet you, and thank you for all you've done to help my daughter."

"Can't say I've done much. She's the talent, and honestly, she's done more for me than I can ever thank her for."

She blushed, hoping the dim club lighting would hide her giddiness.

"We should get dinner tomorrow while we're still here," Elliot suggested.

"We'd love that." And she meant it, because it was true. She couldn't wait to spend time with Cheryl and her family and talk about all that had changed for the better.

As they fell into a comfortable conversation, a small voice broke the air from behind her. "Um, excuse me. I'm sorry for interrupting."

Jolene turned to find a withering blonde with pink-striped hair. She scratched the bend in her arm over a long T-shirt.

"Oh, Dee?"

"You remember me?"

"Of course. How are you?" Jolene touched her bicep and Dee recoiled. A shot of fear trickled up Jolene's arm.

"I'm good. Wow, look at that." Her bony finger touched the *Music Heals* necklace around Jolene's neck. "What's it mean?"

It was apparent Dee used drugs to cope with life. Maybe it wasn't fear Jolene felt touching her, rather a similar past. Jolene looked up at Gavin talking to her family with confidence and ease.

She scooped the necklace and gazed into the engraving. "Something I held onto to remind me to keep pushing forward. I wear it every day so I won't go back."

"To what?"

"A life on the run filled with drugs and addiction." Dee's thin lips flattened as tears threatened in her gray eyes. "Are you in trouble, Dee? Do you need help?"

Dee shuffled her sneakered feet as the crowd chatter roared around them.

Jolene squeezed the trinket knowing she no longer needed it as a reminder to move forward. Gavin was her strength and future. Her salvation. She yanked the ball chain and it snapped.

"Here. You keep this as a reminder to move forward. Okay?" She tucked it into Dee's palm and squeezed.

"W-wow…thank you. Would you mind signing my CD? I know it's a lot to ask, but…"

"Sure."

"It's back with my stuff." She pointed to a table near the backstage entrance.

Gavin's gaze met hers from the corner of her eye. "Yeah, I can do it really quick."

Dee led her through the crowd to a table by the exit, weaving through the comments of the duo's performance.

They were amazing.

Can't wait to tell my friends.

Do you think Marcus is single?

Dee dug through her book bag and handed over a marker

along with the album. "He was wrong about you. You seem so nice and caring."

"Who?"

The marker squealed across the plastic case when an arm banded around her mouth, yanking her back.

"I'm sorry. I had no choice."

A pounding headache and raging music assaulted Jolene's ears. The air whipped through the crack in the windows as the sound of the New York evening pierced her brain.

"Here."

Zane's voice snapped her upright followed by dizziness. She slumped and cracked her eyelids open. He handed something to someone in the backseat. She shifted to find Dee snatching it from his hand. *What the fuck?*

Dee squealed in excitement. Her dark sadness from before had disappeared at the unmistakable sound of a crinkling plastic baggy followed the fizzle of a flame. *Her trophy for luring me.* The scent of burning vinegar woke Jolene's senses and clinched her gut.

"W-Where..."

"Shut up," Zane barked. Motion sickness ensued as the car weaved in and out of traffic.

"Pull over...I need to..." She flipped forward holding her abdomen.

"In here, bitch." He shoved a plastic bag at her.

"Where are you taking me?"

"You make me do things I don't want to because you lash out."

The car darkened, passing through a tunnel then the *whoosh, whoosh* of the highway alerted her they were leaving the city.

"Stop, Zane...please..." A hurl of soda water escaped, dripping into the bag. A familiar brain buzz dulled her alertness into fear and numbness. She looked down at the crease in her arm. The area showed a small pinprick and dried blood. "You poisoned me."

"I'm making sure you won't run."

"He will come...for me." She gagged.

With one hand on the steering wheel, he snatched her hair with the other, pulling her close to his face. The sting led to no pleasure this time.

"You're mine. No one knows where you are."

He tossed her away, and fear paralyzed her, allowing the fogginess to take her under.

"I d-don't l-love you."

He swiftly slammed her face against the dashboard. Stars and blinding pain filled her sight. "Shut the fuck up. SHUT UP! You have that ready yet, Dee?"

"Yeah," her voice squeaked.

"Then do it."

Jolene weaved in and out of consciousness as her nose dripped blood.

"Maybe we shouldn't. She's really nice, Zane." The quiver in Dee's voice reminded Jolene of her times of desperation. Her own pleading when she told Zane she didn't want to sleep with Trip. The times when she felt she didn't need to get high.

"Fucking do it, or you're next! Here." Jolene's arm became pinned across the seat back "Tie her up so she doesn't move."

A rope secured her wrist to the driver's side headrest followed by a rubber tourniquet tightening around her bicep. "No! Please!"

Another knock to her head and darkness swept over her as she felt a piercing sting in the crease of her arm.

This was it.

This was the end.

THIRTY-THREE

GAVIN SIPPED HIS DRINK AS ETHAN DRONED ON ABOUT A RECENT hook-up after parting ways with Jolene's family. He craned his neck to search over the crowd. *Where is Jolene?*

Brad cut his way through the jungle of people. His face impassive as usual but an odd tension exuded from his body.

"Gavin, you need to come with me," he whispered.

"Everything okay? Where's Jolene?"

Ethan stood abruptly when Gavin straightened.

"There's been an incident." Brad weaved through the crowd toward the back entrance of the stage and they followed.

"You said this was taken care of." Gavin pushed passed him and turned the corner to the back of the stage wing. Dmitry held his shoulder, blood seeping through his suit.

"How the fuck did this happen?" He knelt in front of the big bouncer.

"The security tape showed a man matching Zane's description as he came in the back door. He has Jolene."

Dmitry winced. "He was quick. Pushed through the door and shot me. He had a silencer. Before I could grab my gun, he snatched her from the stage entrance." He pointed behind Gavin. "And fled out the exit."

Rage empowered his muscles, and he shot up and busted through the stage door. "Ethan, have everyone questioned when the police arrive. No one leaves here until we get something that will lead us to her."

"Gavin," Brad called. "How do you know where to go?"

"Get the fuck in the car, Brad." He opened the door to his SUV parked in the alley. His brain flipped through every conversation he and Jolene had.

"We are en route." Brad barked orders into the mic on his wrist along with Zane's description and make of car to the police department.

Gavin peeled out into the city streets and darted through evening traffic. A stoplight beamed yellow, and he hit the gas, charging through it. *Where would he take her? Think. Think.*

"Where is she?"

"I don't—" Then it hit him.

"He has this place off the highway, not too far north of Manhattan."

Gavin barreled right to take the Holland tunnel. The tires squealed. In the distance, a dark cloud loomed ahead.

He nearly shattered the steering wheel as the heel of his hand landed. "What the fuck, Brad? You had one job. One fucking job and it was to protect her."

"I don't know what happened. He took her before I could get through the crowd."

The cloud hovered over the entrance to the bridge and a shit storm of fate and failure awaited him on the other side. As they sped across the tunnel threshold, rain pelted the windows, blinding his course. Gavin revved the engine and weaved in and out of traffic.

"Slow down! You wanna get us killed?"

Zane had Jolene. His heart hammered in his chest to get to her.

"GPS a cabin or trailer housing into your phone."

"What?"

"That's where he's taking her. He has some place north of here."

He typed. "There are several in the area."

Fuck! "Pick one! And what did his car look like? Where do we turn?"

A muffled voice came through his earpiece. "Stay on 78...wait...Turn!" Brad shouted. "I see them!"

A beat up gray Chevy appeared up ahead, a small vehicle in the distance. "Are you sure?"

"Yes. His plate came through and police are on their way."

The car curved across the expressway. Gavin spun the wheel to play into the hydroplane as the tires squealed to find cement.

Cars ahead blocked the toll road, and he hit the gas to speed to an open lane. A crash echoed off his car as the gate splintered through the air.

"Here...here...here!" Brad pointed as the exit skidded past them.

The SUV thumped over the barrier markers as mud flew from the wheel in his rearview. Tires gripped the pavement as they found themselves on a wet and foggy road.

She would be okay. She had to be.

Brake lights signaled in the distance. Hope spurred his heart. Could it be them? It halted at a stop sign and Gavin barreled alongside it.

"Not them," Brad said holding the oh-shit handle as the car raced forward. Splattering globs of rain smacked the glass as the windshield wipers swished side to side to keep the rain at bay. Weaving around each corner, Brad notated the turns. He knew this area well from his time as a police chief.

"We'll find her. I promise."

One more bend and the car came into view before jetting off. Fear gripped him, sending his mind into overdrive, and he went to hit the gas before the car fishtailed out of control. *No! Please! Not again!*

"Gavin, listen to me!" *Sarah yelled through the pouring rain and the raging blood in Gavin's ears.*

"Don't tell me I'm not a good father. This is all your fault!" *he boomed.*

"My fault? You were supposed to pick her up. How could you forget your own daughter?"

Whines sounded from the backseat as Gavin glanced in the rearview mirror. "Enough, Nicolette. Enough!" *His child recoiled in her seat. Her sniffles and hiccups told him she was scared.*

"You brought this upon yourself, Sarah. We were never meant to have a child!"

Regret smacked him in the face. How could he say that out loud? Their arguments had become increasingly constant over the last few months, and Gavin found himself running away from his problems, especially when it came to his daughter.

He weaved around winding roads to his parents' estate. He needed to drop them off and cower away into a world of drinking and women. He and Sarah were never meant to be together, and it pained him to admit it. She was his college sweetheart, but having a child together too soon ruined them. Before he knew it, his life had unraveled, and even though Nicolette's smile threatened to overcome the darkness, it failed.

"Don't talk to her that way. And it takes two, Gavin. We both brought her into the world. That doesn't excuse you for being like your own father! We deserve better!"

Gavin's hand went out and slapped her. A blinding admission flooded his chest as she sobbed. What had he done? Nicolette's wailing increased as the storm sent a thunderous boom above them.

"Fuck, Sarah...I'm..." *He went to reach for her.*

"Get off! Pull over!"

"Don't be ridiculous."

"Let us out!" *She grabbed the wheel swerving the car right, the rain being too much for the speed Gavin traveled. Blinding truck lights killed his sight as he swung the wheel to the left. The truck's horn blared and clipped the back end sending the car spiraling out of control. The last thing he heard was the crushing metal of the car against a tree and the blood curdling screams of Sarah and Nicolette.*

"Gavin! Look out!" Brad's shouts brought him back as the car in front of them smashed into a guardrail, sending the car over an embankment.

Gavin slammed on the brakes, skidding to a halt, seconds before following the car's path. He jumped out of the SUV, crippled with fear. Flames burst into the wet air followed by a man's scream. That terrible night overtook him as his feet remained glued to the pavement.

Brad ran ahead, and Gavin scrambled to follow. He slid down the hillside with strength and determination. He could rewrite his history and fucking save her.

"Jolene! Jolene!"

The driver's side had scorched up in flames as gasoline permeated the air. They didn't have much time. Jolene and another passenger were passed out from the impact. Gavin tried the door. The flames heightened and the smoke billowed around them as the summer storm winds picked up. Sweat and rain dripped into his eyes as he coughed and searched for something to help. He grabbed a rock and smashed the window to bits. Brad followed suit.

Glass fragments pelted the area and covered Jolene's lifeless body. Her arm was tethered to the headrest. He leaned over the window and paused at Zane's burnt body hunched over the wheel.

"Gavin, hurry!" Brad yelled pulling the passenger from the back.

Gavin moved to untie her, but the rope was knotted tightly. The flames heated the small area and smoke stung his eyes. "Come on…" he grunted, pulling at the unmoving knot.

"Jolene! Baby, I'm here."

He tried again as the flames engulfed Zane's body and caught the sleeve of Gavin's shirt. The fire crept up his arm. "Agh!"

He backed out of the car as Brad returned, patting his arm with his jacket. "Jesus, you're burning."

"She's bound. Do you have a knife?"

Brad made quick work with his switchblade and dove into the car and pulled Jolene out.

Gavin snatched Jolene and climbed the hillside, cradling her.

"Baby...Bluebird...wake up, please." He took her chin as he begged. Her eyes were swollen shut, and blood seeped from her broken nose. Her lips were blue. "Jolene, I'm here. I'm fucking here. Don't die on me!"

His ear went to her chest. A faint heartbeat thrummed. He pinched her nose and blew air into her lungs. *Once. twice.* He blew again until a rumble of coughs escaped her. Her eyelids remained closed, and her body flopped about. He tucked her into his arms, rocking back and forth, as tears ran down his face.

"You'll be okay, Bluebird. I promise."

THIRTY-FOUR

"DADDY!" NICOLETTE BOUNCES FORWARD ON SMALL LEGS AND LEAPS
into Gavin's arms.

*He scoops her up, inhaling her baby powder essence. Her little arms
wrap around his neck. Peace calms his tormented heart. She is just as he
remembered. Beautiful, soft, and full of life.*

"I've missed you."

She giggles, a sweet sound. "I love you, Daddy."

"I love you, too."

"Don't cry. Grandma told me to tell you, I'm safe."

His body shakes as he looks into her bright blue eyes. "She did?"

*She nods with purpose, and he kisses her delicate cheek. Her smile
casts warmth over his body.*

*"What's this?" He touches the golden crown, surrounding her wild
mane of white curls.*

"I'm a princess and you are the prince!"

"Well, I wouldn't say that."

"No, Daddy, you need to be the prince."

"Okay," he says.

"No! I mean it!" she squeals in his ear.

"Okay, okay, princess."

Her little hands are warm as they touch his cheeks. Her arctic blue eyes sparkle with sincerity. "You need to save her."

Confusion and a sick feeling rapidly flow through his veins and twist his stomach. "Save who, Nicolette?"

"Save her, Daddy. She needs you. Be the prince."

Gavin jackknifed off the bed in panic. "Nicolette…"

"Relax, Gavin. You've been through a lot." Rick darted toward the bed.

He shrugged him off, Nicolette fading away into the dream.

"Save her, Daddy."

He found his arm wrapped in gauze from fingers to shoulder. "What the fuck?"

"You were burned pretty bad."

"Where's Jolene?" He flipped his legs off the bed. Sweat slipped down his spine and forehead.

"Relax."

"Where the fuck is she, Rick?"

Gavin yanked the IV from his arm and stumbled out of the room. Dizziness threatened to cause him to crash to the ground as he limped into the hallway.

"Whoa, big guy. I'm sure the nursing staff could do without your ass flashing the hospital."

He spun to find Ethan chatting it up with a blonde nurse. She giggled and went to Gavin, helping him into the chair outside the hospital room door.

"You need to be in bed," she chirped, checking his bandages.

"Where is she, Ethan? Did she…is she…?"

Ethan's lips thinned, and Gavin gasped for air. Ethan knelt beside him, as the overwhelming feeling became too much. Gavin's entire body quaked, and he no longer cared who saw the vulnerable side of him. He couldn't live without her. He was too late.

"She's okay, man."

"What? W-where is she?" Gavin tried to get up and fell back into the chair.

"Settle down. She's gonna need some time. She's not well."

"How long have I been here?"

"A few days. You don't remember?"

A car crash. Flames burning. Holding Jolene's comatose body in his arms. He couldn't put anything together after that.

"You put up a fight every day with the nurse staff." Ethan chuckled. "They wanted to tie you to the bed, but I told them you weren't into that."

"Fuck you, Ethan."

"Calm down. You can see her once you get a grip." He looked up and spoke to Rick. "Help me get him into bed...again."

A few hours later, Gavin walked achingly to Jolene's room, his IV bag on a rolling stand.

Her father stood from a seated position and greeted him. "Gavin."

He shook his hand and looked over at Jolene. Her hair had been wrapped in a greasy bun and bruises marred her face. She gingerly moved her head toward Gavin's voice. "How is she?"

"A few broken ribs and nose but she'll make a full recovery."

"Thank God."

"Gavin?" she whispered.

"I'll leave you two alone for a minute."

Gavin sat on the edge of the bed. His good hand stroked her face. "Yes, Bluebird. I'm here."

She shuddered as sobs escaped. All he wanted was to hold her, but he couldn't in her frail state. He snatched a tissue from the side table and wiped her tears. Purple and blue bruises were spread across her beautiful face. He wished he could kiss the pain away.

"When you're better, we will go far away from here and just *be* for a while."

"I'm so sorry..."

"There's nothing to be sorry about. You're safe now. Zane is gone."

"Did he...?" The tears flowed from her eyes.

"Yes. Died at the scene. Just sleep, love."

"I can't."

"Yes, you can. I'm here and will keep you protected."

"No, I can't do this anymore." She groaned in agony as she pulled her hand away and wrapped her arms across her abdomen.

"What can't you do?"

"Be with you. I can't keep putting people in danger. I-I..." Her breath hitched. "I'm nothing but damaging to those I love."

"That's not true."

"Look at you." She gestured at the bandaged burns running up his arms.

"That's nothing. It'll be fine." He scooted closer to cup her battered face. "You are everything, Jolene. You are perfect. You are my whole life."

"He drugged me, Gavin..."

Her words came out even. He grasped her hand as the simmering rage still burned within. He wished he could have beat that fucker into a bloody pulp for all the wrongs he'd committed.

"...Stuck a needle in me. I've been sick for days. I want to use again, and that poor girl—"

"Who?" *What girl?*

"Dee. The girl in the car, and he made her do it. She didn't want to, and I couldn't stop it."

"You're getting worked up." He loosened his grip and patted her hand. She laced her fingers with his.

"I need you to understand. She was *me*. Dee did what Zane told her to in order to get a fix. Don't you see? That's the life of a junkie. Rehabbed or not, that urge to obey to get something in return will always be there."

"You need time, Bluebird. You're not thinking clearly."

He swallowed, trying to help her understand the past didn't make her who she was today. It didn't define her, rather formed her into the woman he cherished.

"I can't be with you, Gavin. I need to fix what's inside."

He touched his forehead to hers, wrapping his hands gingerly around her face. "I would never hurt you."

She breathed out. "It's not you I'm afraid of. It's me."

"I can help—"

"I'm so sorry. I can't..."

The door creaked open, and Gavin spun around. Her father and Marcus stood in the entryway.

"But, Jolene..."

"You need to go." Her head moved away, her face toward the windows, and she slowly turned to her side. Marcus' hand landed on Gavin's shoulder.

He remained still for a moment, looking over Jolene's worn body. He loved her more than she loved herself. If only he could kiss away her fears and help her see she was worthy of love.

But his will to control her halted him. His entire life revolved around controlling people because *he* felt in command of the outcome. Control meant conquering his desires no matter the obstacles standing in his way. But in that moment, it was something entirely different. Control was never supposed to be about bending the will of others, it existed to bend his own.

He cleared his constricting throat. He would wait and allow her the time she requested. He stood and kissed her head.

"You will always be my Bluebird. I love you."

Marcus helped him to the door. "She'll be okay. Just give her time."

"Time she needs with me." He ached all over. In his bones, his head, and his heart. Control would prove to be a difficult task to achieve when his entire being fought against it.

"No, time she needs for herself. Even after rehab her lone goal was to get her father's love back, even though it was always there. She never found her true soul. She found the one she thought he would accept."

The sting of tears blurred his vision. She needed to find her wings so she could soar through the clouds on her own.

If you love someone, set them free. If they come back, they're yours; if they don't, they never were.

But if she never returned, he would always be hers.

THIRTY-FIVE

THE DAY GAVIN PACKED HIS THINGS AS A TEENAGER, THE DECISION to be alone had become a paramount feeling. A mountain to climb, to call his own. It pushed him to succeed in life, providing a false layer of power. He would not fail. Of course, living with Rick gave him a place to stash his things and concentrate on a future, but it was Gavin himself who made it possible. All he had to do was stay on task, check the proverbial boxes until his decision to pursue a career in the music industry had been solidified. He had a give-no-fuck attitude about who he might hurt along the way, as long as he came out on top. The burn in his gut and twisting in his chest always pushed him forward.

Now, the will to fight sputtered out from an empty gas tank with no station to fill it. He was exhausted from fighting. His goals were blurred and intangible. And love couldn't be held onto.

As the cab stopped, he shifted his unburned hand into his pocket and paid the cabbie. He gazed up at his home. The *For Sale* sign blew in the breeze, and the attached "sold" decal mocked him. He once had great pride in his house, now sold to a holdings company who would eventually sell to the highest bidder. A house filled by Jolene's love.

As he trudged up the stairs, the mountain of stress to pack and find a new place to live beat down on him. He fumbled with his keys, and they dropped on the cement with a *chink*.

"Fuck…" he murmured and bent over to snatch them up. The door creaked open as he hooked the loop on his finger.

"What the hell? How did you get…"

"You're early." Liam clicked the door behind him after he'd entered.

"Early? I fucking live here, Liam."

"Let's go to your office and I'll explain."

Liam paced along the windows as Gavin sat on the leather couch. "You're a saint for what you did for Jolene, and her album is creeping up the charts on iTunes."

The pain shooting through the nerves in his injured arm made him too tired to understand what and *why* Liam was here.

"And?"

"You did it. Captured your career and fell in love. Now you can have this all back." Liam yanked a trifold white paper from his inner coat pocket and handed it to him.

Gavin unfolded it and read his signature for the sale of the house. "Why do you have my closing papers?"

"The MI Holdings Company is rescinding the offer."

"MI?"

"Mayne Industries," Liam said with a pompous tone.

"You bought my house?"

"To protect your assets. You were in a bad way, and I knew you wouldn't come to me for help. I bought your property as a safeguard until you got a foothold. This house was everything you worked for. When Omega went down, I intervened."

He slouched into the couch, the paper burning his hand as the black script of his signature, *Gavin Mayne*, leapt out at him. The shadowed hold his family had on a boy they threw away disintegrated as his emotions caught up with his head and he began to comprehend what Liam offered him.

"You did this for me? What do you want, Liam?" Gavin clamped his jaw, unsure of which emotion to express. Anger? Happiness? Relief? Love?

"I want you to be happy. I want to be a part of your life."

Liam swiped a hand through his hair, an awkward, nervous gesture Gavin had never witnessed. Maybe he wasn't alone.

"Why tell me now?"

Liam sighed and sat next to him. "Because I have a huge amount of respect for you. You wouldn't have taken my help or believed me if you knew sooner. And…"

"And what?"

"I saw Father's face after Mother went. It seemed he was there to make sure she was gone." His fingers absently circled the vacant spot on his finger where their father's ring used to be. "It got me thinking."

"About?"

"About life. Marriage. Women." He smirked to himself. "I always thought, even though Father was a tough man and cheating husband, surely he cared about Mother. Why else would he keep her? Why not let her go? He had this strange pull over her, like he did us. I'll never know, but when I saw a quick nod to the doctor and him leave the room—minutes after she passed—it hit me. He was there to make sure it happened, like finalizing a business deal. Now I know why my marriages keep failing. Because I *am* him."

A silence of comfort rather than disparity blanketed the two brothers.

"My entire life has been proving to him I could be successful. A lifetime of blind trust bonded me to him. I thought being like him in all aspects—women included—would make him say he loved me." He looked at Gavin. "And what's funny is the reality I lived in for almost forty years flipped completely when Mom passed. I now feel like you. I'm *happy* to feel like you."

"Wow, you're really fucked up over this."

"More like awake."

"What does this have to do with this house?"

"Maybe it has to do with Jolene. Kate was an employee of Mayne Industries."

Gavin didn't know anything about Liam's recent wife other than her name. "You're kidding?"

"Kate was my assistant, and even though I tried to avoid her, something called to me. Kate was the one. Yes, I know…wife number three, but believe me, I would've done anything for her, even invest in a failing start-up."

Gavin's eyebrows shot up. "You hired me to impress your wife?"

"I knew you would help Corrine, and then I could be the hero. *'The man with a list of screw ups saves his niece's business.'* I thought it would bring Kate back." He laughed and patted Gavin on the shoulder before moving to the door. "Be good to Jolene. You and she will make it."

"She left," he admitted, regretfully.

"She'll be back. I know it. There were no agendas with her or you, and that is a beautiful thing. I watched my brother fall in love and do something for someone other than himself."

THIRTY-SIX

THREE MONTHS LATER...

THE DAYS WERE SHORTER AND STILL TIME PASSED SLOWLY. JOLENE sat on a bench overlooking the serene pond and massive oak tree at the rehab center. She attempted to bottle up the foreign feeling in her soul lurking behind drug hazes, stubborn pride, and purposeful misplacement in the world. While the feeling of personal acceptance and love was welcomed, she never fully filled in the missing piece: *Gavin.*

She scribbled in her journal. A hodgepodge of feelings, questions, and random song lyrics filled each page, the final passages all leading to him. She had a hard time differentiating the powerful longing as real or simply an addiction to him. Today was her last day on the property and she still didn't have the answer.

A longhaired man moved into her periphery, and a smile widened on her face so large it hurt. *Marcus.* She slouched back against the bench.

"It's not contagious, ya know?"

He laughed at her attempt to relive the first conversation they had when they'd met at this very spot years ago.

"What isn't?" He played along.

"Addiction."

He sat down and held out his hand. "Marcus."

"Jolene." She tapped a finger to her chin. "Musician type, right? The ladies should look out for you."

A deep laugh escaped as his boyish smile filled her bones. "You should have listened to your own advice."

"Good thing I didn't."

He grabbed her hand, and she willingly laced her fingers with his. The friendly vibe rippled up her arm. Marcus had given up the music scene to stay nearby with her family. He visited every day and helped her through her losses and rediscovery of life.

"How's Dee?" he asked.

"She's good. Left yesterday. It was great helping her find the strength to go to her family for help."

Before Jolene left New York for the North Carolina facility, she found Dee in the same hospital. Jolene urged her to attempt a clean life and shared personal stories of her own struggles. She became somewhat of an older guardian to Dee as they went through the program together. The experience fostered forgiveness for what Dee had done. And perhaps it was a way for Jolene to finally let go of the fear of Zane. Maybe it was a way for her and Dee to close the door on him forever.

"You never cease to amaze me, Jolene. Last day here, huh?"

"Yep." Her lips smacked in apprehension.

"You ready?"

"Pretty much. I'd be delaying the inevitable of being in the real world again by staying." She moved a hand over her journal. *Gavin.* She missed him, and her writings were the only thing keeping them tied.

"Are you writing again?" He snatched her leather-bound confessions and flipped until he stopped at the red ribbon marking a section. "You have enough material to make us a new album."

"It feels weird. They're all about him."

"Ah, the muse." He scanned the pages. "Damn, Jolene. These lyrics are hot."

She snapped up the journal from his hands, and if she could have ingested it she would have, anything to get Gavin back inside her. Her toes curled as blood shot south. Writing about her desire helped suppress the compulsion to crawl to him.

"Have you spoken to him?"

"Only in here. Things I'm afraid to say out loud."

"Do you think it's time you did?"

"What if I fuck up again?"

"You might."

She scoffed. "Gee, thanks."

"We all fuck up, but it's what we learn from those errors that makes us better. You can't live your life behind these walls for fear you might stumble. The scars give us character. Makes us stronger. And you"—he dotted her nose—"are the strongest human I know."

She exhaled what felt like years of torment and conflict. Marcus could always cut through her wonderings and musings.

"I have something that will cheer you up and make you see this all happened for a reason."

She cocked her head. "Okay."

He scooped his phone from his back pocket and tapped the screen. He handed the device to her.

iTunes displayed, and her song "Bluebird" had cracked the top ten.

"What? This can't be."

"Gavin said festival managers are awaiting your return and interview requests are stacking up; the media's clambering to hear your story."

"*Our* story. You've spoken to him?"

"Once or twice. He's been managing our work while you've been getting better. And he's back at Eco."

"Why haven't you mentioned anything?"

"He didn't want me to, said it was for the best. He's even lined up a manager to take over."

All the warmth in her body turned icy. "He's letting me go."

"What do you mean?"

"The other manager. I waited too long, Marcus. I should've called him."

"I don't think that's it."

"Then why line up someone else to manage us?"

"He was giving you space, Jo. The time you need to figure this out."

And when would that time end? Would she ever figure it out? She glanced at the phone screen and touched the album cover. Their song...his song...the one that made her a success. He was rooted so far into her heart, it squeezed the lyrics right out of her, and now she might be too late.

THIRTY-SEVEN

"LET'S SET HIM UP FOR NEXT WEEK." GAVIN TUCKED THE CONTRACT for his new artist, Charlie Snow, into his desk drawer.

"I think I can squeeze him in." The sound of shuffling papers transmitted through the receiver as Kyle narrowed down a time slot. "It's gotta be Thursday. Early. Say, seven o'clock?"

Gavin smiled at Kyle's enthusiasm to fit in a new act around Eco's thriving musician schedule.

"He'll be there."

They disconnected and Gavin's chair squeaked as he leaned back. The last few months had turned things around for him. Several offers had been given to new musicians, and he and Corrine had hired a robust staff of sound engineers, managing interns, and a full-fledged marketing department. The investors, thanks to Liam, had pumped money into building a new studio with state of the art sound equipment and funding for touring schedules.

Jolene's song had hit number three on the iTunes charts. He never expected it when Kyle insisted on releasing it. Hell, he didn't even notice with everything going on. Once the news of

Jolene's accident and his heroic effort to save her hit the news wire, the music industry wanted to capitalize on it.

He swiped the framed photo of Jolene from his desk. He'd taken it the night they released the album. The lights bounced off her creamy skin as her red lips pursed out toward the microphone as she sang.

Bluebird.

He missed her, wanting to tell her the news and hold her until the world disappeared around them. But Marcus said she was doing well and getting herself where she needed to be, which, in turn, kept him from reaching out.

He picked up his phone, and his hand shook over the call button like it had every day for the last three months. He wanted to hear her voice. Her throaty laugh and honest talk to set him straight, but he couldn't. He'd promised. He set it down.

The song "Jolene" by Ray LaMontagne played from the phone, and his stomach sank. *She's calling.*

He made his way to the kitchen. "Hello?"

"Gavin?" Her raspy voice threaded through his veins like wildfire.

"Hey…"

"How are you?"

"I'm good. Are you okay?"

"Better than okay." A lightness came through the phone. She seemed happy.

"That's great. How's Marcus?"

She chuckled at his diversion. "He's good. Said you've been keeping tabs on me."

"I needed to be sure you were doing well."

"Yeah, he said as much. Thank you."

Sweat beaded on his forehead as he created a path in the hardwood. "Jolene, I—"

"I've been writing," she blurted out. "And all my songs are happy ones. Go figure."

"As they should be. Marcus said you've been feeling better." Silence fell between them. What could he say when she appeared content without him?

"They're happy because they're about you. I try to write about recovery, and you're there. I try to write about finding myself, and you show up in the words. I write about the unknown, and you know what?"

"I'm there." Like she was for him, every fucking day.

"Yes. And I found me because of you."

He gripped his chest at the buttons of his shirt. "What are you doing, Bluebird?"

Her pet name spilled out before he could stop it. Her breath hitched through the receiver, sounding so close.

Knock, knock.

"Shit, hold on." He strode to the door and opened it wide. There stood his angel, her mermaid hair blowing in the October breeze.

"Jolene..." The name flowed like a prayer as he met her emerald-green gaze. He swallowed as the intense need to grab her and keep her locked in his house forever contracted his muscles.

"Gavin."

He pulled her across the threshold and slammed a kiss on her red lips. Her skin and her kiss relieved the thirst he'd craved. "I will never hurt you. Never leave you. I am incomplete without you."

"God, I've missed you so much. I thought you'd given up on me."

He backed away. "Why?"

"Marcus said you lined up another manager for us and..."

His finger went to her lips. "Never, Jolene. I was making sure you were comfortable. I didn't want to pressure you."

She smiled under his finger and sucked his digit. The heat of her tongue punched his groin. Still so sexy.

"No pressure, Gavin."

"Fuck, Jo..."

"If I wait another minute to feel you, I'll die."

He raised her up and kicked the door shut behind him. He nipped her lips as his dick hardened. "Open to me, Bluebird."

She did, and he tasted the sweet flavor of Jolene. His tongue couldn't push in far enough as she groaned and fisted her hands in his hair. He carried her into the kitchen, setting her on the island.

His forehead met hers. "Stop. Stop. Too much."

"What?"

He squeezed his eyes closed to focus on letting his muscles relax. His temperature had shot through the roof as the last few months of control were whittled away.

"We need to slow down. *Fuck*...I'll lose all the control I fought to sustain."

She lifted his face and kissed him softly. Her smooth bow lips sent waves of heat to his toes. She was in his house. In his arms.

"Don't hold back, Gavin."

He traced each facet of her face, skin, and hair with his fingers. "I have to. Only for a little while."

"Until what?"

"Until I can believe you are here. The last few months were empty without you, Jo. I thought I'd lost you."

"Never lost. Only finding a path back to you. Every day I walked the grounds of the rehab center and settled on a bench overlooking a pond. With my journal in my lap and ink in my pen, I wrote and wrote, scribbling nonsense until my hand hurt. And do you know why?"

"Tell me," he whispered.

"Because I hoped for a different result. Something telling me I could live my own experiences. All the things I missed when I was younger. But that never came. Instead of writing about the past, I'm writing about a future with you, because you are my wind, Gavin. You make me soar. You own me."

Her fingers trailed his neck and disappeared under his collar.

"I love you, Jolene. I can't stop."

"I can't either." She pushed the buttons through the holes, opening his shirt wider, allowing it to fall to the floor. Her eyes widened. "Your burns…"

He looked down at the marks, which streaked up his left hand, forearm, and shoulder. His prior tattoos of tribal designs had become severely distorted, as though the fire had burned away his past, leaving the angel of Nicolette's remembrance on his chest, unharmed.

"They're…"

"They don't hurt anymore."

"They're beautiful. They look like mine." She removed her short-sleeved yellow shirt. Her breasts, covered in a lace see-through demi, bounced heavily. Her existing nipple poked forward as she took his hand to touch her arm. "We match."

"Jolene…" He kissed her long and hard. A powerful feeling flipped his heart, leading his mind into dark territory. He needed to claim her. He wanted to hurt her and bring her pleasure. If this was what love felt like, he was more fucked up than he could have ever imagined. He broke away.

"Don't stop," she whimpered. "I feel it too, Gavin. Show me."

"How?"

"Hurt me. I need the sting and the pleasure. I have gone without all of you, and I'm not going to settle for anything less."

Visions of her tied and beaten red shot his dick into a rod of steel. "We're not ready. You went through trauma."

"I trust you."

He opened his eyes and met desire so deep his heart nearly burst into flames.

"I want to hurt you."

"Then do it. It's the only way I can feel all the emotions you create in me." Her lips singed his jaw with each peck. "Fire." *Kiss.* "Ice." *Lick.* "Happiness. Sadness. Pain. Pleasure and love."

He swallowed as his Dominance ticked up after being buried for months. "Are you sure?"

"Yes."

"Choose a safe word, Jolene."

"I won't say it."

He chuckled at her defiant ways pushing him closer to the edge. "Doesn't matter. You might someday. Maybe today. Maybe tomorrow. But you need to have something to ground you and warn me I'm pushing too hard."

"O-okay."

"Well?"

Her eyes closed feeling his light touch. "Flame."

"Interesting choice."

"It's everything we are. It's what you saved me from. It's what I feel when you touch me. It is our safe place."

"Do you feel it now?"

"Yes."

"I do too. Even when we were apart, Jolene, you were in my blood, my skin, my heart."

He lifted her from the island and placed her gently on the floor. He pulled her skirt off to find she had nothing on underneath. "Oh, Jolene. You came all the way here without panties?" He knelt and pushed his tongue into her folds.

"Yes." She gasped and wrapped her leg around his shoulder. His tongue lapped up her wetness to taste everything. Her fingers gripped his hair as her hips undulated into his movements. "Feels so good…"

One long lick and he placed her foot on the ground and removed her ballet flats. He took her bra off and lifted her back onto the island. She leaned back on her hands and spread her legs wide.

"Good God, Jolene." He fingered her entrance. "Bad girls get pain. Is that what you want?"

"Yes, please."

"Up on all fours and don't move."

Her eyes widened with her smile, and she shifted on the island. Hands flat. Knees on the marble. He rubbed her ass as she pushed it up. "I will be right back."

He disappeared into his office and shuffled through the boxes in his closet, grabbed what he needed, and returned. Her skin was blushed all over as her hair cascaded down to the dimples above her round ass and down the sides of her body. "Fucking perfect, Bluebird."

A shimmer of arousal coated her pussy, and he held himself back from licking her raw. He would take his time to appreciate the gift and reconnect with her the way they were meant to.

He held out the implement he'd chosen.

"See this?"

Her eyes darted to each end. A round plume of soft feathers on one side and the other held a flat leather keeper.

"Yes."

"Pain and pleasure, Jolene. I promise to always bring you both. The thing you need and the thing you desire. When the two merge, you will know I am always with you. Do you understand?"

"God, yes."

"Close your eyes." She did. He floated the feathers over her tender skin. Arms, legs, back and face. She sank into the softness with a purr. He ran the feathers over her nipple. Her succulent tits swelled. "You like this."

"So much."

"Tell me how it feels." He continued tracing her flesh.

"Loving and tender. You know how to draw out the soft spots within me."

He moved behind her, the plume never leaving her skin. Her body shuddered as he inserted two fingers into her wet core. In and out. Slow and deliberate. His control waned as she rocked into his thrusts.

"It feels go good..."

She rocked faster, and with each smack against his knuckles, he knew she controlled her own climb. He let her fly. The way she wanted to. Pleasure flooded his veins, and he relinquished his need to control and let her find her own orgasm. He set the crop down and tugged her nipple while kissing between her round ass cheeks.

"Gavin...it feels so good."

"You want it." Her wetness coated his fingers as they drove into her hot flesh.

"I want you."

"I know. I can feel you. So fucking beautiful, Jo. I've missed your greediness." He licked her crevice until his tongue met her spine. The heat crawled off her body, tingling his tongue. "Find it, baby. Come when you're ready."

He twisted his hand and curled his fingers along the ribbed area inside her throbbing core. She sped up her rocking motion.

His other hand met her clit. The rise to her orgasm crept steadily with each pass. He wanted to fuck her, but this moment was hers.

Moans escaped her lips as her head tipped back. Her hair flowed down her back, and she grunted his name. She quickened as she fucked his fingers.

"It's coming...I'm..."

"Yes, Bluebird. Soar."

"Yes!" She cried out as warm juices dripped from her pussy all over his hand. *Fuck.*

Her head dropped between her shoulders and she caved onto the island. Sobs sounded as he leaned over to hug her. It was beautiful. Her release. It was everything.

"Gavin...I can't handle it..."

"Shhh. I'm here, Jo."

"I love you so much it hurts. It never felt like this before. It is beautiful pain."

He moved around the island and kissed the tears from her cheeks. Seeing her that open, so in the moment, hurt so much it pleasured him. Never had two powerful sides merged to create the man he'd always hidden. Pain and pleasure. Control and chaos.

"It is. And I love you too." He kissed her and snapped up the implement, crop side out.

Her brilliant eyes widened in excitement. "How much, Jolene?"

"As much as you think I can take."

He moved behind her and smacked her ass with his hand. She yelped. Dominance filled his chest. "Good answer. Are you ready?"

"Always."

THIRTY-EIGHT

G AVIN WALTZED INTO THE BEDROOM WITH A LIME SPRITZER . J OLENE was propped up on a mound of pillows, freshly bathed, wrapped in a robe, and sated. Just the way he loved her.

He handed her the drink and snuggled up next to her.

"How's Ethan?" she asked.

He cocked an eyebrow. "Not the man I'd hoped you would be thinking about."

Her raspy laugh filled the room, and he smiled. "How is he though?"

"Good. Working for some promotions company. I had a connection who needed some help."

"What about The Resort? Were you able to get something going?"

"Slowly. It's been a rough couple of months."

"I was thinking about how we can help him get back on his feet."

"Already taken care of." He smiled and nudged her nose with his. He wanted to keep the world at bay for a few hours…or days.

"Tell me."

"I will once it's figured out."

"Still so bossy."

"You like me that way."

"You make it hard not to." She pulled the robe closed and stretched her legs. Her blue painted toenails wiggled as she released a sigh of comfort. "This is nice."

"Hotel Gavin, at your service."

"This is worlds better than that flea bag hotel I was in."

"It was rehab. It's not meant to be a luxury resort."

"That's not what I read in a celebrity magazine. The talent gets all the goods, apparently. Isn't that what the manager does? Finds the top of the line rehab centers for their talent?"

He plucked the glass from her hand and set it on the nightstand. She squeaked in amusement and sank into the bed. He hovered over her.

"I'm giving you the six-star resort treatment."

"Six stars?"

"Yes." He kissed her with each reason. "Plush bedding, free wifi, a spa, air conditioning…"

"Thank goodness for central air. What else?"

"Guest fitness."

"Is that right?"

"You'll get a free workout everyday you're with me." He ground his hard-on against her cleft.

"A must have…" Her breath hitched. "That's five, what's number six?"

"My heart."

Tears slipped from her eyes and down her cheeks. "This hotel must only allow one guest."

"Yes, Bluebird. Live with me. Marry me. Be with me forever. This is our home when you are here."

"Gavin…I…"

He swallowed and fear caused his hackles to rise. "I'm sorry, Jo. Too soon?" He shifted and she stopped him.

"No. It's…I haven't had a home in forever, and the way you

say it…like I live in these walls hits me"—she touched her chest —"here."

"You do. You live inside and outside these walls. You live in my soul. We can go anywhere together. Achieve the impossible. Shit…I sound like a fucking sap." He smiled, shyly.

"I like when you show this side of you." Her hand tickled the side of his face. "One minute you're my dark and wicked King of Kink, and then you're this tender being that makes me safe. Two sides to complete the whole package. You're blushing, Mr. Mayne."

He laughed, feeling his insides turn to mush. "I can't help it. It's weird to feel this soft side."

"And I love it."

"So…" he prompted. "Will you come home?"

She turned her lips inward and bit down. Her skin flushed a rosy pink as she appeared to try to form words. "Yes. I will."

He pushed out the breath he'd been holding. "Thank God. If you'd said no, I was going to tie you to my bed until you changed your mind."

"Well…we could still do that."

"You were made for me," he growled and kissed her. "Thank you for saving me."

"We saved each other."

EPILOGUE

"You know I don't play for 'team sub'," Ethan complained. Jolene spun in the front seat of the SUV as Ethan tugged at his blindfold.

"Leave it on. It's a good look for you. 'Ethan the Master' turns 'Ethan the submissive,'" Gavin said smirking in the rearview.

"Screw you."

"It will be over before you know it." Jolene smiled at Gavin.

Ethan tilted his head back against the headrest. "That's what they tell all the subs."

The Range Rover crawled to a stop in the meatpacking district of Manhattan. Over the last several months, between small tours and travel, Gavin had somehow managed to find time to put Ethan's surprise together.

Jolene smiled as she set her hand on his where it rested on the gearshift. As each day passed, their flame grew brighter, and he became more like the man he'd always wanted to be.

Gavin took her face and kissed her long and hard. His toes curled and the familiar burn ignited in his gut. Would he ever tire of her? *No way.*

"Eh-um. I can hear you," Ethan whined.

"Sorry, Ethan," she said as Gavin gazed into her green eyes.

"Okay, smart ass, you can take it off." Gavin turned off the engine, and Ethan scooted forward to glance at the slate gray steel walls of the building.

"Where the hell are we?"

"You'll see." They exited the car, approached the door, and Gavin punched in a key code. The lock snapped back.

They walked through the door and Candy, the receptionist from The Resort, greeted them. She sported a blonde pixie cut, corset top, and mini skirt. She squealed in excitement. "Ethan! Welcome to West Eden. Where all dark fantasies come true."

Ethan's mouth dropped. He actually had zero response. Gavin smirked. Ethan's eyes flicked to Jolene then to Gavin.

"Welcome home, Ethan." Gavin held out a ring of keys.

He swiped them. "You're fucking with me."

"Nope. Gavin's been keeping it a secret for a while. Even I didn't know," Jolene admitted.

"Thanks, man." He gripped Gavin in a bear hug.

"I appreciate the gesture, but there are people waiting for you."

Ethan backed away and Gavin could swear his eyes glassed over for a moment. "People?"

Candy pulled him toward the barn doors. "Come on!"

She rolled the doors open and Gavin saw the entire group of past members of The Resort gathered around the entrance. Damien and Brit, two of his past play partners, stood grinning ear to ear. Ten years of kinky wedding bliss between the two of them. Gavin was unsure how they'd made menage their kink for so long but somehow it worked for them.

Damien nodded, and Brit batted her long eyelashes through the white pearl mask she must have insisted on wearing. An homage to the rebirth of the club. That alone brought warmth to Gavin's chest. He was forgiven.

Even though anonymity would remain for the members, the

masks were no longer needed. Through his own experiences, Gavin considered hiding behind a mask unnecessary. He gripped Jolene's hand, and she beamed up at him. He only needed to be himself, inside and out.

Ethan backslapped and hugged his friends. His community. It was joyful to watch him reconnect with them even though it was a society Gavin would leave behind. It would never feel right after betraying their trust at The Resort. He'd promised them they would be safe, and he wouldn't interfere with Ethan's new club.

"Will you miss it?" Jolene asked as if reading his mind.

"No. It was a major part of the man I hid behind. He no longer exists. Because of you."

He toyed with the engagement ring on her left hand. The sapphire glimmered in the light, sending righteousness through his bones. He bent down and kissed her.

Jolene was his present.

Jolene was his future.

And he would never be alone again.

AUTHOR NOTE

Thank you for reading BEYOND THE TRUTH! I hope you loved Jolene and Gavin's story! Please consider leaving a review on your favorite site. Spreading the word is much appreciated!

The next book in the BEYOND SURRENDER SERIES is BEYOND HER DESIRE. Find out how Damien and Brit survive their marriage after tragedy.

Five dangerous stars! It is an all-consuming, pulse-pounding, sinfully sexy tale with the right amount of panty-melting scenes and hot passion.
~Girls Behind The Books Blog

BEYOND HER DESIRE

With his ring, I wed. With his collar, I obey. With my body, I share.

By my own free will, I surrendered my life to my Master. I vowed to honor him through my thoughts, words, and actions. We were linked by love and trust. He would never forsake me. He owned me. Even when sharing my body with other men.

But when tragedy strikes, his control attempts to carry us through. But cracks show in my surrender, and the cracks slowly break us apart. Sharing my body always brought us closer. I had no choice but to invite another man into our marriage.

There is only man brave enough to show us who we are. Fox Baron. An artist, sex god, and my teacher.

But I never expect what comes after. No longer will our metal rings and leather strap hold our future promises, they remind us of the things we wish to forget.

Sharing is a dangerous game and we may not survive.

BEYOND HER DESIRE
Now Available on Amazon

LOOKING FOR MORE?

If you enjoyed BEYOND THE TRUTH, you'll love the sexy, emotional love triangle of how it all began. See how it all started in BEYOND THE MASKS.

Can betrayal and obsession lead to love?

Shane Vaughn has it all. Well, almost. Fame, success, and money can only get her so far. After surviving a devastating heartbreak at the hands of the all-consuming Jacob Andrews, she's demanding no-strings, uncomplicated liaisons from now on.

Where could she find a simple distraction from Jacob? The exclusive pleasure club, The Resort.

The masked Dom with the blue-eyed gaze could work. He was hypnotizing and mysterious, rendering her powerless. A seductively simple decision.

Unless the masked Dom is Gavin Mayne. A pompous, arrogant, and commanding man. A talent director determined to take

Shane's job. But how can he control an Alpha woman? Force her submission and have her kneeling at his feet.

That is until Jacob Andrews demands a second chance. He couldn't let Shane go, especially into the arms of another man. She was the love of his life but will she forgive him for what he's done?

A dangerous combination of betrayal and obsession will surface. But when secrets are revealed, who will be the last man standing?

BEYOND THE MASKS
Now Available on Amazon

BOOKS BY NICKY F. GRANT

BEYOND SURRENDER SERIES

Beyond the Masks
Beyond the Truth
Beyond Her Desire
Beyond Eden (COMING SOON)

ABOUT THE AUTHOR

Nicky's emotionally rich, vibrant stories are set in cities that thrum with energy. Her heroines come up against personal and professional challenges, and are pushed to break new ground and become better versions of themselves.

As a writer, Nicky imbues each of her stories with equal parts love and lust, which she believes are among the strongest emotions we can experience. By immersing her readers into worlds of power and erotic passion, she invites them to explore their own unspoken desires. Her hope is that her stories embolden her readers to realize their fullest potential — be it in the boardroom, the bedroom, or anywhere in between.

Sign up for Nicky F. Grant's Newsletter:
www.NickyFGrant.com
Like and follow Nicky F. Grant on on social Media:
Facebook:
www.facebook.com/NickyFGrant/

Reader Group:
www.facebook.com/groups/grantsgoddesses
Instagram:
instagram.com/nickyfgrant

ACKNOWLEDGMENTS

Robin "Eagle-Eye" Hill – Where do I start? This year has been filled with highs and lows and you always level me out with honesty and laughs. Without you, Gavin and Jolene wouldn't have the beautiful ending they deserved. I mean...I did love the OTT "lifetime" scenes, but alas, they needed cut. Thank you for being my voice of reason. Thank you for your words of encouragement through this book and your perfect friendship. We are God-maids for life (or maybe Mer-Desses haha). <3

To the Goddesses! Thank you for your daily laughs, companionship, and cheerleader support for this book and my kooky ways. You are my tribe. I love you more than you know.

Heather Bentley – You and Robin are linked to the same brain! Thank you for beta reading this monstrosity LOL. You both hit on the same items/scenes that needed a little more finesse and care.

Amanda Walker – LOVE, LOVE, LOVE this cover! You, lady, have brought the essence of this story to life through your artful design.

Saya – Again, your critique and care for this story brought out the best in these characters.

Samantha and Marit – Thank you for being the Alpha readers on this book during it's infancy. Without your feedback, I would not have been able to push through to complete Gavin's book as well as giving him and Jolene the Happily Ever After they deserved.

To my fellow author tribe: Emma Scott, Michelle Windsor, April Moran, CE Johnson, Erica Lynn, Grea Warner, Wende Dikec, Jen Sako, Cin Medley - without your uplifting posts, conversations, and knowledge – I would have quit writing. I love you ladies so much!

To my husband. This year was really difficult for so many reasons and you, my champion, brought life back into me. You held me in the dark when I couldn't walk through it and led me to the light when I could. You are my whole world and now you are also the sun. I love you more than words and you are the story book of my life. We will always live our Happily Ever After and beyond.